Teacup and Sorcery

Rosie Reed

Teacup and Sorcery by Rosie Reed

All rights reserved. This book or any portion thereof may not be reproduced or used in any manner whatsoever without the express written permission of the publisher except for the use of brief quotations in a book review. Fonts used with permission from Microsoft.

Copyright © 2023 by Julie Farrell

Chapter One

Have you ever had a conversation with your cat? Oh, you've probably *talked* to your cat. But has your cat ever talked back? Well, stick around, because a talking cat is imminent. And if that's not exciting enough, other forthcoming attractions at Paws for Tea include murder, magic, and the man who broke my heart ten years ago.

And when I say man, I do, of course, mean vampire.

Scanning my gaze over the marvellous moggies dotted around my aunt's cat café, I counted them for a third time. Okay, there was the tiny tabby curled up on the windowsill, the tortoiseshell washing itself near the counter, and the three cute kitties darting up and down the multi-level climbing frame. Along with four other adorable fur babies, that made nine cats, present and... not quite correct.

There should only be *eight* cats at Paws for Tea. So, who was the fat and fluffy ginger puss sitting on a bookshelf, blinking his big green eyes at me? And why did I have a strange urge to chat with him?

It was probably my latent witchiness. I'd never been able to suppress my magic. My senior witch grandmother had once told me, *"If you don't learn to control your magic, then your magic will control you."* But magic had taken my parents from me as a child, so I'd turned my back on it. *And* on my grandmother. And on my hometown of Royal Windsor.

Now I was back in Windsor under a cloud. Last week, my dream job as a London journalist had turned into a nightmare when I'd made a stupid mistake and been fired by my editor – who also happened to be my ex-boyfriend. Coming home to my friends and family had seemed my best option.

A trill voice called out, "Waitress!"

Uh-oh, time to stop counting cats and get to work. This was my first shift here in ten years, but thankfully the group at the table in the corner were my only customers, so surely I could cope with that.

And hopefully they'd forgive any mistakes I might make, because Paws for Tea was so lovely. The atmosphere was warm and cosy – like sliding into a snug bath after a winter walk. None of the furniture matched, in fact, some of the chairs looked as if they'd been acquired from a bric-a-brac stall. But it was clean and, more importantly, there were sweet cakes and even sweeter kitties. Customers were discouraged from picking up the cats, but they tended to jump on your lap the moment you sat down. And they didn't usually talk.

The fat and fluffy ginger puss clambered off the bookshelf and followed me over to the table, where a middle-aged man and three women were talking in hushed tones.

"Hey Amber," the cat said. "Remember me?"

Oh fudge cakes, it did speak to me. You heard it too, right?

But now wasn't the time to reply. Not unless I wanted these good people to think I was crazy. Ahahaha.

Gripping my trusty notepad, I smiled at the customers and launched into journalist mode. "Can you give me an update on the situation here?"

The middle-aged man spoke gruffly. "We'd like to order some drinks."

"Uh-huh? And what are your top tips for beverage buying? You don't mind if I quote you, do you? What are your names, ages, and addresses?"

The four customers stared at me as if they'd been put on pause.

The cat propped his front paws on my shin. "Get a grip, Amber, you're not a journalist anymore."

"How do *you* know that?" I spluttered.

One of the women – a horsey-looking posh lady – glowered impatiently. "Are you talking to that cat?"

"Of course not, that would be crazy, ahahaha." I composed myself. "What can I get you?"

They did that awkward English thing of eyeing each other up to see who should go first, giving me the chance to look at them properly. The three women consisted of the horsey posh lady, a curvy middle-aged woman in a bright-pink suit, and a brunette in her forties dressed in a gypsy top.

I broke the impasse and spoke directly to the woman in the gypsy top. "Yes, madam?"

Her voice was as calm as windchimes. "I'd like an almond-milk skinny chai latte with extra cinnamon and star anise."

I hovered my pen over my notepad, narrowing my eyes. "How many drinks is that?"

"One. It's a latte made with almond milk and spices. I can't have dairy because I'm lactose intolerant."

"Oh right." I tried to make a joke. "I'm sure the feeling's mooooo-tual, ahahaha."

She didn't laugh at my cow impression.

I attempted to jot down the complicated chai latte order, but the curvy woman in the pink suit interjected. "I'll just have a glass of water, love. That's nice and simple, isn't it?"

"You'd think so wouldn't you... Tap water or bottled?"

"Tap water is fine."

"Ice or no ice?"

"No ice."

"Fruit slice?"

"Er, okay."

"Lemon? Lime?"

"Um... lime."

"Pint or half-pint?"

She spoke through gritted teeth. "Just get me a glass of tap water before I die of thirst."

I smiled sweetly. "All right, you only had to say."

The horsey-looking woman held a menu aloft. "It says here you do speciality coffee. What do you offer?"

Oh blimey, I had no idea! I'd only arrived back last night, and I'd spent the entire time catching up with Aunt Vicky and my best friend Harry.

The cat padded his paws into my shin. "Say something about quantum physics, Amber. That always impresses people."

I gazed at him. "What on *earth* do cats know about quantum physics?"

"Oh, cats know *everything* about quantum physics. Fish, cream, and quantum physics – that's what we're all about. *And* the laws of washing in a sunbeam. You see, quantum phy—"

"That's enough about quantum physics now, thank you, puss."

The man sneered. "Are you talking to that cat about quantum physics?"

"Of course not. Ahahaha."

Right, apparently no one could hear the cat but me. It must be my magic. That, or I was going insane – it could be either. Or even both. Ahahaha.

The horsey woman looked down her nostrils at me. "*Do* you have speciality coffees?"

"Yes. We have um… quantum cappuccino."

"Quantum cappuccino? Whatever's that?"

"It's, er, fifty percent coffee, fifty percent milk, and… fifty percent froth."

She tucked her bobbed hair behind her ear. "Don't be ridiculous. I'll have a glass of white wine."

The man tutted. "It's a bit early, isn't it? I'm not paying you to come here and drink wine."

"Why *are* we here, Tony?" the pink-suited woman asked. "I'm dying to know."

"Well, you'll have to delay dying for a bit longer," Tony said. "We're waiting for Billy to arrive."

I brandished my trusty notepad. "And what would *you* like to drink, sir?"

He sat back in his chair, stretching his legs under the table. "Bottle of beer, please love."

The horsey lady pointed accusingly. "You said it was too early to start drinking!"

The bell above the door tinkled so I left them to argue amongst themselves.

Oh *yes*, this was more like it. The young woman in the doorway smiled at me like a ray of sunshine, soothing my heart. "Amber?" she said. "It's me – your cousin Evelyn."

"Oh, Evelyn!" I pulled her close for a hearty hug, melting into her tender arms. "When you phoned this morning, it was like Fate herself had sent you."

She held me tight. "As I said, my boyfriend's on secondment in Windsor, so it was the perfect excuse."

It was so exciting to discover I had a cousin – well, we were second-cousins really, because her granny was my granny's niece. But it was wonderful, nevertheless. This was the first time we'd actually met, but over the phone Evelyn had told me she was a novice witch who lived in a quaint English village called Maiden-Upon-Avon. As we broke the hug, I saw she was wearing her magic wand in her hair bun, but other than that, she looked quite like me – high cheekbones and big brown eyes. I had long dark red hair, whereas hers was brown, but I could see the family resemblance. I hugged her again, so glad to see a friendly face.

Like most people who came in here, Evelyn was instantly captivated by the kitties, and she couldn't hide her excitement as a cat called Chunk trotted over to say hello. Chunk was a big black puss with yellow eyes and a playful personality. He nuzzled Evelyn's hand, purring and mewing – making her grin with joy. Being with these lovely animals brought peace and happiness to everyone who met them. And the tea and cake were the cherries on the top.

Evelyn tickled Chunk's velvety ears. "Where's your aunt, Amber?"

"Vicky's in the basement, mixing up the marzipan."

"She bakes her own cakes?"

"Everything's homemade here."

Something fluffy rubbed against my legs. Oh, it was the talking ginger cat. The sight of his cute face nuzzling my shin filled me with affection. As I bent to stroke him, he stood on his back legs, raising his front paws up, like a child in need of a hug.

"Mew, mew, purr!"

Unable to resist, I picked him up and held him close. He propped his front paws on my shoulder, meaning he was facing behind me, purring in my ear. I stroked his fluffy back, taking comfort in his soft body. "Hey, lovely puss."

My breathing gently fell into line with his purring. For some reason, I had a special affinity with this lovely cat.

Evelyn glanced around the café. "Oh wow, magical paintings, cool!"

I turned to look at the paintings of various Windsor landmarks that adorned the walls of the cat café, created by my talented childhood bestie, Harry.

As well as painting 'formally', Harry loved to scribble on napkins or bits of paper during conversations – before modestly revealing an almost-perfect sketch of a tree, a feather, or a close-up of an eye. His doodling had often got him into trouble at school, where he'd spent many-a class drawing caricatures of the teachers. They'd called him a distraction. But the truth was he'd made my schooldays bearable. I adored that angel.

But… "I don't *think* the paintings are magical, Evelyn. Brilliant and talented as Harry is."

She threw me a knowing smile as we drifted over to inspect Harry's artwork. The talking ginger cat seemed happy in my arms, so he came too.

Evelyn was unable to keep the excitement from her voice. "Look closer."

Oh wow, she was right… Suddenly Harry's paintings seemed even more lifelike than usual! I scrutinised a beautiful oil-painting of Windsor's lush riverside. The crystal blue water, bright green grass, and egg-yolk sun all looked… real.

"That's amazing," I whispered. "The river actually seems to be moving."

The cat was still looking over my shoulder, so he turned his head from side to side. "I can't see."

I hoiked him round, hooking him under one arm, then I reached out to touch Harry's painting. "It's wet! My finger's actually gone in the water, and – ow! That swan just pecked me!"

The cat wriggled. "Let me at him, I could easily fight a swan that size for you, Amber."

I sucked my damp finger. "That's so weird. Harry never told me his paintings were magical." I turned to face Evelyn. "What's going on?"

She tenderly squeezed my shoulder. "There's something I need to tell you."

The cat spoke proudly. "*I* know what's going on. You're finally seeing things as they really are. I mean, just as an example off the top of my fuzzy head, you're standing here having a chat with a cat."

I kissed him on the top of his fuzzy head. Although I was eager to hear Evelyn's explanation, I couldn't help but wonder what *other* magic I might find in Harry's artwork. I edged further along the wall and found a display of photos – also by my talented friend. I reached out and eased my finger into a black-and-white print of a tea set on a table. Being very careful, I nudged the table with my finger and it moved an inch!

I spoke in hushed reverence. "That's incredible…"

As the cat wriggled his back paws, he tickled my ribs, which had the knock-on effect of *me* jabbing the teapot in the photograph. *Uh-oh*...

The teapot wobbled precariously. Oh fudge cakes!

I winced at the crash of smashed crockery. Oh blimey, the pictures were not only real – but really breakable!

Evelyn was chuckling. "I'm sure Harry won't be too upset."

Speaking of people being upset, raised voices from my customers made us both look over.

Tony slapped the table hard. "I just don't understand you, Judy. I've done what you wanted."

"Have you?" the pink-suited lady asked. "That would be a first!"

Evelyn gestured to the notepad sticking out of my apron pocket. "Do you need to make their drinks order?"

"Yeah, but this is my first shift here in ten years, so it might take a while. Do you want to sit down?"

She ran her thumb across my cheek with tender affection. "Wouldn't dream of it. I'll help you – come on."

I gently popped the talking ginger cat down on the floor, but as Evelyn and I scooted behind the long wooden counter, he jumped up onto a tall stool. "I'll supervise." He blinked innocently. "Meow, meow, purr, purr."

I wiped the counter pensively. "Wait a minute, I do know you! You're Marmalade Sandwich, all grown up!"

Affection twirled inside me like a sycamore seed. I'd met this cat ten years ago, before I'd gone off to London. He'd been a tiny ginger ball of fluff then, and all he could say was 'meow' and 'purr'. He'd actually *said* the words, not just made the sounds. No one else had been able to hear him speaking then, and apparently they still couldn't now. I wondered if he was my familiar. And if he was, what did that mean exactly? Why was I suddenly encountering magic everywhere?

I turned to ask Evelyn, but she was inspecting my notepad with a frown.

I cringed as I re-read what I'd written.

Hippy woman: non-cow milk, star nancy? I don't know what this woman is talking about, just keep smiling.

Pink Suit woman: tap water before she dies of thirst.

Horsey woman: white wine/quantum coffee.

Cranky man: beer.

The water and beer were easy so, while Evelyn got started on the coffees, I took those over to the table.

During my decade working as a journalist, I'd got good at 'reading the room', but it didn't take a genius to detect a thunderstorm's worth of tension zapping between these four.

The chai-latte lady decapitated a sugar sachet. "Tony, what *is* this all about?"

Tony drummed his fingers on the table. "I've told you, we need to wait for Billy to arrive."

The bell above the door tinkled and a young arty-looking man strode inside. Could this be Billy – as if on cue?

I opened my mouth to greet him, but he pushed past me and halted at the table. "Judy, I need to see you."

The pink-suited lady was surprised. "What are you doing here, Vincent?"

Not Billy then…

"I think we all know the answer to that, Judy." Tony grumbled. "Well, Vincent, you're here now, so you may as well sit down. I've got something to say and you all need to hear it. We're just waiting for my son, Billy. *Oof!*" Tony rubbed his abdomen and winced.

Judy squeezed his hand across the table, speaking tenderly. "Take one of your heart pills, love. You're getting stressed."

"Stop fussing. I'm fine." He pulled a pill bottle from his pocket.

I edged away and joined my cousin behind the counter. She was frothing up what was probably dairy milk in a metal jug at the coffee machine. "Er, I think she wanted…"

Evelyn raised her voice above the whirring. "Amber, this thing that I need to tell you. It's… your grandmother."

My insides froze. "Oh fudge cakes, where? She's not standing behind me, is she?"

Evelyn stopped frothing. "It's unlikely."

"Good." I fiddled with a teacup. "We've been estranged for years. Last time I saw her she kept saying I needed to train as a witch and fulfil my magical destiny. Oh *no*, she's told you to come here and talk to me about that, hasn't she?"

"Actually, Amber…" Evelyn held my hand. "I'm sorry to tell you this, but… she's dead."

As reality skidded to a halt, a million emotions surged into my heart. Regret, sadness… perhaps a tiny bit of relief? Oh yikes, and guilt for feeling that.

Evelyn was still speaking. "…. and she wants you to have her wand. You've already got an affinity with it – you saw Harry's magical paintings because of its influence."

I swallowed my tears, trying to make sense of all this. "I lost touch with my grandmother years ago. How… how did she die?"

Evelyn's eyes were full of kindness. "The Beings of Magic committee believe Vermilitrude Eldritch was murdered."

"Murdered? Who by?"

"We don't know yet. But you're the only beneficiary of her will. Why don't you just hold the wand?"

She held it aloft. To humans, it probably just looked like a long wooden pencil with a cluster of glass gems at one end instead of an eraser. But as I gazed at it, it seemed to detect my presence and began to gently vibrate – lighting up its gems and emitting streams of red, yellow, purple, orange… all the colours of the rainbow.

It was captivating. I reached out to take it, but a small piece of paper that had been tied around it fluttered to the floor. I bent to pick it up.

The note tingled in my hand.

"What does it say?" Evelyn asked.

I was about to unfold it, but Tony suddenly groaned and coughed loudly.

I stuffed the note into my apron pocket and rushed over.

The others were on their feet and panicking around Tony, who was desperately gurgling, as he gripped his throat with one hand, and clawed the air with the other.

"Does anyone know the Heimlich manoeuvre?" The pink-suited woman shrieked. "Lydia, loosen his collar!"

"What happened?" I frantically asked.

The chai-latte woman wrung her hands. "He took his pill and started choking!"

The pink-suited woman grabbed her glass of water. "Tony, drink this!"

She helped him glug the water down, but instead of helping, it actually increased his frenzied coughing fit. "Gah-gagggarrghh!"

"Perhaps we ought to call an ambulance," the arty man muttered.

"I'll do that." But before I could move, Tony suddenly lurched into me and grabbed my T-shirt in his fists. His breath was hot on my cheek. As I leaned back, he forced out two words. "Fine... lettuce..."

"*Which* lettuce?" I whispered.

But it was too late. The life drained from him and he collapsed into me like a concrete slab. I wasn't strong enough to hold him and I stumbled backwards – my shocked legs giving way.

Evelyn grabbed his other side, and we awkwardly lowered him to the floor.

In the stunned, stifling air, Evelyn crouched to check his pulse. Her voice was barely a whisper. "He's dead."

Well… what a fine welcome back to Windsor! A talking cat, a murdered grandmother, and now a dead customer. Surely nothing else could go wrong today? Oh fudge cakes, why did I have to go and tempt Fate like that!

Chapter Two

Aunt Vicky ran upstairs from the kitchen to find one of her customers dead, and my cousin Evelyn on the phone to the emergency services.

Vicky was one of those compassionate women who operated on a wavelength of love. She always dressed beautifully, and today her long blonde ponytail trailed down the back of her navy-blue dress. She was a psychic, but presumably she hadn't seen *this* coming, or she might've given me a bit of warning. She spoke calmly to the shocked customers. "We must wait here until the police arrive. Let's all take a seat on the other side of the café."

I gently corralled the cats out to the back, where they had their own indoor and outdoor living spaces. Then, with all the kitties safe and snug, I drifted over to where Tony's shocked guests were sitting at a table near the window – as far away from the dead body as possible. It was strange to think of life continuing as normal out in the streets of Windsor. In here, life had changed in a matter of moments. Permanently for Tony.

Evelyn was a trainee therapist, so she and Vicky set about taking care of the pink-suited lady, the chai-latte woman, posh horsey lady, and the late-coming arty guy.

I was feeling like a spare part when the keen waitress in me noticed the empty spaces in front of them. Here was my chance to do something useful while we waited for the police to arrive.

I clambered onto a spare chair. "Ladies and gentlemen, as a proud Englishwoman in a crisis, I must do what my grandmothers and great-grandmothers did before me. And that is... get the kettle on. Yes, I shall make us all a nice cup of tea!"

The hippy lady coughed politely. "I'd like an almond-milk skinny chai latte with extra cinnamon and star anise."

I sagged. "I don't recognise this country anymore."

Vicky helped me down off the chair. "Come on, we'll make the drinks together."

After we'd distributed five teas and one skinny chai latte, the bell above the door alerted us that the police had finally arrived.

The already tense mood buckled further as a scowling plain-clothed detective strode in from the street. I hadn't yet met Evelyn's boyfriend, Detective Inspector Alex Taylor, but he was now sucking up all the attention in the café. He certainly caught the eye, and I would've probably lingered on him longer, had my focus not been absorbed by the other detective behind him.

David Van Danté. Oh my fudge cakes! My heart thrashed violently in my chest as a decade of buried feelings rushed up, almost knocking me over. My skin prickled with terror. Would he remember me? Did I want him to? Of course I did, and *that* was precisely the problem.

I'd first met David ten years ago, when we'd solved a murder together. I should've known he was trouble when I'd found him crouched over a dead body, but somehow I'd let him convince me to lie to the police for him – to give him an alibi. Obviously he hadn't actually been the killer, but during our investigation he'd rubbed my fur up the wrong way, rattled my heart like a teacup on a saucer, and... shown me a good person under that attractive and cocky exterior. Then he'd gone and spoiled it all by doing something stupid like transforming into a vampire.

Vampires had killed my parents. If only he'd been honest from the start.

But actually, it was even more complicated than that, because David Van Danté might very well be the man of my dreams – and I wasn't simply speaking metaphorically.

Ever since my teens, I'd been having a recurring dream about a man whose face I couldn't see, but who warmed my heart and radiated pure love into my soul. I'd never felt such intense closeness to anyone in real life, but my dream man's presence was like coming home. My best friend Harry always got excited about my 'dream man', saying it was a prophecy and that one day I'd meet him in person.

But David *couldn't* be my dream man, because he'd turned out to be my mortal enemy – a vampire. And not only that but he'd clearly been mixed up in something illicit back then – something to do with his missing brother and a cache of stolen diamonds.

Despite our romance being doomed from the start, David and I had parted amicably. We'd both been due to leave Windsor to start our dream jobs anyway, so I'd snogged him 'goodbye' on the backseat of

Harry's tour bus – just to find out what it was like to kiss a vampire. (It was delicious).

Then, after that, my life had changed forever – it was like a tender piece of my innocence had been lost. My experience with David had shown me that dream men don't exist. And worse still, when I'd left Windsor, my beautiful and comforting recurring dream had vanished forever. *That's* how he'd broken my heart, you see. By stealing my dreams.

I had often thought of him over the years, wondering how he was, hoping he was doing well. But I certainly hadn't expected him to walk into my aunt's cat café on my first proper day back in Windsor! And I was dismayed to discover he was even more enticing than *ever* – dressed in his tailored black suit, and sizzling with super-cool vibes. He was six-foot tall and dashingly handsome, with dark hair, high cheekbones, and pale skin. How dare he come in here looking so gorgeous after all this time!

His manners had always been impeccable, and I watched as he greeted Evelyn with a handshake and a, "How do you do."

His voice was still deep and low, but now with extra gravel that instantly grated on my nerves – in the most glorious way. He was *my* David Van Danté, but even more so. Gah!

But… I sensed a difference in him. A darkness. He was a vampire, of course, but it was more than that. Oh, *yes* that was it. On his top lip was a sneery smirk that hadn't been there before. He'd always been a bit cocky, but in a playful way. Now he looked jaded. Had life made him cynical? Was that the cause of the smirk? Whatever the reason, it made him look smug and aloof.

It also made me want to kiss him. Double-gah!

I pushed away the urge to rush over and say hello. Apart from the fact he was here to investigate the death of Tony, what would I say to him after all these years? And how embarrassing that I was back working here again. I realised I was wringing my hands, so I thrust them firmly by my sides, refusing to let his presence ruffle me up.

Too late.

Clutching a notepad, David stepped over with Alex to inspect the dead Tony.

Gosh, *I'd* only been doing that very same thing just twenty minutes ago. Standing in front of the *living* Tony, notepad in hand.

I'd taken him a beer. But that hadn't killed him, had it? Oh fudge cakes, surely not.

Alex crouched next to the body and lifted the tablecloth that Vicky had respectfully covered Tony with.

Tony's guests – still sitting on the other side of the room – held their breath as one, waiting for Alex to take control.

And then he did. He stood and spoke across the café. "Right, everyone, I'm DI Taylor, this is DS Van Danté. What happened?"

Was this all part of Inspector Taylor's cunning psychology? See who speaks first…

The pink-suited lady's voice was strained. "Tony took one of his heart pills then started choking. He has a bad heart, you see. That's why he takes the pills. He must've got over-excited and had a heart attack."

David held pen to notepad. "And you are?"

"Judy. Tony's wife."

Alex held poor Judy in his glare for longer than anyone was comfortable with. Then he knelt and opened one of Tony's eyes, gazing into the void. "Tony who?"

Judy bit back her tears. "Tony Royal. Owner of the famous Royal Boutique B&B down the road."

David wrote this down, then glanced up at Alex. They gazed into each other's eyes for a few seconds – as if they could communicate telepathically – then Alex exhaled heavily and pulled on a pair of disposable gloves. He removed the pill bottle from Tony's fist, read the label, and sniffed the contents. "Hmm, smells like *chilli*. Do heart tablets usually smell like curry?"

"Don't think so, sir," David said, also having a sniff. "Is there such a thing as anaphylactic shock from a chilli allergy?"

"Bag up the pill bottle, Sergeant. Get the pills and drinks tested. The pathologist's report will tell us the cause of death." Alex added an aside to David. "But my money *isn't* on a heart attack."

"Perhaps poison, sir?"

Despite Alex and David trying to speak quietly to each other, you could've heard a pin drop in the café, and if *I'd* heard Alex's last utterance, then Tony's fellow diners surely had too. And it didn't take a genius to guess what he was implying: 'One of that lot over there must've killed Tony. It's our job to figure who and how.'

The customers-turned-murder-suspects eyed each other up, probably wondering which of them had done the deed. As was I. Was that a flash of guilt across Judy's face?

The two detectives got down to business. David took notes as Alex did the speaking. "Mrs Royal, perhaps you can explain why you were all meeting here this lunchtime?"

Judy wrapped her hands around her teacup. "Tony invited us all here for lunch. Well, he asked Lydia to invite us."

"Lydia?" Alex asked.

"That's me," the horsey lady said. "I'm Lydia Drake-Countford, the receptionist at The Royal Boutique B&B. Tony asked me yesterday evening to invite everyone for lunch today at midday."

Alex checked his watch. "I see. And what was the purpose of the meeting?"

Lydia fiddled with a button on her blouse. "We never found out. Tony didn't tell me, and he started choking before he could get to the point. And before that, he wanted to wait for Billy to arrive and–"

"Billy?" Alex interjected.

Lydia didn't like being interrupted. "Tony's grown-up son. From his first marriage."

Without taking his eyes off the suspects, Alex spoke to David. "Make a note to speak to Billy Royal, Sergeant."

David continued writing. "Yes, sir."

Alex's stern gaze shifted to the arty-looking guy. "And you are?"

He pushed his long fringe out of his eyes and spoke nervously. "Vincent Varney. I'm an artist. I'm exhibiting my collection at the gallery in The Royal Boutique B&B."

"Gallery?" Alex asked suspiciously.

Judy gestured to Harry's paintings on the café walls. "Similar to here, we have a gallery in our dining room. I'm an art dealer. Vincent is my current commission."

"Vincent wasn't actually invited," Lydia said, glancing at her long fingernails. "He barged in. But Tony said he could stay."

Alex transferred his blank expression to the chai-latte woman. "And *you* are, madam?"

She absentmindedly rubbed her black crystal pendant. "Hyacinth Meadows. I run the Turret Sanctuary."

"Which is?"

"A spiritual B&B and healing centre located next door to The Royal Boutique B&B."

"You run it by yourself?"

Her voice was laced with pride. "Yes. Well, with my angels."

"Angels, really?" Alex glanced at David. "Getting all this down, Sergeant?"

David's smirk grew even sneerier. "Yes, sir. Angels, of course."

Alex folded his arms across his chest. "So I assume you and Mr Royal were in competition with each other? If you ran neighbouring B&Bs. Why did Mr Royal want *you* here?"

Hyacinth rubbed her crystal again. "I don't know. Lydia arranged it all last night. She said Tony had requested that we all meet here for lunch at noon. That's all I know."

Alex glanced at the dead Tony, then spoke to Judy. "Mrs Royal, who are your husband's solicitors?"

She hesitated like a contestant on a quiz show. "Er, Wordsworth of Windsor, up the road. But I can tell you now, Inspector, my stepson Billy is heir to my husband's money and The Royal Boutique B&B."

Alex didn't hide his surprise. "You don't jointly own the B&B?"

"No. I bought it for him. I'm successful as an art dealer, so he runs it himself and keeps all the profits. It's his."

The entire café – including the people, fixtures, and fittings – exhaled as Alex and David went into a huddle for a chat, investigating the body again. I exchanged a look of worry with Aunt Vicky. Despite this being the end of the line for Tony, our involvement in this case was clearly just beginning.

Chapter Three

Everyone clambered to their feet to stretch their legs – and to dissipate the sense of squashed guilt that a grilling from Inspector Taylor brought forth.

I turned to admire Harry's paintings again and, as Judy and Hyacinth stood with their backs to me, they didn't realise I was listening.

Judy sounded frantic. "Hyacinth, they think Tony was poisoned! You won't tell them anything, will you?"

Hyacinth squeezed Judy's trembling hand. "Your secret's safe with me. Although I am surprised you went through with it."

My ears strained to suck-up more info. Was I about to overhear a confession?

But Evelyn made me jump as she stepped over. "Did you make yourself a cup of tea, Amber?"

"Oh... I'll make one now."

Halfway across the room, Marmalade Sandwich hopped onto his back legs, demanding another cuddle. I picked him up and nuzzled my face into his neck, making him purr. He was so cute, for goodness cake. But I did fancy a cup of tea, so I carried the cat over to the counter and popped him on a tall stool, then scooted around to make my drink.

Alex's voice was loud above the chatter of the crowd. "We'll now take witness statements and fingerprints. It's quick and harmless, but we'd appreciate your cooperation. Sergeant Van Danté, you take that side of the room, I'll take this side."

Oh fudge cakes, if I'd stayed on the other side of the café, I could've avoided David. But safely behind the counter, I watched David step over to speak to Judy.

He spoke professionally. "I'll start by asking you a few questions, Mrs Royal."

To my amazement – and David's – Judy suddenly became angry, shouting furiously. "Do you think this is funny!"

David held out his hands to placate her. "Of course not, madam."

Overcome with fury, Judy raised her hand to slap him, but David intercepted, catching her wrist gently. "It's all right," he said flatly.

This defeat enraged Judy further. "Get your hands off me!"

"Excuse me, madam, but—"

Alex stepped over. "What's going on?"

"Sir, it's all right. Mrs Royal's upset and –"

"Of course I'm bloody upset!" Judy shouted. "My husband is dead and *he* thinks it's funny! Look at him, smirking – but my husband is dead!"

David was defensive. "Sir, I—"

"All right, Sergeant, I'll deal with this."

"But *sir* –"

"I said, I'll deal with this. Thank you, Sergeant."

Alex turned his back on David. "I know this is a difficult time for you, madam, but I won't tolerate aggression towards my officers. Now, I'm going to ask you a few questions. If you'd like to come this way."

David stood there, humiliated. My heart surged with sympathy.

But oh *no*, He looked like he was about to come over to the counter. I grabbed a handful of chocolate-coated coffee beans and frantically shoved them in my mouth. But not even the choca-mocha fix could help soothe my David-induced tension. Right, there was only one thing for it. I'd have to leave Windsor forever.

David glanced over. I ducked behind the counter.

Marmalade Sandwich paused, mid-wash. "Amber, where are you?"

"Down here. I'm going to sneak out before he sees me."

The cat scampered over to look at me. "How are you planning to sneak past him?" he mewed. "He's standing just a few feet away."

"Oh puss of little faith! I was a journalist for ten years. I know how to stay low, sneak into places, sneak *out* of places... Just watch and learn."

David was now eyeing-up Alex and Judy so, with my gaze firmly fixed on him, I slipped out from behind the counter, planning to run away and join the circus and never come back. Unfortunately, I was so focused on avoiding David that I failed to notice the tray of dirty plates I'd left there earlier and, as I swept past it, I knocked it to the floor with a *crash, bang, wallop, clatter!*

Despite having my back to everyone, I knew all eyes were on me. The silence sucked at my ears. A plate rolled across the café like a wagon wheel from a flaming coach crash.

"Who put that tray there?" I asked haughtily.

Someone coughed politely. "I think *you* did..."

Right, time to leave. I stuck my nose in the air and continued my journey to the door, which meant I didn't see the discarded slice of cheese on the floor – until I was already sliding on it like a skater on a rink-full of marbles. I twirled my arms, stumbled, and yelped. But somehow managed to stagger upright. Oh... well that could've been worse.

And look, the cheese-skate had delivered me safely to the café door. Perfect. Determined to escape with some pride intact, I reached for the door handle, yanked it towards myself, forgot to move out the way and went down like a felled tree as the door hit me in the face.

I lay on the floor, watching the ceiling go round and round. Should there be stars indoors like that?

And as if things couldn't get any worse. David's handsome face came into view as he crouched by my side. Before he even said anything, I was showered with the waft of his manly scent. It was a mixture of sandalwood and chocolate-chip cheesecake, which shouldn't go together, but on him, it smelled divine.

"Hello, Amber," he said coolly.

I pushed myself up to my elbows. "Oh hi, David. What are you doing here?"

He fished a stray lettuce leaf out of my hair, then helped me sit up. Blimey, his touch was electrifying.

"I'm here with the police," he said. "But what are *you* doing here at Paws for Tea? Apart from causing chaos." He smirked at this last comment. No wonder Judy had tried to slap him. His smug smirk made you want to punch his lights out.

"What am *I* doing here? Oh…" Okay, here was the chance to make myself sound more interesting and successful than I really was. Some nearby discarded sandwich inners caught my eye. "I'm a cheese… sculptor."

Unsurprisingly, his voice was tinged with doubt. "A cheese sculptor? Really?"

"Yes. I re-create works of art with huge blocks of cheese, and I was here getting supplies. You might've seen my *Mona Cheese-a*? Or my *Girl with the Cheese and Onion Earring*?" I paused for a beat. "I also sculpt with onions."

David gazed deeply into my eyes. Most of the time, his eyes were a dark-chocolate brown, but sometimes, like now, they flashed icy blue. "So… that article in the Daily Snoop last week was written by a different Amber Eldritch?"

Yikes, he'd been reading my articles! "Oh. Yes. That was me actually, yes."

"And you're *not* a cheese sculptor?"

"Not exactly." I put on a pretend-fanfare voice. "Surprise!"

"Are you ready to stand up?" He wrapped his arm around my back. "Oh, you're trembling."

"Am I?" I tried to sound casual. "Probably just the shock from the fall."

He hoisted me to my feet then studied me intensely, making me feel like a squashed fly. The trouble was, it seemed natural to hug and even kiss him – and I soooo wanted to. But too many things had been left unresolved and they'd been festering for a decade. You couldn't just start snogging someone after so many years of fester.

Still gripping my arm, he smirked knowingly. "It really *is* a surprise to see you, trust me."

"*Trust* you?" I laughed scornfully, pulling my arm away. "Your sense of humour's still intact, I see."

"Why's that funny? Do you have trust issues?"

Wow, it was like an entire decade had vanished into thin air. "I don't trust *you*. You once used your handsome charms to persuade me to lie to the police for you – after I'd found you crouched over a dead body."

"Shh, please!" He lowered his voice. "I obviously wasn't the killer – I'm sure you knew that straight away."

"Well, maybe not *straight* away."

"Anyway, *you* tried to use my involvement in that whole thing to get a scoop for your newspaper. But luckily for me, I saw straight through that little trick."

I threw a hand to my hip. "Yeah, you can't trick a vampire."

"Are we making this species-related now?"

"I couldn't at the time, could I? Because you conveniently forgot to tell me you were a vampire until you 'vamped-out' right in front of me."

"Saving *your* life. But…" He glanced at the counter. "Do you work here? I've read quite a few of your Daily Snoop articles over the years."

"Have you?"

David chuckled – and not in a warm and encouraging way. "Yeah, they're always very… interesting. Especially that one last week, about the dog who won the local mayoral election. What was the headline again? *Poli-tricks and the Pooch*. Did you come up with that yourself?"

Oh fudge cakes, I really wanted to wipe that smile off his face. "Yes. And that was in fact my final article for the Daily Snoop."

"They didn't fire you for it, did they?" He caught my expression. "Oh they *did*? Amber, I'm sorry…"

I gestured to the smashed plates on the floor. "It's fine. I decided I'd rather spend my life causing chaos in my aunt's cat café. Obviously I don't feel like a failure in the slightest, and Vicky's sofa's very comfortable, thank you."

He winced. "The story did sound a little far-fetched, even for that notorious tabloid."

"I had a very reliable source. Deep Stoat…"

He buried his face in his hand, trying to control his laughter. "Deep *Stoat*?"

I wanted to be angry, but I laughed too. "I guess that should've got alarm bells ringing. Anyway, I thought *you'd* gone off to join the Met Police in London?"

"Yep. I've just spent the last ten years working as a royal protection officer."

Woah, what? "You... you're a bodyguard for royalty?"

"I *was*."

On auto-pilot, I reached out and squeezed a rock-solid bicep. *"Phwoaar..."* Oh fudge cakes, did I say that out loud? I pulled my hand away and wiped my mouth in case I was drooling.

"Finished?" he asked, raising a cool eyebrow.

I started to reach back. "Well, if you're offering another squeeze..."

He laughed at my pretend perviness. Well, *he* thought it was pretend. I held up my hands then made a show of lowering them to my sides. "Sorry, it's probably not polite to grope policemen at a crime scene, is it?"

He sighed wearily. "It's better than being slapped."

Compassion filled my chest like honey. Judy's extreme response had obviously hurt David more than he was letting on. "So why aren't you working as a royal protection officer anymore?" I asked. "What happened?"

"I also got fired." He glanced over to where Alex was taking fingerprints. "I can't talk about it. Not here."

Oh dear, that didn't sound good. Whatever had happened to him, the fallout was obviously the snarly smirk that was now etched on his lips. I wanted to know everything.

But the horsey woman Lydia started arguing loudly with Alex. "It will utterly ruin my fingernails, Inspector!"

David leaned closer. "Amber, is there somewhere quieter we can go?"

Gulp! "Quieter?"

He held up his notebook. "I need to take your witness statement."

"Oh... I'll make you some tea. Let's go over to the counter."

I slipped behind the counter and grabbed a couple of cups and saucers.

David tickled Marmalade Sandwich's ears. "Hey, cute kitty, I feel like I've met you before."

Marmalade Sandwich sniffed him. "We've met – I never forget a smell."

That had presumably sounded to David like, "Mew mew mew."

"Aw, are you talking to me?" David asked.

"Yes I am indeed," Marmalade Sandwich said. "Not that anyone listens."

I noticed David had a nasty scar running from his hairline to his eyebrow. My imagination went into overdrive. "Where did you get that?"

He touched it with his long fingers. "Oh... I came off my motorbike."

The teacup in my hand rattled on its saucer. Get a grip, Amber, there's nothing remotely appealing about a motorbike-riding, handsome police officer vampire, whose big brown eyes were currently fixed very much on me.

He leaned his elbows on the counter. "Amber, can I ask you something?"

Oh cripes, he was going to ask me if I'd thought of him over the years, of the kiss we'd shared on the backseat of Harry's tour bus, of the love that might've been had he not been a vampire and had we not both been leaving Windsor to start our dream careers.

I put down the teacup. "Yes?"

He clicked the top of his biro. "Did you see any of *them* acting suspiciously when you took their order?"

I glared at him. "There was certainly a lot of tension, yes."

"Did any of them tamper with Tony's bottle of heart pills?"

"I was focusing on taking their order." *And trying to avoid discussing quantum physics with a talking cat.*

"All right. Well, if you think of anything…" He wrote down his phone number and tore off the page. "Give me a call, okay?"

I stared at his phone number. "Um, yes. And now some tea, Sergeant Van Danté…" I reached out and accidentally knocked the teacup from its saucer. We grabbed it at the same time, and David ended up grasping my hand, sending zings up my arm.

He gazed into my eyes. "It's all right. I know it's a shock. The death, I mean."

"It is…"

Alex's gruff voice broke the spell. "Sergeant, if you've got a moment?"

David threw me a toothy smile, then went off to exchange notes with his superior officer.

Marmalade Sandwich was washing again. "What a turn-up. Now, Amber, I expect you'll be wanting to read that mysterious note that was attached to your grandmother's wand, yes?"

"All right. But first, let me drink my tea. I really need it after that."

Chapter Four

I finished off my cuppa and finally felt ready to read the mysterious note that had fallen from my grandmother's wand. Turning my back on the hubbub in the café, I pulled the expensive notepaper out of my apron pocket and unfolded it like an ancient relic. The spidery handwriting had been scrawled in a hurry. It was a Windsor address.

Marmalade Sandwich stood on a box of teabags and peered over my shoulder. "I know where that is."

"What? You can't read, can you?"

"Oh-ho, very bright me. Would you like to hear my theory unifying relativity, quantum physics, and mackerel?"

"No thank you."

"Suit yourself." He sat down, licked his paw, and ran it across his ear, turning it inside-out.

I chuckled and flicked it back for him. "Stop being so cute."

"But you will go to the address on the note?" he asked.

"Perhaps later. Some stupid idiot dropped an entire tray of dirty plates on the floor. I'd better clear it up."

Sweeping the smashed crockery actually helped me relax a bit, but the tension in Paws for Tea increased as the paramedics arrived and started prodding and poking Tony's body. My nerves felt all jumbled up. I'd hoped to come back to Windsor for a *break* from stress. Everything I'd been through recently was suddenly shunting up behind me and making me feel faint.

I decided to pop outside for a breather, so I told Aunt Vicky I'd be right back, then grabbed my handbag and slipped out to the street – successfully managing not to draw attention to myself this time.

The entrance to the cat café consisted of two sets of doors, to ensure the cats didn't wander outside to the road. Hopefully Marmalade Sandwich had found his way out to the garden at the back of Paws with the other kitties. Much as I already loved him, I got the feeling he might try to convince me to go to the address on the note, and I couldn't handle any more excitement today. I just wanted to stand here and catch my breath.

Wow, had it really been ten years since I'd last stood here? Paws for Tea was located in the heart of Windsor town centre, on the corner of two streets. Across the main road was the imposing and majestic eleventh-century world-famous Castle. Across the other road was a maze of winding narrow cobblestoned streets, inviting tourists to explore the quirky shops, old buildings, and traditional pubs. Windsor was like the Mother Town of Mother England. And despite feeling like a failure for being back here, I couldn't help but take comfort in her.

As always, the streets of Windsor bustled with locals and tourists alike, but I never felt stressed here like in London. May was my favourite month, and the town looked stunning – so green and bright. A warm sunbeam soothed me. My tension slowly melted like a lolly at the seaside.

Ahh, yes. It was nice to be home.

I hoiked my handbag onto my shoulder and – Hold on… why was it heavier than usual?

My cardigan was covering the top of the bag and, as I pulled it away, I realised Marmalade Sandwich was sitting there like a hen on a roost. He smiled sheepishly, which is impressive for a cat. "So… that note."

"I can't carry you around sitting on top of my handbag like that."

"You used to when I was a kitten!"

A memory spiralled back. "What you *mean* is, you used to sneak into my handbag because you were so tiny, and by the time I found you, it was too late."

He gazed at me with his big green eyes. "Pleeeeease let me come with you."

I stroked his soft face. "I'm not going to the address on the note. I just came out for some air."

"So why did you bring your cardigan and handbag?"

Gah, blast that cat's logic. "Because… I might take a stroll to The Long Walk. The greenery helps me think."

"Then I'll come too. Look… have you got any money on you?"

"Why?"

He gestured with his nose. "Buy one of those cloth tote bags in that souvenir shop over there. I'll fit in one of those."

I glanced across the road at the charming little building that was surrounded by tourists from all over the world. The shop was adorned with Union Jack flags, and the large windows were crammed with souvenir tea towels, tea sets, and T-shirts. The merchandise took up half the pavement too, which was where the tote bags were hanging, along with matching purses and keychains.

"Look, Marmalade Sandwich, I know you're –"

"Pleeeeeease."

I kissed him on the head, stifling my laughter. He was adorable. "All right."

Soaking up the holiday atmosphere in the shop, I bought one of the overpriced cloth Union-Jack-emblazoned bags, and Marmalade Sandwich hopped inside. "Oo, yes, I like this. You might buy a snuggly blanket too, but this is fine for now."

He popped his head out the top, and I carried him on my shoulder towards The Long Walk – the lush, two-mile tree-lined avenue that connected the town to Windsor Great Park.

But before I was able to head down The Long Walk, Marmalade Sandwich spoke frantically. "Turn left here – go down that road."

I halted. "Why?"

"It's the address on the note. Go on, Amber. Pleeeeease."

As I gazed down the leafy road, the peacefulness struck me like a feather pillow. "All right, but I'm not going inside the address. We'll just have a look."

The rows of thatched cottages with their pretty gardens looked like something off a biscuit tin lid. I inhaled the beautiful surroundings, enjoying the green trees and blue sky. As I walked onwards, the narrowing street became even more rural – fronted by a lush village green and a large cricket pavilion. And beyond that, the spectacular fields rolled for as far as the eye could see.

Marmalade Sandwich's purring became erratic and excited. "Down the end there!"

I eyed up our destination. "The one all on its own?"

"That's right."

It looked like a perfectly charming cottage. What could possibly go wrong?

Oh dear…

I unlatched the dainty wooden gate and strolled down the garden path towards the thatch-roofed, crooked cottage. The red-brick building was surrounded by a well-established English country garden, with a lush green lawn, a divine-smelling lilac bush, and flower beds overflowing with wallflowers and bluebells. I halted on the stone doorstep and looked for a bell, but couldn't see one.

"Push the door," Marmalade Sandwich whispered.

Wondering why I was listening to the advice of a cat, I gently pushed the wisteria-framed oak door, and was dismayed to discover it was unlocked.

It creaked open ominously.

"Go on, Amber," Marmalade Sandwich urged. "Step over the threshold and see what's inside."

"What's *likely* to be inside?" I asked. "My destiny? The secret to all my problems?"

"Could be," the cat said. "But *I* thought we might have a rummage in the fridge to see if they've got any tuna."

I called out from the doorstep, where my feet seemed keen to stay. "Hello?"

How would I react if someone actually answered? Only one way to find out.

I stepped inside.

Chapter Five

The front door of the cottage led directly to a living room with a comfy sofa and a wooden dresser. On paper, it should've felt cosy and rustic, but this wasn't on paper, this was my life. The curtains were closed and, in this dim light, the weathered ceiling beams cast eerie shadows over the scuffed floorboards. And if that wasn't bad enough, I couldn't shake the feeling that I was being watched.

The big stone fireplace in the centre of the room also had snuggly potential, *if* there'd been a roaring fire crackling with flames. But instead, a chilly draft whooshed down the chimney, sending shivers through the room – and down my spine. Marmalade Sandwich flattened his ears against his head and lowered his face so that only his eyes were peeking out of his bag. "I'm not sure about this, Amber."

"It was your idea!" I squinted into the dimness. "Is there anybody there?"

"You sound like you're conducting a séance," the cat mewed. "We don't want to contact any dead people. Especially not if *we're* about to join them!"

I pulled him close. At least there shouldn't be too many hiding places for assailants to spring from. The cottage seemed to be a typical two-up/two-down affair – the ground floor consisting of just this living room and the adjoining kitchen. In the shadowy darkness, I could see a flight of wooden stairs leading upwards. I dreaded what might be lurking up there.

Not that I could investigate – my feet had glued themselves to the living room floorboards with fright.

It wasn't just my imagination working overtime. Even though I'd tried hard to ignore magic all my life, this was undeniably a witch's cottage. Now that my eyes were adjusting, I could see a crystal ball nestled on an ornate writing desk, as well as a handful of ivory runes, a deck of tarot cards, a spell book, and a magic mirror.

I steeled myself, unglued my feet, and picked up the spell book, blowing off the dust.

As my handbag gently trembled, I realised my granny's magic wand must be inside. Had Evelyn put it in there at the café? Or did wands have a life of their own? I really hoped it was the Evelyn option.

"Hello?" I said again.

"Ah, Amber, you came."

"Wah!" I yelped and jumped, making Marmalade Sandwich hiss.

But I knew that voice. An upper-class older lady who I'd once known rather well. Oh dear...

In the dim light, I squinted at the figure who was now flickering into existence. She was dressed in a long silk Edwardian gown, including a bustle at the back and a high lace collar. On her head she wore an impressive hat adorned with an ostrich feather.

Yes, I knew her. I hadn't seen her for years. Decades. But I knew her.

Vermilitrude Eldritch. My grandmother.

"Granny, you scared the life out of me!"

"Tactless as ever, dear." She inspected me. "Amber, why are you wearing an apron? You look like you're about to scrub the scullery."

"This is my waitressing uniform." I lowered Marmalade Sandwich's bag to the sofa and self-consciously took off my apron.

She tutted. "London life hasn't treated you well, has it? Where do you get your hair done? Billingsgate Fish Market?"

I ran my fingers through my long locks. "I don't think it looks that bad, but I've been… Hey, wait a minute, I thought you were dead?" I reached out to touch her, but my hand went straight through. "Oh…"

She raised her chin. "Yes I am. Still, life goes on."

But not for you. "I was very sorry to hear about your demise."

"Don't tell lies, of course you weren't." She took off her hat and tried to hand it to a maid. There wasn't one there, so she simply dropped it. The hat disappeared. "And anyway, being sorry won't bring me back to life, will it?"

I stepped over and pulled open the pretty curtains. Ah, that was better – now I could see the magical cottage properly. "Isn't there a spell that can bring you back to life?"

"Magic can't help me now. What I need is for someone to solve my murder. Because if my murderer isn't caught, I won't be able to re-materialise in the magical land of Marvelton. I'll be stuck haunting Windsor forever. Would you like *me* for company for eternity?"

She certainly knew how to spur me on. "And I suppose you want *me* to investigate?"

She clutched her pearl choker. "Good heavens, no! What on earth do *you* know about investigating murder?"

"I've investigated a few as a journalist."

She scoffed. "Amber, you worked for a tabloid newspaper and wrote articles with words containing fewer syllables than a game of charades! I've known teapots with a higher IQ than some of your readership. If I wanted to find a woman who could write a headline like *Farewell to Charms! Death of Senior Witch Spells Trouble*, I'd ask *you*. But when it comes to solving my murder, I'd prefer to rely on the experts."

I flopped down on the sofa. "You mean the police?"

She floated closer. "Oh good heavens no!"

"It's all right, puss, it's safe to come out now." I delved into the tote bag, but Marmalade Sandwich batted my hand away. "Ow!" I focused on the ghost of my grandmother. "Why not involve the police?"

Vermilitrude sounded offended. "Humans? Meddling in magic! Oh my goodness me, Amber. You've a lot to learn about life."

"Or *death*, in your case."

Still inside the bag, Marmalade Sandwich had gone all floppy. I carefully unwrapped him and cradled him in my arms. "It's all right, my lovely little kitty."

He cautiously looked around, sniffing the air. I'd never known him this quiet before. Vermilitrude had really affected him. Perhaps they'd met before.

"So you think your murderer was magical, Granny?" I asked, sitting back against the sofa cushion.

"I'm sure of it. And furthermore, so does the Beings of Magic Committee."

"What's that?"

"It's a committee. Made up of Beings of Magic."

She was always like this. Trying to catch me out. "Okay, and what have they discovered so far?"

She rolled her eyes. "They're still consulting their telephone-directory-sized rule book to find out what needs to be done. It may take some time. But you must stay out of it, Amber. You're not trained in magic, and I fear my killer might come after you if you start poking your nose in."

That suited me fine. "All right, I'll steer clear." On my lap, Marmalade Sandwich blinked at me. I tickled him under the chin, enticing a smile.

"I wasn't scared or anything," he protested.

"I know. You're a big brave cat."

My granny huffed and disappeared. I froze for a moment, waiting to see if she planned to return. When she didn't, I relaxed and exhaled. Now that the curtains were open, I could really appreciate the – wahh!

Vermilitrude re-appeared on the sofa cushion beside me, making *me* scream and Marmalade

Sandwich bolt to the other side of the room, where he scrabbled under the writing desk, yowling.

Vermilitrude continued mid-conversation. "But in the meantime, my dear, I do have a little job for you, which will require your journalist skills. You can start straight away."

I headed to the writing desk. "I haven't decided if I'm sticking around Windsor yet. Granny, where's your... um... body?"

She patted her tight bun. "My outer flesh was removed by my niece, Joanforth Eldritch. She cast it back to Marvelton, and I'm keen to re-join it."

"I see." I peered under the ornate desk. A pink nose and two green eyes looked out at me.

I held out my hand for Marmalade Sandwich to sniff, as my granny continued to talk. "I've left you this cottage in my will. *And* a substantial amount of money – which you can inherit once my murder has been solved."

I swivelled to face her. "That's very generous, thank you."

She shrugged. "Yes well, all my *other* relations have successfully managed to make their *own* wealth."

I ignored this jibe. "Murder seems endemic at the moment. There was a murder at the cat café just now. A man called Tony Royal – the owner of The Royal Boutique B&B."

"Oh how dreadful, my dear. I hope you're not too upset."

"Well–"

"Because I need you clear-minded and focused on the mission I'm about to set you."

Keeping low, Marmalade Sandwich poked his face out cautiously. I stroked him on the head. "It's all right, puss... Granny, this is rather a lot for me to take in."

"A lot for you to take in? How do you think *I* feel?"

My journalist's mind took over. "Look, I won't rush off and start investigating, I promise. But what happened?"

She held her fingers to her forehead like a swooning gentlewoman – which she most certainly wasn't. "Yesterday afternoon, I was hit over the head with a wuthering windchime."

"You were killed by a... windchime?"

"Not just any old windchime. A *wuthering* windchime."

I knew I'd regret asking, but... "What's a wuthering windchime?"

She spoke theatrically. "It's a rare magical crystal that – when combined with a secret spell – can create a chime *so* lethal, it can kill from ten paces!"

I winced. "I guess the secret spell's *not* so secret now, if your killer has it?"

"Precisely. There's layer upon layer of magic involved in my murder – so I don't want you or any humans involved. It's dangerous."

"But you can't think of who might've *done* it?"

"I cannot. They must've come up behind me when I was working at my writing desk yesterday. I heard the chilling chime, then... woke up dead."

I shuddered at the thought. Poor granny. "That's awful."

"Yes. What a time! My murder, this Tony's murder, and one dog theft – whatever next?"

My ears pricked up. "Dog theft?"

"My corgi, Colin. He didn't come home yesterday. Amber, this is the mission that you must accept. You must find him. I'm terribly worried for his safety."

I stepped back over to the sofa and rummaged in my handbag for my reporter's notebook. Lost dog? This was local paper stuff. I could do this in my sleep. "When did you last see him? Is he microchipped?"

Vermilitrude fiddled with a brooch on her lapel. "Yes, he's microchipped – the local dog walker sorted all that technical wizardry out for me. In fact, *he* was the person to last see Colin. The dog walker, Billy Royal. He collected Colin yesterday afternoon for his walk. Find Billy and you might find Colin."

I paused, pen over pad. "That's a coincidence. His father's just been murdered at Paws."

"Billy's father is the dead Tony?"

"Yep. And the police want to talk to Billy. What time did Billy pick up Colin?"

She drifted closer to me. "The same time as always. He always comes at eleven in the morning to walk Colin for an hour. Then he comes again at four in the afternoon."

I wrote this down. "So you last saw both Billy and Colin at four yesterday afternoon?"

"That's correct. Billy collected Colin at four. I sat down to continue work on an important project, then about half an hour later, I was hit with the wuthering windchime. Next thing I knew, I was dead! I used every ounce of my lingering psychic energy to summon my niece, Joanforth, who... *ahem*... tidied me away to Marvelton. I told her we needed you here, so she used my crystal ball and discovered you'd just arrived in Windsor and were staying with your Aunt Vicky. Fate herself must've intervened!"

I chewed the end of my pen. "Perhaps Fate might've been a bit more forceful and stopped you from being murdered?"

"Shh! Don't question Fate. She gets insulted when criticised."

"And Colin?"

"He never returned, poor little pup. Joanforth went over to Billy's house, but she said there was no answer. I do hope Colin's all right."

"Yes. And Billy too."

She glanced at her fingernails. "Well, I suppose so."

My energy rose. This was like being a reporter again. "So, to summarise: Billy collected Colin for his usual walk at four yesterday afternoon. Half an hour later, you were murdered. And neither Billy nor Colin have been seen since."

"Precisely."

"And today, Billy's father, Tony Royal, died at Paws for Tea. Surely that can't be a coincidence."

She drifted away. "I'm glad I can rely on you to find Colin, Amber. You can move in here – use it as your base. The place is all yours."

"I'm perfectly happy sleeping on Vicky's sofa." I glanced around the beautiful cottage. "You don't haunt here, do you?"

"I have limited psychic energy, which gets used up every time I appear in my ghostly form. When it runs out, I'll disappear. Then, when I've replenished it again, I can come back. It's like clockwork. I can move around Windsor, but not leave the town. Like I said, I eventually want to re-materialise in Marvelton."

"Marvelton. Yes, there's a name I haven't heard in years."

It was a faraway land where my mother had taken me as a child, full of magical beings. That made me think of something else. "Granny, why isn't my mother a ghost, but you are? And my father?"

Her face hardened. "Some people come back as a ghost. Some don't."

My mind alighted on the other dead body I'd seen today. "Oh wait, if ghosts exist, is it possible for us to talk to the ghost of *Tony*?"

She considered this. "I'll search around and see if he's contactable. But if he's not a Being of Magic, then it's unlikely."

"That's a shame."

Her ghostly form faded slightly, so I dropped my notebook into my bag and stretched, starting to feel strangely peaceful. Now that the sun was shining through the windows, I took in the quaint surroundings. On the other side of the living room, Marmalade Sandwich had emerged from his hiding place and was flopped in a sunbeam, having a wash.

But, cute cat and dead grandmother aside, it was a lovely warm room. To one side of the stairs, a glass cabinet full of antique ornaments stood grandly, and a clockwork sewing machine on a rickety table stood next to that. I'd always loved making my own clothes, and after a decade of 'fast-fashion' I had a sudden urge to sew. Perhaps I'd try making something next time I came here.

My granny materialised next to the beautiful old writing desk. "Amber, come here and pick up my magic mirror."

The ipad-sized ornate mirror was heavier than I'd expected, and I almost dropped it as – in the reflection – my long red hair arranged itself into a 'just stepped out of the salon' style.

Oh wow, perhaps magic did have benefits after all. I couldn't stop running my fingers through my luscious locks.

Vermilitrude spoke primly. "And upstairs you'll find a magic wardrobe."

I put down the mirror. "A magic wardrobe? It doesn't lead to a magical land, does it?"

"It gives you your dream outfit. It was given to me by the Royal Wizard of Marvelton. You can go up and try it, if you like." She looked me up and down. "You certainly couldn't do any worse."

Ignoring my grandmother's criticism, my gaze swept across the cluttered writing desk, landing upon a mesmerising find – a silver pendant in the shape of a cat, adorned with delicate amber stripes.

I held the cat pendant aloft in my trembling fingers. "Where did this come from?"

"Oh I don't know, dear, there's lots of junk I've accrued over the years. You can have it if you want it."

I would have it, because it was already mine. My childhood best friend Harry had given me this pendant as a gift for my twelfth birthday. He'd saved all his pocket money and gone to a magic market in Marvelton to buy it. I'd never known it to be magical exactly, but wearing it had always made me feel safe and secure. And the cat's amber stripes had always glistened in the light, as if they were moving.

Since I'd made the firm decision to turn my back on magic after it'd taken my parents from me, this had been the only magical item I'd tolerated. Then, when I'd left for London all those years ago, I'd somehow been parted from the pendant. I had no idea how it had turned up here. But I was delighted to be reunited with it.

I kissed the little stripey cat, then fastened the silver chain around my neck in front of the large mirror by the front door. The cat pendant seemed to smile – as pleased at the reunion as I was.

Vermilitrude appeared in the reflection behind me. "Amber, I've been thinking, I'm worried my killer might be lurking – and they *might* have their eye on you. I want you to train in magic – just a few spells for your own protection."

I gazed at myself in the mirror. "I'd really prefer not to."

"As I've said before, if you don't learn to control your magic, then—"

"My magic will control me."

"Precisely. So it's decided. You'll train."

I turned to face her. "Wait a minute, I think I missed that discussion."

She swept her hand theatrically through the air. "No discussion necessary. You're now a novice witch. And for that you'll need a tutor."

"I'd always assumed you'd teach me." That was one of the many things that had stopped me from training…

"I'm dead, Amber. I'm sure I did explain about my limited psychic energy?"

"I know." I grabbed my granny's wand from my handbag. *My* wand. "Look, I'm not making any promises. But how about my cousin Evelyn?"

Vermilitrude sounded impatient. "She's only a novice. You need someone who's studied all the theory."

Only half-listening, I sat at the clockwork sewing machine and found a scrap of lace. "Like who?"

"A senior-witch or even a vampire would do."

I paused from feeding the lace under the sewing machine's needle. "A vampire?"

"Yes. All young vampires study their M-Levels in Theoretical Magic. What are you doing with that lace?"

I ignored her question. "But vampires and witches don't get on. Everyone knows that."

As I guided the fabric under the sewing machine's jabbing needle, I thought about a tale I'd almost forgotten – or tried to. Long ago, in the olden days of magical history, witches had worked well with vampires. Vampires possessed no magic of their own, or at least, it was very limited. But they were skilled at creating spells, so the witches had used their abundant magic to enact the vampires' spells.

But when the witches had realised they could create their *own* spells, the vampires had grown resentful and attacked the witches! The result had been a magical battle that had almost destroyed all sorcery. Peace treaties had been drawn up, but the two species were always wary of each other, even after so many centuries.

And anyway… "Vampires killed my parents," I said quietly.

Vermilitrude's voice was almost tender. "I believe it's time to forgive and forget, don't you agree, Amber?"

I pressed the pedal of the sewing machine with my foot, feeding the lace under the needle. "But what magic can vampires do? I thought they just went around biting necks and sucking blood."

"They can fly."

"As a bat?"

"Or as a raven. Or just as themselves."

"What about mind control?"

She let out a strained laugh. "That's a myth."

Marmalade Sandwich leapt on the table and mewed frantically. "I know who can tutor you, Amber!"

"What's he saying?" Vermilitrude demanded.

"Um, something about quantum cream, I think."

Marmalade Sandwich leapt up and down excitedly. "No, not cre... well, if you have any? But, listen, Amber, I know the perfect vampire to tutor you." He turned to Vermilitrude and gave a big meow, then suddenly jumped into my arms and started to nibble my neck, making me squirm with laughter.

"Tell me what he's saying!" Vermilitrude commanded.

Determined to be understood, the cat jumped back onto the sofa, then hissed, baring his fangs.

"Do *you* know a vampire who might tutor Amber, little cat?" Vermilitrude asked.

"Little?" I muttered.

Marmalade Sandwich nodded. He held one paw against the opposite leg, exposing two claws.

Vermilitrude squinted at the cat. "First word, two syllables? Right... first syllable...?"

With the flamboyancy of a seasoned actor, the cat gestured outside.

"Garden?" Vermilitrude guessed. "Er... window?"

The cat mimed waking up, stretching, and yawning.

Vermilitrude frowned. "Day? First syllable is day? Right, second syllable?"

The cat mimed turning the handle of a film camera.

"Cinema? No... television?"

"Video," I said flatly.

Marmalade Sandwich touched his nose with his paw, indicating this was correct. He drew his front paws together to indicate 'shorter'.

"Day... vid?" Vermilitrude said pensively.

Marmalade Sandwich sat back on his fluffy bottom, stuck his paws in front of him, and mimed driving, while purring loudly for the engine noises.

Vermilitrude didn't hide her confusion. "David Car?"

I couldn't take it anymore. "Oh for goodness cake, he means David Van Danté!"

"Oh I was rather enjoying that." Vermilitrude tried to tickle the cat, but her hand went straight through him. "Now, Amber, who is this David Van Danté to whom your cat is referring?"

"He's a vampire I knew ten years ago – just before I left for London."

She clapped her hands with joy. "Oh him! Yes, your aunt told me about him."

"You've been discussing me with Vicky?"

"We've met on a few occasions in Marvelton. I needed to ensure you were well, my dear. And yes, your cat is quite correct to suggest this vampire. Did he ever become a police officer?"

"He did. And he's back in Windsor."

"Well then, it's settled. Splendid." She inspected the circle of material in my hand. "What've you made there?"

I slid the lacy armband around my bicep, then slipped my wand underneath. It was the perfect fit. "I suppose it's a symbol of the magic flowing through my veins."

She smiled approvingly. "Very good, Amber. Off you go then."

I gathered up my cute kitty and left, *almost* feeling ready to embrace my inner-witch, but still not quite. And I certainly *wasn't* ready to ask David Van blooming Danté for any favours. His smirk would engulf his entire *face* if he knew I wanted his help. No, what I needed right now was a chat with an angel to help me get my thoughts in order. And luckily, I knew precisely where to find him.

Chapter Six

As I headed back to Paws for Tea, my thoughts zoomed like electric eels in a tank. My grandmother was a ghost. She'd been murdered! She wanted me to find her missing corgi. To train in magic. To ask David to train me... No way.

But what about Tony's murder? I wondered what the police were focusing on right now. Would they be trying to figure how Tony's pills had been tampered with? Whether chilli could really be fatal?

Oh fudge cakes, I'd forgotten to tell David about Tony's last words. *Fine lettuce*. What did *that* mean?

I needed to talk everything over with a trusted friend, and here he was. My heart surged with joy at the sight of Harry outside Paws for Tea, back from his latest tour and polishing the front of his bus. My childhood bestie was an angel, and he always wore his feathery wings out proudly for any Being of Magic to see. He had an angelic face and golden curls, but an impish manner. His deep blue eyes always contained a spark of mischief. But also he knew when to be serious. Such as now.

He wrapped me in his arms *and* wings for a big hug. "Are you all right, Bambi? Oh... you've got a cat in a bag. Who's this?"

I introduced him to Marmalade Sandwich, who licked his hand with his sandpaper tongue, mewed a bit, then pounced onto his shoulder – chasing after Harry's long white wing feathers.

Harry laughed and flapped his wings to make the cat jump around with glee. It warmed my heart to see them playing together.

After my parents had died, my granny had become my legal guardian and – because I'd been keen to turn my back on magic – she'd packed me off to an expensive boarding school for girls. Harry had been the only boy there, because his parents were art teachers.

We'd been through a lot together, both feeling different to the other girls – not least because we were Beings of Magic, and *my* magic kept going off beyond my control whenever I got emotional. For example, my untamed magic would make me fade to almost invisible whenever I felt I wasn't being *seen* by the other girls – making me feel even more insecure and freakish. Not good for a lonely teenager.

Over the years, I'd managed to get a grip on my wayward magic by tensing up and stuffing it down to my knees. Unhealthy, yes, but I hadn't known how else to control it. Other than training as a witch, of course.

My grandmother was right really. Magic was always there bubbling under the surface and, if I didn't learn how to control it, it would consume me.

Anyway, Harry was proud to be a Being of Magic. He was a snazzy dresser too. Today he was wearing a gold leopard-print suit with a red velvet shirt. I was so proud of what he'd achieved in the last decade. Being the skilled artist that he was, he'd designed the branding of his tour company himself. Purple with gold writing, emblazoning the words *Magical*

Mystery Tours of Royal Windsor down the side of the bus. He'd purposely chosen an old 1950s London Transport bus to fit in with Windsor's nostalgic vibe.

And it was a bus with a big personality. It's fairly common, isn't it, for people to joke that their car has a mind of its own, but they usually mean it metaphorically. Harry's bus, Bert the Bus, really did have a mind of his own. He even looked like he had a face. His two big front windows looked like giant eyes, and he always had a spark of life behind his headlights. His front radiator grille smiled wryly as I rubbed his warm metal.

"Hi Bert," I said.

One headlight shone bright for a moment.

"Harry, your bus just winked at me."

Harry was still playing with Marmalade Sandwich. "Bert, stop flirting."

It had all started when, to save money on paying a driver, Harry had bought a Tour Bus Driving Spell from a wizard in Marvelton – meaning the magic could drive the bus while *he* gave guided tours over the microphone.

But the spell had slowly unravelled and, over the last ten years, the bus had developed a cheeky personality – as well as a thorough working knowledge of Windsor. Harry's Being of Magic passengers always enjoyed Bert's eager interjections, and even locals would climb aboard to hear what Bert had to say about the obscure history of the town and its citizens. Unfortunately, the human passengers had no idea about any of that. If humans found out about magic, apparently it made their brains go a bit funny.

I wondered what my excuse was…

With Marmalade Sandwich perched on his shoulder, Harry noticed the pendant round my neck. "Hey, you found it."

I rubbed it affectionately. "Yeah. Did you hide it for me?"

He grinned. "I didn't, I promise."

I studied his face. He had an endearing (read: annoying) tendency to play 'hilarious' pranks on people, then deny all knowledge. But this time, I sensed he was telling the truth.

And anyway, he didn't know about my grandmother's cottage, did he? Or her murder. I was about to fill him in, when Aunt Vicky came out of Paws, carrying a mug of tea. "Amber, I thought you were just popping out for some air?"

Uh-oh, I didn't like the severe tone in her voice. "Have the police finished in the café now?"

Vicky handed Harry the tea, then tickled Marmalade Sandwich on his shoulder. "Aw, hello puss, what are you doing out here?"

"Apparently he's my familiar," I explained.

"Oh right." Vicky accepted this unquestioningly – she was fully entrenched in the magical community. "No," she continued. "The police are still in there testing everything. Inspector Taylor is insisting we close for the next few hours."

I clutched my cat pendant. "But has everyone been let out? Am I in trouble for sneaking off?"

Harry leaned against Bert. "Perhaps Sergeant Van Danté can put in a good word for you, Bambi. Wasn't it nice to see *him* again?"

I ignored Harry and spoke to Vicky. "Where's Evelyn?"

"She's gone for a visit to the Castle. Oh, and Inspector Taylor said our Merrie May Ball can still go ahead tomorrow night."

"No reason why not," Harry said. "We've worked hard for it."

A group of tourists strolled past in the sunshine, heading for the Castle across the road. Harry handed them a leaflet. "Roll up, roll up, for the best bus tour in town!"

Vicky glanced at the cat café and sighed. "I knew something bad was going to happen when I woke up with a headache. I should never ignore my headaches. And later, I've got that tall dark handsome stranger coming – or so my crystal ball said. Hey, wait a minute… what if that tall dark handsome stranger was a prediction about Sergeant Van Danté, Amber? I saw you two chatting."

Why did all roads lead to David Van Danté today? A quick subject-change was required. "Um, I've got something to tell you both. It's my grandmother… she's been murdered."

They stared at me, wide-eyed and open mouthed, like a couple of hooked guppies.

Marmalade Sandwich mewed on Harry's shoulder. "Gentle as a brick through a window, Amber."

Harry's brow furrowed with confusion. "*Tony* from The Royal Boutique B&B was your grandmother?"

"No, Harry. *Evelyn* told me about my granny's murder just before Tony died. There was an address attached to her magic wand, so I went there."

Marmalade Sandwich jumped into my arms. "That was my idea."

I hugged him. "Yes. And the address turned out to be Vermilitrude's cottage. She's haunting it. And she's given me the task of finding her corgi. Also... she's very generously left the cottage to me."

Vicky squealed with excitement. "Oh Amber, that's wonderful news. Of course, I'm sorry to hear about Vermilitrude – she was almost like family to me."

My dad was Vicky's brother, and Vermilitrude was my mum's mother, so they weren't 'officially' related. But I could imagine my granny getting involved in everyone's business, whether they were her relatives or not. Whether they *wanted* her to or not.

Vicky was still speaking. "...but I know she'll be okay in Marvelton when she finally gets back there. But your very own place in Windsor – how fab. I thought you'd be sleeping on my sofa for ages!"

"Oh... I don't know if I'm ready to move in there yet, Vicky."

"Nonsense. I love having you, but you can't be comfortable squashed into my living room. This is a sign for you to spread your wings."

She gestured to Harry's out-stretched wings, and chuckled.

Harry started asking me questions, but we were interrupted as Judy Royal came marching towards us, still dressed in her tight pink suit, followed by a journalist and photographer.

Marmalade Sandwich scrabbled into his tote bag. "It's all right, puss. They won't hurt you."

The journalist was brandishing his notepad and scowling in that hungry wolf way I'd come to know well. He was only local news, but he looked like a man in need of a juicy story. "Mrs Royal, can you tell my readers what happened at lunch today? Was your husband murdered? Did this café poison him?"

Judy shielded her face with her hand. "Leave me alone!"

I darted forward and grabbed her arm. "Come with us. Harry, let's go!"

"Yes," Harry shouted. "Fire up your engine, Bert!"

Clearly annoyed at the comment about the café poisoning Tony, Vicky stepped into the journalist's path. "*I* can give you a quote. Or how about a nice cup of tea – if you dare!"

Judy, Harry, and I rushed towards Bert's back entrance, which – like all models from its era – was permanently open. Bert revved his engine and, with a squeal of tyres, sped off...

...leaving us on the pavement. That was the trouble with half-sentient magical buses.

Harry wolf-whistled and Bert slammed on his brakes, stopping in the middle of the road to a cacophony of beeping.

Harry, Judy, and I ran onboard, out of breath, but safe.

Sensing that he now had passengers, Bert launched into his tour spiel. Harry had told me he always went through an auto-sequence that he couldn't turn off. "Congratulations on choosing the Enhanced Bus Tour Spell. Please read the user manual carefully to guarantee years of fun bus touring. I have hundreds of functions to assist you in all your bus-touring needs. Please set the clock on the dashboard and I will set an alarm to remind you of your first tour."

Harry stroked Bert's soft upholstery. "No tour, thank you, Bert. Just drive."

"Please set the timer on the dashboard and I will…"

Harry grabbed a spanner and tapped a vertical handrail in a threatening way. Bert went quiet for a moment. Then he started humming. "Hum, hum, hummm. Hum, hum…"

I ushered Judy into a seat and smiled sympathetically at Harry. Apparently Bert spoke twelve languages and sometimes made random announcements in Swahili.

Thankfully Judy was oblivious. Poor woman had already suffered enough.

I rested my hand on her shoulder. "Are you okay?"

She pulled a hanky from her handbag and blew her nose noisily. "Thank you for helping me."

"I hope everyone will enjoy today's tour of Windsor!" Bert announced.

Harry spoke through a fixed grin. "Just drive around. Please."

"But I tour therefore I am!"

I ignored the bickering between bus and angel, and focused on Judy. "I really am sorry about Tony. You must be devastated."

Her voice juddered. "The last thing I needed was those vultures circling. If there's one thing I detest, it's journalists. They're like animals, the way they swarm then pounce."

I shifted in my seat. "We're... they're not all bad."

She narrowed her eyes. "You're not one, are you?"

"I... I'm a waitress in a cat café, ahahaha." But if I *had* been investigating her story, my next question would be... "But, um, how come you went back to Paws for Tea?" *To the scene of the crime...*

Marmalade Sandwich popped his head out of his bag and mewed at Judy. "Amber, I think she did it! I can smell her guilt."

Judy tickled his ears. "Aw, what a sweet cat. Tony knows I love cats. That's probably why he gathered us all at the cat café. Oh blimey, can this really be happening?"

Mental note: she just totally avoided my question.

Harry sat opposite us. "Such a dreadful thing to happen to your husband."

"Yes. And that policeman was so rude to me. I'm sure he thinks I had something to do with it."

Bert sped round a corner, so I gripped the armrest. "Really? Why would one of the best homicide detectives in the country think that?"

She glared at me. "I don't know." She glanced out the window, then did a startled double-take. "Wh...what...?"

Oh no... Bert was taking off! My heart thrashed with fear as the street fell away and became bright blue sky.

"If you look to your left," Bert said jovially. "You'll see–"

Judy sounded terrified. "Is this bus flying?"

I let out a shrill laugh. "Your grief is making you hallucinate!" I hissed at Harry. "I thought humans couldn't see magic."

Harry whispered sharply. "No, but they can see if they're in a flying bus!' He spoke through a maniacal grin. "Can we have all four wheels on the ground, Bert?"

"Oh all right..." The bus landed with a bump, jolting us in our seats. "I can do wheelies. Let me show you!"

"No!" Harry and I both shouted.

Bert grumbled. "Here I am, an almost sentient magical bus, and they just want me to drive around."

"Behave," Harry said. "Or I won't pump up your tyres later." He slung an arm casually over the back of his seat. "So, Judy, do the police know *how* Tony died yet?"

Judy wove her hanky through her fingers. "I suppose they're finding out. But it must've been his heart. He had a bad heart. That's why he always took his pills – three times a day, just before meals."

So if someone had wanted to kill him, they might've added a little extra something to those pills? But Inspector Taylor had smelt *chilli*.

I twirled my hair around my fingers, hoping to seem innocent. "Did Tony have a chilli allergy? Is that what might've killed him?"

"No. He enjoyed a curry as much as the rest of us – no problems."

It was a mystery for sure. But it wasn't for me to figure out. I'd been tasked with finding Colin the corgi. Allowing myself to enjoy the journey, I watched Windsor rumble by outside – glad to be back on solid ground. Bert drew up at a set of traffic lights and I gazed at a row of pretty Georgian townhouses. "Have you lived in Windsor long?" I asked Judy. "You and Tony?"

She smiled tenderly. "We both grew up here, but we only met ten years ago. He's always had this burning ambition to open a B&B, so I helped him make his dreams come true."

"Financially?" Harry asked,

"Yes. But emotionally too. And it's been my pleasure. He's the love of my life." Her smile faded and she snuffled into her hanky.

Okay, she did seem genuinely upset about Tony's death, but as a journalist I'd met plenty of people who were skilled in the art of deception – most of my colleagues at the Daily Snoop, for example.

Marmalade Sandwich propped his paws on my chest, mewing in my face. "Amber, I'm bored. Play with me. Pleeeeeease?"

How could I resist that cute little face? I rummaged in my handbag, scrunched up a piece of paper from my notepad, and threw it down the bus. Marmalade Sandwich leapt off my lap and ran after it in a frenzy, batting it under the seats.

Judy chuckled through her tears. "He's ever-so sweet. Tony would've loved him."

I set my expression to sympathetic. "How did you two meet?"

"Tony was a busker by the railway arches." She chuckled at the memory. "He always played his saxophone there, and we got chatting as I went back and forth to the car park. There was one time when I didn't have enough change for the parking machine, so he lent me the money from his busking cap."

Harry spoke encouragingly. "So you fell in love, bought the house, and converted it to a B&B? It sounds like you were happy together."

"When I met Tony, the bailiffs were knocking on his door and social services were sniffing around Billy, who was only twelve. Billy's mum had left the year before, you see. I moved in and – without wanting to brag – I turned them both around. I paid for Billy to go to a good college in Hurley."

"How generous," I said. "Billy must've been grateful."

Judy declined to answer. Her silence spoke volumes. He wasn't grateful in the slightest.

Marmalade Sandwich batted his ball up the bus aisle, gleefully chasing it. I threw it again, and he ran off, puppy-like. That reminded me... "Judy, have you seen Billy with a corgi recently?"

"I've seen him with lots of dogs over the years. He's a dog walker."

"Yes, that's what my granny said."

She frowned. "Your granny?"

"She's lost her corgi." She'd also lost her life, but best not to mention that.

Judy's eyes were full of compassion. "I am sorry to hear that. But I haven't seen Billy for a day or two. We were waiting for him to arrive at the café just before Tony... died."

After a respectful silence, Harry probed for more details. "And you and Tony lived at The Royal Boutique B&B together?"

"Yes, in the beautiful attic." Her voice was tinged with pride. "My art gallery is in the dining room. That was Tony's idea. Immerse the guests in lovely art as they eat their breakfast – what a treat! Tony makes a great full English. He's quite famed for it."

Harry threw the paper ball for Marmalade Sandwich, who scuttled after it. "And you're an art dealer?"

A smile danced on her lips. "I am. Tony's always let me get on with my career."

And where did the arty guy who'd turned up uninvited fit in? "And Vincent is your in-house artist at the moment?"

"It's an honour for me to represent him and showcase his talents. I'm so impressed."

"What sort of paintings does he do?" Harry asked, wings flapping eagerly.

"They're lovely local landscapes inspired by Constable. All greenery and merrie old England times, you know?"

"They sound amazing," Harry said. "I'm a massive art-lover, especially of landscapes of the English countryside. I'd love to see them."

Judy's face lit up at his enthusiasm. "You're welcome to pop in anytime. I owe you one for rescuing me from that awful journalist."

Bert spoke cheerily… in what sounded like Mandarin. I had no idea what he was saying, but he pulled himself up outside Paws and turned off his engine. The journalist and photographer had gone, so we said goodbye to Judy.

I watched her entering Paws for Tea, still wondering why she'd gone back there. Did she have a motive for killing her husband? If she did, I hadn't discovered it. Perhaps Harry and I could visit her art gallery later. Have a little look around. At the paintings, of course…

But for now, I had a cottage to move into.

Chapter Seven

We followed Judy into Paws for Tea, but she was nowhere to be seen. Perhaps Inspector Taylor had taken her down to the kitchen to chat. I didn't get the chance to look around though, because the place was crawling with uniformed officers, dusting for fingerprints and testing for poison.

I explained to a scowling constable that I was here to pick up my belongings, and he granted me access to Vicky's flat above the café. The truth was, I'd barely unpacked, and I only had one suitcase anyway, so I was in and out in a matter of minutes. Harry and Marmalade Sandwich came with me to the local supermarket for some essentials, and then we walked to my new home.

I stepped into my granny's – into *my* cottage and put down my suitcase in the hallway, waiting to be heckled, criticised, or bossed around. But the place was empty. My ghostly grandmother must've run out of psychic energy. Phew!

Now that her eerie presence had gone, I saw that the walls were painted with soft pinks, and the warm sunlight streamed in through the windows, casting a gentle glow over the space. Perhaps I could be happy here. It was admittedly better than Vicky's sofa – grateful as I was for her kind hospitality.

And it was extremely nice of my granny to leave me this place. She'd always been kind, despite being stern and critical – I realised that now.

Marmalade Sandwich wriggled out of his bag and trotted off for a sniff around.

Harry carried my shopping through to the kitchen. "Come on then, make yourself at home…"

I'd already seen the living room, and Harry was currently in the kitchen, filling up my fridge. So I decided to find out what upstairs was like. At the top of the creaky wooden staircase I found a surprisingly modern bathroom and, across the small landing, a big bedroom containing a four-poster bed, a writing desk, and an amazing view over Windsor's rolling green fields.

The bed looked invitingly comfy – covered with squashy pillows and snuggly blankets – and I realised that Joanforth must've changed the bedding when she'd been here dealing with Vermilitrude's outer flesh. I sat down tentatively on the bed and gazed at a bookcase against the wall. It held leatherbound spell books and a few well-thumbed novels. Jilly Cooper and Jackie Collins. Granny, you dark horse!

Marmalade Sandwich trotted into the room and leapt onto the bed. "Oh yes, very nice. I can see it now, you and me, snuggling up of an evening… me purring, you tickling me behind the ears."

I held him close for a cuddle. "That sounds nice."

There was a soft knock on the door. "Settling in okay, Bambi?"

"You don't have to knock, Harry."

As he sat down with me, a spring went *boing*, making us both laugh. He was like a sunbeam on a rainy day. He held my hand. "Tell me…"

Blimey… and Aunt Vicky was supposed to be the psychic. But somehow he always knew when I needed to talk.

I let out a light laugh. "It's been an interesting day. An interesting week!"

Harry gently combed his fingers through my fringe. "Yes, but would you really want *boring*?"

I winced. "Maybe just for a short while."

"I'm here for you, Bambi. Whatever you need, just ask."

"Oh Harry…" I hugged him tight, realising too late that Marmalade Sandwich was now being gently squashed between us. "Mew-eew!"

"Sorry, puss." I pulled away and squeezed Harry's hand. "You've always been here for me. Even when I've been working myself into the ground over the last decade, you've been at the end of the phone. I don't think a day's gone by when we haven't spoken. Not since the day I met you."

His wings fluttered gently. "I don't know what I'd do without you, Bambi." He grinned playfully. "Who else could make me laugh so much that my tea comes out my nose?"

I chuckled at the memory. That had happened to us both more than once. "But two murders, one failed career, one missing dog… and…"

"And one heartbreakingly handsome vampire policeman? Did you like seeing David Van Danté again?"

I felt myself glow a little. "No."

"Rubbish, of course you did."

Feeling like a teenager at a sleepover, I hugged a squishy pillow close. "I'm not interested in David Van Danté. I've got far too much to untangle at the moment. The last thing my heart needs is the man who convinced me to lie to the police. Look at the trouble *that* got me in."

He raised a playful eyebrow. "If my memory serves me well, you kissed him on the backseat of my bus."

"Well... he's a good-looking chap – you can't blame me for that. But he's a vampire and everyone knows witches and vampires don't get on."

"Who says?"

"Everyone. It's common knowledge."

Harry's eyes sparkled with mischief. "I think you should ask him out on a date."

"No! That ship's sailed. He's probably married."

"He's not."

My heart skittered. "How do you know that?"

"I asked him."

I spluttered with disbelief. "You did *what*?"

Harry became animated. "Yeah, after I got back to Paws earlier, I sidled up to him when he was dusting for fingerprints. I said, *Hi David, remember me*? He seemed really pleased to see me and shook my hand heartily. That bloke's got a *very* manly handshake."

I sat up primly. "I don't care."

"So, you're not interested in what we spoke about?"

"Certainly not. What did you speak about?"

He leaned forward excitedly. "I said to him, did you like seeing Amber again? He was like, it was a surprise."

"Oh great, so I'm a surprise. Like... an unwanted tax bill."

"No. He said it *was* a surprise, but it was a shame it was under those circumstances. And then he said, when he'd heard that the murder had taken place at Paws, *you* were the first thing he thought of. But he assumed you were a big London journalist, living your dream."

I traced my fingers over the pattern on the duvet. "I was until a few days ago."

"That's what *I* said. And then he said, and listen to this, Bambi, he said, *Is she... how is she?* And it's so blinking obvious that he was about to say *Is she married*."

I stifled my grin. "Not necessarily."

"So *I* said, she's fine – apart from being fired, dumped by her boyfriend, and moving back to her hometown to sleep on her aunt's sofa."

"Thanks for painting such a great picture of my life."

He waved this away. "And then I said, how about *you*, are you married? And he said..."

In my attempt not to lean forward in anticipation, I leaned too far back and fell off the bed. "Wah!"

Marmalade Sandwich peered over the edge. "You made me jump."

I crawled back onto the squashy duvet. "I'm fine, carry on..."

Harry was enjoying this tense moment of gossip. "And David said.... *no*. But his parents want him to get married – apparently they're quite traditional vampires. So, I don't see why it shouldn't be *you* who nabs herself a handsome groom."

I stroked Marmalade Sandwich vigorously, making him purr double-time. "What an imagination you have."

Harry shrugged coolly. "You know *my* view – I'm still convinced he's the man of your dreams."

My heart throbbed with tender pain. "I don't have that dream anymore. You know that."

"Well anyway, I've arranged for you two to go on a date tomorrow night – a romantic meal in a swish restaurant."

My blood froze with terror. "You haven't, have you!"

"Nah, not really. But you'd like to, wouldn't you?"

Oh fudge cakes, yeah! "Harry, I'm not a teenager at a sleepover. I'm a thirty-two-year-old woman."

An impish grin swept across his face. "Does that mean you're too old for a pillow fight?"

Before I could answer, he reached for a pillow and, in one swift motion, thwacked me on the side of my body, making feathers explode into the air – and knocking my David-induced tension away. "Wahh!"

I was still hugging my pillow so I automatically thwacked him back – catching him on the wing and causing a few of his own feathers to waft. I screeched with happiness, as we whirled the pillows at each other, and even Marmalade Sandwich joined in, mewing with joy and standing on his back legs to swat the pillows, springing around like a lamb.

Harry retreated to a corner of the bed, holding up his pillow like Peter Pan fighting Captain Hook. "Do you relent?"

"Never!"

"Right!"

I braced myself for the impact, but to my surprise, Harry threw the pillow aside and leapt on top of me, tickling me in the ribs and making me squirm with giggles. Begging him to stop, I tried to tickle him back, but he'd pinned my arms. So instead I dug my elbows into the slippery duvet and crawled out like a soldier on army manoeuvres – desperately gesturing for 'time-out' but unable to speak for laughter.

Harry laughed too, but a wave of intense emotion overwhelmed me and I suddenly burst into tears. "Oh *no…*"

"Bambi!" Harry pulled me close for a full-body hug.

I sobbed on his shoulder. "Sorry, sorry… I don't know why I'm crying."

Harry spoke kindly into my ear. "Hey, if this was a film, *I'd* be David and that would've been really flirty. It definitely would've resulted in a snog!"

I chuckled and sniffled, feeling better for the cry – and his wonderful kindness. "Hey, come on, help me tidy up these feathers. Then I guess I'd better unpack."

He kissed me hard on the forehead and we set about picking up the feathers together. They'd wafted quite far, and I found myself in front of a sturdy wooden wardrobe. "Harry, this must be the magic wardrobe that Granny was talking about."

Harry joined me. "What does it do?"

I ran my fingers over the varnished mahogany door. "She said it gives you your dream outfit."

He threw me a grin. "Go on, what've you got to lose?"

Excitement fluttered through me like a giant butterfly sneeze. Okay, here we go then... As I stepped inside the old wardrobe, the door gently creaked behind me. It was comforting in the dim light, surrounded by the scent of old pine and even older magic. Once my eyes had adjusted, I saw that the wardrobe was empty apart from a long golden chain hanging from the ceiling, which was adorned with an ivory handle dangling down. It was very much like a Victorian lavatory chain, and the word *Pull* was even inscribed on the end.

I batted the handle, Marmalade Sandwich style, and it swung on its chain.

"You all right in there, Bambi?" Harry called. "What's happening?"

"I'm going to pull the chain. If the floor opens up and I fall down a rabbit hole then..." It would fit right in with everything else that had happened so far.

In response to its chain being pulled, the wardrobe gently rumbled like a distant summer storm, prickling my body with static electricity akin to a million mini-lightning strikes.

I knew *that* feeling. It was magic. But had it done anything to me?

I stepped back out into the room. "Well?"

Harry squealed with excitement. "Oh my word!"

I stood in front of a full-length mirror and grinned. I was now dressed in skin-tight black jeans, a purple velvet top, and knee-high black boots with chunky heels. Even this *wardrobe* wanted me to embrace my inner-witch. And I had to admit I liked it.

Harry stepped behind me in the reflection. "You look very cool, Bambi."

Spirals of glee whooshed through me and I laughed out loud, feeling wonderful for the first time in… in years really.

Was *this* magic? This feeling of bliss? Whatever it was, I felt ready for my next adventure. And for the first time in ages, the future was looking really bright.

Chapter Eight

It didn't take me long to unpack, so Harry and I had a quick cup of tea, then strolled back into town to have a look at Judy's art gallery.

Marmalade Sandwich insisted on coming too. "Pleeeeeeease, Amber!"

How could I refuse that?

He hopped into his bag, and off we set. It was easy to find The Royal Boutique B&B, but to get to it, we had to walk past the establishment next door. The sign on the wall proudly declared: *Turret Sanctuary*.

That's *right*, the chai-latte woman, Hyacinth, had said that she and Tony were neighbours. But, actually, they were more than neighbours, because it looked like – several years ago – one magnificent Victorian townhouse had been transformed into two separate guesthouses. The B&Bs were almost identical at the front – both still boasting the original decorative windows and cream-coloured walls. Delicate wrought-iron balconies graced the upper levels of both B&Bs, providing panoramic views of the street below, where Harry and I were gazing up from. What a lovely couple of establishments.

I hitched Marmalade Sandwich's bag up my shoulder. "Shall we go and look at Judy's gallery then?"

Harry cupped his hand around his ear. "Where's that chanting coming from?"

Intrigued, we left the street and made our way down the side driveway of Turret Sanctuary, squeezing past a battered old Volkswagen Beetle, and finding ourselves in a large garden surrounded by a high wall. It was a beautiful green space with gnarly trees and an atmosphere of calm.

I lowered Marmalade Sandwich to the grass. He slunk out of his bag cautiously, testing a paw on the damp lawn then shaking it, before trotting off to look around.

I spoke quietly, feeling soothed by the gentle sound of birdsong. "Hyacinth said this was a healing sanctuary. She said she runs it with her angels."

"I don't think so," Harry whispered. "I'd know if there were other angels around."

I watched Marmalade Sandwich amble over to a hexagon-shaped brick structure that was integrated into the garden's boundary wall. He sniffed it, then rubbed his face against the rough stone.

I spoke pensively to Harry. "How strange to have a random two-storey turret embedded into the wall. Was this all once part of the Castle?"

"Nah," Harry the tour guide said. "The turret's just a folly – a decorative structure that the wealthy Victorians were fond of."

Regardless of its real age, the turret was captivating, with a quirky, old-world charm. Green plants with little purple petals flowed from the cracks of the weathered red brick. How lovely that nature flourished in even the stoniest places.

We couldn't see Hyacinth or any guests, so we made our way over to a disused well in the middle of the lawn. As I peered into the dark cavern, I saw a metal grille covering the hole, with foliage growing through the slats. Life had found its way down there too.

Harry leaned over the rim of the well. "At least no one can accidentally fall down it, mentioning no names, I'm looking at *you*, Amber Eldritch."

"Me? I'm not that clumsy, am I?"

Harry stifled his laughter. "David told me about the tray of plates you dropped earlier. And – cheese sculpting, was it, Bambi?"

I glanced casually around the garden. "Sounds like you two had a right ol' chinwag."

Before he could answer, I pointed to a glass extension to one side of the garden. "That must be the back of The Royal Boutique B&B."

Of *course*, they shared a garden because the two B&Bs had once been one big house.

I inhaled the crisp fresh air. "How nice for their guests to all mingle together out here." A dark thought struck me. "Hey, Harry, I wonder if any of the guests might've wanted Tony dead!"

Harry cringed. "The police have probably thought of that and need statements from them all."

We drifted over to The Royal Boutique B&B's glass extension and looked inside. "Tables, chairs, and paintings on the walls. Bambi, this is our destination!" Harry reached out to open the door.

"Wait. We'd better go around the front of The Royal Boutique and not just walk in. Anyway, where's Marmalade Sandwich got to?"

Over on the opposite side of the large lawn, he was sniffing an old greenhouse.

The cat mewed at me. "Psst, Amber! There's people in here."

Rather than finding gardeners inside the large old greenhouse, actually, six people were sitting on benches at a wooden table, wearing eye goggles. Chemistry equipment had been neatly arranged on the table – glass beakers, a Bunsen burner, and bottles of blue liquid.

Hyacinth stood to greet us, pushing her goggles up to her forehead. "Welcome, friends."

"What's going on here?" I asked.

She gestured proudly. "This is where I hold my crystal-growing workshops."

I tried to keep up. "You run workshops as a sideline to the B&B?"

"It's my passion," Hyacinth explained. "I was put on this earth to teach people the Way of the Crystal. I used to be a schoolteacher, but I left when my angels told me to spread the word about crystal healing and transcendental meditation."

I pointed to a bottle of blue liquid. "What's that?" *And had she been sniffing it?*

Hyacinth held up the bottle so we could read the label. "Nickel sulphate solution. It makes beautiful turquoise crystals when heated to thirty degrees. Would you like to join us? It's very quick and easy to make a crystal, and my guests are always welcome to create their own during their stay– as they're doing here. I offer jewellery-making courses too, so they can attach their crystals to a necklace or a bracelet, like mine."

She held up the black crystal hanging from a cord around her neck, rubbing it lovingly. This woman really liked crystals – that was clear.

"It's beautiful," I said, captivated by the gold flecks gleaming in the black stone.

"Thank you, I got it when I was travelling in East Asia a few years ago. That's where I learned all about spirituality." She looked at me properly. "You were at the cat café."

"That's right. We heard the chanting and thought we'd come and have a look."

She held her hands together in 'prayer' pose. "Oh yes, we always start our sessions by chanting to the angels. Hmm, my angels are telling me *you're* very stressed, young lady. They're suggesting that you should connect with nature on a deeper level and cleanse your chakras."

I glanced at Harry, who was sniggering. "I'm sure my chakras are quite clean, thank you."

Hyacinth sprang to life and gestured to an ancient oak tree on the far side of the garden, near The Royal Boutique B&B. "See that magnificent oak? It holds all the distilled power of humanity's true and ancient essence – the answer to life, the universe, and our place in it."

"Really? All that in one tree?"

"Let me show you." She strode off, so we followed, halting with her in front of the building-high oak.

She was right in some ways: the tree did emit an aura of tranquillity, just standing there like that, with its baby leaves rustling in the gentle breeze. It gave me a sense of timeless stability. Its roots went deep into the earth and its branches reached up to the sky. I exhaled peacefully.

Hyacinth spoke calmly. "Just one hug, and you'll feel energised and 'at one'."

I shot her a side glance. "You want me to hug a tree?"

"Yes. And then you can ask me anything."

"Ask you about what?"

"The true nature of life, the universe... anything. That's why you're here, isn't it?"

"We just heard the chanting," Harry explained. "But... Amber would love to hug a tree, wouldn't you, Bambi?"

Marmalade Sandwich rubbed his face against the oak's bark. "Yeah, go on, Amber. Hug the tree, hug the tree, hug the tree!"

"Oh what a sweet cat," Hyacinth said. "I think even *he* wants you to hug the tree."

I spoke through a gritted smile. "Whatever gave you that impression?"

Harry draped his arm around my shoulders. "Everyone wants you to hug the tree, Bambi. It's unanimous."

"All right..." Feeling utterly stupid, I wrapped my arms around the massive trunk, pressing my cheek against the rough bark. "There, I've hugged it. Okay?"

Hyacinth patted me on the bottom. "Spread your legs. Give yourself to the tree!"

Harry sniggered. I turned my head to see him holding Marmalade Sandwich. Both of them were watching keenly. "How does it feel?" Harry asked.

"I'm not feeling much but a face full of bark."

"No, no – be at one with the tree." Hyacinth massaged my shoulders vigorously. "Just relax."

My voice juddered at her touch. "That's easy for you to say."

"Look, here, I'll rub my sacred crystal and count to a hundred."

"A hundred?" I asked. "Are we playing hide-and-seek?"

"Just make it ten," Harry said. "She's happy with the quick version."

"Very well." Hyacinth rubbed her crystal theatrically. "One... two... three..."

She continued counting, so I embraced the moment – and the oak tree. As I waited for this endurance to end, a trickle of relaxation began to seep through me... Hmm, that was actually quite nice. Yes, Hyacinth was probably mad, but... I *was* somehow soaking up the strength of the tree, the naturalness of it. It made me feel strong, grounded, and calm.

Checking Hyacinth wasn't about to do anything weird to me, I closed my eyes and listened to the sounds of an ancient forest rustling in my ears. The chirping birds sang a sweet melody like Mother Nature's own orchestra. And still I hugged the tree. My tension thawed further as the sun's rays caressed my face through the canopy of green baby leaves.

Mmm, gentle woody freshness soothed my nostrils, as I unwound into the lovely new space inside of my soul. Space that I hadn't even known was there.

"Nine... ten..."

I stood up and inhaled deeply. "That was beautiful."

Hyacinth smiled knowingly. "It never fails to make me feel better. That's why I love this place so much."

Still cradling Marmalade Sandwich, Harry spoke to Hyacinth. "How long have you been here?"

She raised her face to the sun. "Three years. I was a stressed-out teacher at an expensive college."

"Not Eton?" I asked with dread. I'd once had an encounter with a former Eton boy. Why did *everything* remind me of David? Gah!

Hyacinth spoke calmly. "No, it was a few miles away, in a little village called Hurley."

My ears pricked up. "Hurley College? That's where Judy said Billy Royal went. Did you know him? It's just I think he might know where my granny's missing corgi is."

Hyacinth ran her fingers over the oak's rough bark. "Billy was never in any of my classes. I always taught the bright and talented pupils. But I knew *of* him from the other teachers. And I'm sorry to say, Billy was a troublemaker. And *he* wasn't the only one."

Oh dear, it didn't sound like she'd had much fun teaching there. "Why did you leave?" I gently asked.

She clutched her crystal. "The truth is, I was about to have a… a breakdown. And this is what my angels told me to do. Of course, it's dreadfully bad karma about Tony. I'll go next door later and do a cleansing ritual for Judy. Fancy him having a heart attack in the middle of lunch."

"I don't think the police know the cause of death yet," I said.

"Oh? Well, it looked to me like he was having a heart attack."

Harry spoke sarcastically. "Are you a qualified doctor?"

"I'm a certified level three crystal healer and reiki master. All fully accredited from the ashram I attended in Phuket." Hyacinth glanced behind us and groaned. "Oh *no*…"

I turned to see Inspector Taylor and Sergeant Van Danté heading this way. Yikes! I'd spent too long as a journalist, and my guilty instincts took over. I grabbed Harry's arm and dragged him behind the lofty turret, leaving Hyacinth to welcome the police.

We could hear the conversation from here.

Alex spoke flatly. "Ms Meadows, I'd like a follow up chat with you."

She sounded nervous. "Of course, Inspector. How can I help?"

David spoke next. "When I interviewed you earlier, Ms Meadows, why did you fail to mention this?"

There was a rustle of paper as David held something up.

"Oh, er... I haven't got my reading glasses, what is it?"

Inspector Taylor was getting agitated. "It's an application for a tree preservation order made by you. You're trying to get a tree preserved in your garden – presumably this big oak here – because Tony Royal has been applying for permission to cut it down. Apparently, it blocked his light, its roots were damaging his property, and he wanted to build another extension on his half of the garden."

Harry and I exchanged a look of surprise, then listened to Hyacinth's reply. "That's all true, Inspector. But, you see, I regularly use *my* part of the garden to lead meditation and crystal healing sessions with my guests in the warmer weather. This is my sacred space. I asked the angels what I should do, and they told me not to cut down the oak tree."

"Did they indeed?" Alex asked blankly.

"They did indeed. Tony's planned building work would not only be noisy, but it would've blocked out the natural light for the turret. You see, my guests have the option of staying in the main part of my B&B or in the self-contained turret, which has its own bathroom and kitchen, and the top floor offers spectacu –"

"You can save the sales spiel, Ms Meadows." That was David.

I stepped back to look at the turret, thinking it must be a fun and quirky place to stay, but I trod on a twig, which cracked loudly.

Harry and I froze like thieves in a spotlight. We exchanged a look of panic, but there was nowhere to run, so we flung ourselves against the wall.

Alex and David swaggered around the corner, halting side-by-side.

David's eyes flashed blue. "Amber, what are you doing here?"

I ran my fingers over the turret's brickwork. "Wow, Harry, isn't this a nice... wall?"

"It's lovely."

"And... look at those pretty white flowers down there."

"That's wild garlic," David muttered, in a 'don't push your luck' tone of voice.

"Oops, sorry, Sergeant, sore subject." I lowered my voice. "Hey, you don't think Hyacinth knows about vampires, do you?"

The already-chilly weather around Inspector Taylor plunged to arctic. "Vampires?" he asked David.

I quickly jumped in. "It's nice to meet you, by the way, Inspector Taylor. We didn't get the chance to speak earlier because of the... because of the... you know... But my cousin Evelyn speaks very highly of you."

Blimey, he was hard to read. His expression remained utterly blank. "Don't try and get round me. What are you doing here?"

"We were just passing," Harry protested.

"And we thought we'd pop in," I added.

David folded his arms across his chest. "I assume you're not here to interfere in this murder case?"

"Of course not." I looked him firmly in the eye. "And you can believe me because I would *never* lie to the police. Not for anyone."

David's top lip curled into a snarl. Blimey, he was attractive. "Leave this for the police to investigate. I really mean it."

Yikes, from the stern look on his face, he really *did* mean it! "You've got a very suspicious mind, Detective Sergeant Van Danté – I have no interest in solving this case. I've been tasked with finding a lost dog. Colin the corgi. I don't suppose either of you know anything about *him*?"

I wilted in the glare of both detectives.

"We're investigating a murder," David said. "Why should we know anything about a lost dog?"

I raised my chin. "I just wanted to check all my sources. As a journalist, I like to deal in hard facts."

Inspector Taylor snorted. "Oh really? I would've thought as a journalist you don't deal in facts at all."

"Very funny, Inspector Taylor."

"Am I laughing?"

"How does one tell?"

Inspector Taylor shook his head and walked off. Sergeant Van Danté shot me a warning look, then followed.

Harry was grinning. "Wow, Bambi, did you find that as thrilling as I did?"

"No, I did not." *Oh fudge cakes, Yes I did!*

I shushed Harry as Alex spoke to Hyacinth again. "We're going to have a look around, Ms Meadows."

"Oh er, do you have a warrant, Inspector?"

"Madam, I'm investigating a murder – *that* is warrant enough. Let's go, Sergeant."

I picked up Marmalade Sandwich and popped him in his bag. "Come on, Harry, let's leave the police to their investigation. We've got some paintings to look at."

Chapter Nine

We headed back to the street and entered The Royal Boutique B&B's front entrance.

Despite retaining its outer Victorian charm, Tony's guesthouse had been renovated with modern fittings and furniture. Unusually for a B&B, there was a reception desk at the entrance, as well as a small waiting area, where two cream leather sofas stood proudly on the laminate flooring, lit by expensive, decorative lamps. The bowl of complimentary chocolates did not go unnoticed to my roving eye.

This was all very swish. In my experience of the typical English bed and breakfast, the owner would usually greet guests by bustling out of the kitchen, tea towel in hand and grumbling about the weather. If the owner was female, she'd still have her hair-rollers in – if he was male, he'd have his slippers on. They'd thrust your room key into your hands, tell you not to be late for breakfast at seven, then get on with the hoovering while you struggled up the narrow staircase with your luggage.

Harry and Vicky would've accused me of exaggerating the 'faded charms' of the traditional English guesthouse for comic effect, but it was no exaggeration that The Royal Boutique B&B was extremely upmarket. Had Tony wanted his B&B to be more like a hotel? It certainly emitted a sophisticated and corporate air. But unlike a corporate hotel, the reception desk was rather cramped. In fact, it was barely more than a wide lectern, holding a phone, a signing-in book, and a chilli plant.

Chilli plant? Hmm...

The horsey woman, Lydia, was sitting behind the cramped desk, painting her nails. She glanced at me and Harry, then gestured towards Marmalade Sandwich in his bag. "No pets allowed in the rooms."

Despite being an angel, Harry always gave as good as he got – especially around snooty people. "We don't want to stay here."

"Good. We're fully booked."

He leaned on the desk. "We want to see the art gallery."

The phone *briiinged* into life. Lydia waved at Harry. "Be a poppet and answer that, would you?"

His eyes twinkled with mischief. "Of course..."

Oh dear, I knew that look. He picked up the phone and put on a stupid voice. "Good afternoon, this is the employment bureau of ironic workers. Looking for a plumber with hydrophobia? We're your agency. Desperate for a florist with hay fever? We can find one for all your sneezing amusement. Or what about a receptionist who sits around on her arse painting her nails and being rude to customers? I have the perfect candidate right here."

Lydia paused, mid-nail-paint. "Stop that and find out who it is."

Harry listened to the person at the other end, then held out the receiver. "It's Mandy from the Hair Salon."

Lydia glanced at her wet fingernails, groaned, then leaned over the desk and lined up her face with the phone. "Hold it steady for me, poppet... Yes, Mandy? No, I will not change my appointment. No, I cannot be flexible. Yes, I can find another hairdresser – consider it done!" She spoke to Harry. "Slam the phone down in a huff, would you?"

Harry politely listened to Mandy's reply. "Mandy says next time she sees you coming, Lydia, she'll demonstrate exactly what she can do with her curling tongs."

Lydia guffawed. "Oh, that's sweet."

He raised an eyebrow. "Not the way she said it."

Yikes, I'd better intervene before they started duelling. Without knowing what else to say, I delved into my journalist's bag of small talk. "How long have you been working here, Lydia?"

"Or *not* working," Harry muttered.

She sighed boredly. "Two years. And for your information, I'm extremely dedicated and efficient. But given that my boss died in front of me just a few hours ago, I decided to take a moment to have a break. Of course, I usually have someone to paint my nails for me, but I happen to find it very soothing."

I loaded my voice with sympathy. "It must've been such a shock. I suppose it's too soon to start wondering what will happen to this place now?"

She blew on her nails. "I hope we can carry on. Although, of course, like all B&B owners everywhere, Tony was hugely involved. He made all the breakfasts, cleaned the rooms, did the repairs.

And I took care of the bookings and admin." She lowered her voice. "He wasn't what you might call *academic*."

I stepped over to the spotless waiting area. "It sounds like a lot of work for just the two of you. Judy mentioned that she doesn't get involved."

"It is a lot of work," Lydia said, huffily. "Especially recently, since *I've* been the one liaising with the solicitors and the council – helping Tony to achieve his expansion dreams."

I unwrapped a *Royal Boutique B&B* chocolate and popped it in my mouth. "Is this to do with Tony wanting to build an extension on Hyacinth's garden?"

"*Not* Hyacinth's garden – both their gardens, half each." She screwed the lid onto her nail varnish bottle. "But I can't talk about it."

I knew that tone of voice. She was dying to tell me *everything*. I unleashed my inner-journalist. "You're more than just a receptionist here, aren't you, Lydia? I can see that."

"I work my socks off for Tony – but does he ever say thank you? Not once. And the phone never stops ringing. There it goes again."

Harry picked it up automatically. "Hello? Oh, hold on… Lydia, it's your mother."

Lydia waved this away. "Tell her I'll call her back."

Harry spoke into the receiver. "I'm afraid she's been abducted by aliens… Yes, *isn't* it good news? Goodbye."

I tried to steer the conversation back to Tony's death. Not that I wanted to investigate... but it *had* happened at my Aunt Vicky's café. "Lydia, do you know what Tony was planning to announce at Paws for Tea earlier?"

"He didn't tell me – just asked me to invite those people. Strange bunch to invite out for lunch."

"Because he and Hyacinth are rival B&B owners?"

"Yes. And we all know he doesn't get along with his son Billy. I left a message for Billy to come, but I suppose he decided against it."

I tried to sound innocent. "Why don't father and son get on?"

Lydia fiddled with her gold earring. "I don't think Billy ever forgave his father for marrying Judy. I believe he was very close to his mother."

Harry frowned. "But Judy said she'd pretty much saved them from financial ruin."

"Yes, ungrateful little so-and-so."

"*You* don't like Billy either?" I asked, helping myself to another chocolate.

Lydia snorted. "He's a bit rough-and-ready for my liking. A bit..." She mouthed the word 'common' as if it was a contagious disease. "Why are you so interested in Billy, anyway?"

I gestured to Marmalade Sandwich in his bag. "I'm looking for a lost dog. Billy was the last to see him."

She tutted disapprovingly. "You might want to check the local furrier."

I froze with fear. "You're not serious, are you?"

"Billy Royal is a scallywag. I wouldn't put anything past him if there was money to be made. But saying that, the apple doesn't fall far from the tree, does it? Tony was rather unrefined too. Oh, he wasn't bad looking, but not someone you'd take home to mummy and daddy. But I suppose some women are attracted to that oily working-class type. Women with bad teeth and no dress sense!" She guffawed again.

Harry's lips curled into a cheeky grin. "Were *you* romantically involved with Tony?"

Lydia almost fell over in her haste to stand up. "Do you mind, I'm engaged to be married –we certainly were not involved! Just because he wanted to divorce his wife, it doesn't automatically mean it had anything to do with me."

Did I hear that right? "He wanted to divorce Judy?"

She held up her hand. "I've said too much. It's not my place to tell *you* how much Tony and Judy have been arguing recently."

I smiled sweetly. "You're a very loyal and discrete person, I can tell that."

"Well, yes. *I'm* the one who has to stand here listening to Tony shouting at Judy about how much he wants to divorce her. And Judy begging him not to leave. Honestly, after all that woman's done for him. But that was Tony's style really. He used people then threw them away."

This sounded like a raw nerve. "He did a similar thing to… you?"

"Excuse me, who are you?" She suddenly became defensive. "Wait a minute, you're after my job, aren't you? You saw the ad online?"

"No, of course not."

"Well, you can forget it. No matter what happens next, regardless of whether Tony's dead or alive, this job is mine!"

I held up my hands to placate her. "Lydia, I promise, I'm not here to steal your job."

"Then why *are* you here?"

Harry grabbed my arm. "We're here to see the art gallery – Judy said we could. Come on, Bambi, let's go before that phone starts ringing again."

Leaving her seething, we rushed down the corridor and around the corner to our destination. We'd already seen the art gallery/dining room from the garden, but only now could I see what a lovely space it was. Entirely made of glass, it was clean and airy, with modern tables and chairs in the middle and, around the perimeter, large pastoral paintings were proudly displayed on free-standing easels – Vincent Varney's collection, commissioned by Judy Royal.

One side of this lovely room overlooked the large, lush lawn, which flooded the space with sunlight and green hues. The kitchen where Tony presumably made his famous breakfasts could be accessed through an archway, and nearby, a saxophone stood in a stand.

Judy had said Tony played the saxophone, so that must be his. The music-stand in front of the saxophone held a book of sheet music. There was a jam fingerprint on one of the pages.

"He must play during breakfast," I said, inspecting the beautiful brass instrument.

Harry clicked his fingers. "That's *right*. Tony's well-known for it. He always serenades his guests during breakfast once he's served his famous full English fry-ups."

I gazed out into the garden. "You can see why Hyacinth wouldn't want Tony to build another extension. This dining room is *already* an extension, and if he extended further, it would mean cutting down that lovely oak tree."

Harry nodded. "Hence why Hyacinth took out the tree protection order."

I couldn't shake Lydia's anger from my mind. "Harry, why do you think Lydia felt *I* was a threat to her job here?"

He chuckled. "Perhaps she observed your customer service skills at Paws, and thought they were comparable to her own!"

"Oh ha ha, you're hilarious. But seriously, she mentioned that Tony had placed an ad online. Do you think he was maybe trying to recruit someone else for her role? She did say it was his style to use people and throw them away."

Harry pulled out his phone. "Let's see if we can find anything."

I pulled out my phone too and searched online for reception jobs in Windsor. After a bit of clicking around, I found an advert for a receptionist at this very guesthouse. "Here we go, Harry, listen to this.

Permanent, full-time role... heart of Royal Windsor, blah, blah, blah... oh, that's a good salary... administration duties, responsibility for all bookings, total control of reception area..."

Harry peered over my shoulder. "That sounds like a full-time position – like Lydia's actual job."

"I agree. Hmm... what if Lydia somehow discovered this ad online? And after all her hard work on the tree protection stuff, she felt betrayed and...."

Harry's eyes widened. "And she killed him?"

"Shh..." I strained to listen. It seemed very quiet out in the foyer. Was she eavesdropping? "Let's just look at the artwork and get out of here. We can talk about this later."

Feeling like we were in a proper art gallery, we browsed around Vincent's beautiful paintings. Harry launched into tour guide mode. "They're rather dark for rural scenes, but Vincent was clearly inspired by Constable's *The Haywain*."

I stroked my chin like a wise sage. "Oh yeah, Constable's *The Haywain* – that's what I was about to say." I focused on a blotchy depiction of England's rolling hills. "Actually, that dark green colour reminds me of something. Where have I seen it before?"

My thoughts were interrupted by the sound of a commanding male voice speaking to Lydia at reception. "We need to look in the dining room again."

"It's Inspector Taylor!" I hissed.

"And David," Harry said with a grin.

"Shut up and find somewhere to hide."

"Why? We're not doing anything wrong."

After our encounter in the garden just now, I got the feeling that something like 'being innocent' might not matter too much to Inspector Taylor. But there was nowhere *to* hide. The French windows were locked and, to get out of here, we'd need to pass Alex and David.

I eyed up a free-standing easel. Could I hide behind there? I instantly abandoned the idea – there was a huge gap between the easel's legs, and DI Taylor would surely notice *my* human legs conspicuously standing there. Argh, I was panicking! I froze like a rabbit in the headlights as the voices of the two detectives approached. The inspector was in the middle of talking to his sergeant.

"… and I want you to track down Billy Royal urgently. Those text messages between him and the victim were unpleasant to say the least."

David spoke with clipped professionality. "Yes, sir. And as sole benefactor of his father's will, Billy is our prime suspect."

As they strode around the corner and into the dining room, I pretended to be engrossed in one of the paintings. Their steely silence squashed me and my heart thumped in my ears, waiting for the inevitable admonishment.

Finally, Inspector Taylor spoke gruffly. "We seem to be following you two around today."

"We were just looking at the paintings," Harry said breezily. "I was saying how dark they are for rural scenes."

"How *fascinating*," Inspector Taylor said in a thoroughly unfascinated tone.

Not quite ready to face his wrath, I continued to scrutinise the painting in front of me, which depicted a bustling summer fayre on a village green, with rustic folk skipping and dancing. It evoked a wistful longing for days gone by, making me want to say things like 'Verily sirrah' and 'Fol-di, yol-di, leh' – which was weird, because I had no idea what any of those words meant.

But… there *was* something familiar about the shade of green that Vincent was so fond of. Believe it or not, I wasn't actually a Constable connoisseur, so I couldn't claim to recognise similarities between this painting and the work of that great artist. No… it was something I'd *written* once upon a time. But what? My thoughts whirred and clicked into place. "That shade of dark green reminds me of … Can it be? Yes, I think it is."

"What?" David asked, behind me. "What about the shade of dark green?"

I turned to find the penetrating stares of both police officers fixed upon me. Yikes! My heart fluttered and I grappled to gain control. "Oh, it's nothing really. It just reminds me of an article I wrote years ago. It was a silly fluff piece – a ghastly tale of how the Victorians loved this certain shade of green paint, until it started killing people during their tea and cake!"

"*Paint* started killing people?" David asked sceptically.

"Yes. Because it contained arsenic."

Alex became interested. "Arsenic?"

"That's right. The colour was called Paris green. The Victorians loved the shade, so they used it for wallpaper and all sorts of things like that. But the arsenic started seeping out of the walls and into the *people*."

David's tone was inquisitive. "You think Tony's *pills* might've been laced with arsenic?"

"Oh, I wasn't saying that. Why? Have you heard back from the coroner with the cause of death? Everyone's saying it was a heart attack or a strange allergy to chilli. But... why are you both looking at me like that?"

Alex pinned me with his glare. "Do *you* know where to acquire a tin of this Paris green paint, Ms Eldritch?"

"Of course not. But... there again, it wouldn't even need to be *fresh* paint. When I was researching that article, I remember there was a church in London where a coat of Paris green had been discovered under decades-old layers of other paint. And it was still deemed potentially lethal."

"If the parishioners started licking the walls?" Alex asked blankly.

"Or if it was crumbled up and added to the communion wine," I said. "Why? Is it important to the murder case?"

Alex sighed wearily. "No, Ms Eldritch, I'm asking because I want to impress my arty friends. What do *you* think?"

"I think you're a very rude man," is what I *didn't* say.

Actually, perhaps there *was* a morsel of a clue, a tiny little factoid, with which I could wipe the smile off his face. Not that I'd thus far seen Inspector Taylor smile.

Well then, perhaps it would wipe the smug smirk off David's face instead. I practically swaggered on the spot. "Oh, by the way, Inspector, did you know that Tony has been threatening Judy with divorce?"

Alex didn't miss a beat. "That's no concern of yours."

But by his side, David jotted it down on his notepad.

"So you *didn't* know that then?" Harry asked haughtily.

Alex pointed to the door. "Get out."

"But—"

"Both of you. Now."

I hitched Marmalade Sandwich up in his bag. "Fine. Come on Harry."

Harry and I traipsed past the two detectives as if we'd been chucked out of class for giggling – which we *had* been plenty of times as children.

But this time we weren't really leaving. Harry bumped into me as I halted suddenly –then I shoved him into a convenient alcove between the dining room and the reception area. I put my finger to my lips, shushing him.

His wings flapped with excitement. He loved a bit of harmless mischief. We both listened carefully.

David spoke quietly. "Our suspicions were right, Inspector? About Tony Royal being poisoned?"

"Let's not jump to conclusions until we get the post-mortem. But arsenic in paint, eh? We'd better speak to the wife again. And that artist Vincent Varney – see what *he* might know about this shade of Paris green. Right, there's nothing more we can do here, come on."

Harry and I fell over each other in our desperate attempt to scarper. I gripped Marmalade Sandwich tight as we sprinted past Lydia and fled out into the street, where we burst into laughter. It was great to be back home with my bestie – he always brought out the rebel in me, and I loved it!

Chapter Ten

Still trying to calm our giggles, we decided to take a scenic stroll back to Paws for Tea. I'd only arrived back in Windsor yesterday, so this was my first proper look at my lovely hometown and, as we walked, pleasant memories trickled into my mind.

Had it really been ten years since I'd left? It was all so familiar. And being back home somehow made *me* feel more familiar to myself, if that didn't sound too strange! It was giving me the chance to rediscover a long-lost part of myself; a part that I'd forgotten even existed. A spark that I'd buried. A continuous glow of light that had never gone out, but just faded.

Growing up here, I'd hated the fact that Windsor *always* stayed the same. If you ignored the modern eateries and shops selling plastic souvenirs, you could easily be in the 1950s, 1800s… or any era in English history. I now found its timelessness charming. Comforting.

I'd taken this town for granted for my whole life, but actually, people travelled halfway around the world to enjoy what I had on my doorstep. There was so much to be grateful for, if only we opened our eyes to it.

Harry and I strolled down the Castle hill and along the wide path that ran parallel to the River Thames, chatting about everything and nothing as we always did. We'd spoken to each other on the phone every day since I'd left, and he'd visited me regularly in

London. But being back here with him made me feel young and free.

The pathway beside the river was lined with vibrant greenery, spring flowers, and sturdy towering trees. Perfectly picturesque. As always, the grassy banks were covered with hundreds of swans – those giant majestic birds that had once belonged to The Queen and now belonged to The King. Their elegance and grace enhanced my tranquillity. It was good to be home.

At the ice cream van, Harry and I queued with a group of tourists. He got chatting to a nice American couple – Mitch and Molly from Minnesota. "I recommend a Mr Whippy 99 Flake," Harry said. "It's a wafer cornet of soft, whipped ice cream, with half a chocolate Flake bar stuck in the top. It's as English as fish and chips and jellied eels."

The American lady wrinkled her nose. "What's a jellied eel?"

"How do you like the sound of eating salted, slimy elastic bands?" I asked.

Harry chuckled. "I'd steer clear of those. Just stick to the ice cream, I would."

I bought Harry an ice cream, and one for myself of course, and we sat on the grassy bank, watching the swans paddle by. The sun danced on the rippling water like fairy sparkles, making my heart sparkle too. Marmalade Sandwich sat on my lap, keeping a careful eye on the swans, which were twice his size. I scooped a splodge of cold ice cream onto my finger and he licked it off eagerly, darting his warm pink tongue in and out and going cross-eyed as he focused on the task.

He purred contentedly. I understood why: if *I'd* had the ability to purr, I would've done too.

"You're a cute kitty, aren't you?" I said, stroking his ears.

He keenly licked the sides of his mouth, blinking at me with his big green eyes. I decided to take that as a 'yes'.

I gazed at the river. "It's so beautiful here, with all the green and blue – like magic for the eyes. Hey, that reminds me, Harry, why didn't you tell me that your paintings and photographs were magical?"

He crunched his wafer. "You saw them like they really are? That's so cool! It must be because you're embracing your magic."

I wasn't sure if I *was* yet. "I broke a teapot in one of your photos, I'm really sorry."

He laughed heartily. "No worries, I've still got the negative."

"I always said your artistic talents were so good that your paintings came alive. Little did I realise how right I was."

"Oh, that gives me an idea." Harry's eyes twinkled with mischief. Oh dear, I knew that look.

"What?" I asked suspiciously.

Harry touched my wand in its lacy armband. "Bambi, I want to show you something."

I leaned forward. "Okay, what?"

"Follow me. Come on, let's go!" He suddenly leapt to his feet, ran a few paces, then soared into the air.

"Wait, Harry." I quickly gathered up Marmalade Sandwich then, laughing with glee, I ran after him. "Harry, *I* can't fly. Wait for me!"

He was already higher than the tallest trees. He shouted down at me. "Follow The Queen's Walkway – it's like the Yellow Brick Road!"

It was completely *unlike* the Yellow Brick Road. The Queen's Walkway was a tourist route through the streets of Windsor that had been laid to commemorate the ninetieth birthday of our longest reigning monarch, Queen Elizabeth II. It was marked by ornamental brass plaques embedded in the pavement, displaying Her Majesty's 'E II R' royal cypher, so they were easy to follow. Losing sight of Harry, I ran towards the town.

The Queen's Walkway led me towards an alleyway, which I knew was a shortcut to the main High Street. A steep set of concrete steps ran upwards next to the King and Castle pub, so I took them two at a time, feeling more elated than I had for years. I'd completely lost track of Harry now – he could fly fast – but I knew he must be leading me somewhere thrilling. He was always so full of fun. That's why he made such a great tour guide.

Dodging out the way of a group of tourists, I reached the top of the concrete steps and wheeled around the corner to the main street. But I yelped as I bumped into a tall figure on the pavement.

I stepped back, ready to jovially apologise to the older woman who I'd collided with. No harm was done – this lady was thickset and sturdy. But my joy smashed to smithereens as I caught the furious look on her face. "Why don't you look where you're going, you silly girl!"

Dread slunk through my ribcage. Oh fudge cakes, this was my old headmistress at the Severe School for Young Ladies, Miss 'Meatgrinder' Stern.

And suddenly, I was a terrified teenager. "*Miss Stern.*"

She peered over her glasses. "Who are you?"

Was this really happening? The woman who'd ruined my teenage years didn't even remember me. I eyed up the walking cane clasped in her bony hand. But she'd never needed it for mobility. It was a weapon. I knew it well.

And then I was back there. It felt so real, holding Harry's hand in front of Miss Stern's desk. She'd confiscated my cat pendant because I'd been distracted in class. Harry had been making me laugh. We'd been sent here for an extra-curricular lesson: Obedience.

Miss Stern peered over her glasses. "Hold out your hand, Eldritch."

The thirteen-year-old me held my head high. "You're not allowed to hit children. It's not right."

"Very well. I shall contact your grandmother. I'm sure she'll want to know why you've been misbehaving. And she'll undoubtedly instruct me to separate *you* two, once and for all."

I squeezed Harry's hand tighter. At thirteen, I didn't know if my granny would side with me or old Meatgrinder. But I couldn't take the risk. I couldn't lose Harry. He was my sanctuary.

I held out my trembling hand, scrunching up my eyes.

"Palm upwards," Meatgrinder instructed.

Harry stepped in front of me. "No! It was my fault. I was distracting Amber. Punish me. Let her go."

The edge of Miss Stern's mouth twitched. Without looking away from Harry, she said, "You may leave, Eldritch."

Biting back my tears, I headed for the door. Outside the office, I stood in the corridor and listened to the sound of a cane thrashing, then… silence. Harry had refused to give her the satisfaction of crying out.

If this had been a better memory, Harry would've swaggered out to the corridor, and told me he'd grabbed her cane and thwacked her with it. But that's not what happened. He came out with his palm throbbing and his eyes stinging with tears.

"You should tell your parents," I said to him. "They're teachers here."

"They're scared of her." He held up my cat pendant. "But *I'm* not."

I joyfully fastened it around my neck. "How did you get it?"

"Swiped it when she wasn't looking…"

Back in the now, in the street, I touched my pendant. I was glad to remember why I loved it so much. Not just because he'd given it to me, but because it represented the *Harry* part of me. Meatgrinder had tried to take it – to destroy my Harryness. But I was an adult now. And I'd never let anyone ever take my spirit again. No matter how hard they tried.

Miss Meatgrinder Stern was still waiting for an apology as to why I'd bumped into her. Her lined face was etched with a lifetime of anger – just like David's smirk had etched itself there after a decade of cynicism. Perhaps it wasn't too late for David, but Miss Stern's puckered expression represented all her tortured misery – and the misery she'd inflicted on others.

She recoiled as I planted a big kiss on her cheek. "It's been lovely bumping into you again. But I must fly!"

Chapter Eleven

Feeling free of Miss Stern, I ran off down the High Street. But then I halted again as I spied a swan feather on the pavement... Not a *swan* feather, but a Harry feather.

I picked it up and turned to face a tall grey wall. I must've walked past this old wall hundreds of times, but it wasn't usually transparent. Brick walls tended not to be. Now, through the wall, I could make out a street. It was narrow and cobbled, like so many in Windsor, and it was lined with shops and stalls – but something told me they weren't the usual tourist outlets.

My wand tingled in my lacy armband. I glanced at the feather Harry had left for me.

"Are we going in there?" Marmalade Sandwich asked, popping his head out of his bag.

"It looks solid," I said. "But... if *Harry* believes I can walk through a wall, then I guess I should believe in myself. What do you say, puss?"

"I'd say, what does *physics* believe?"

I tickled his cheek. "You would. Right, brace yourself."

I held my breath, took a step forward, and... squeezed through the wall. It was like wading through treacle. Wow! I popped out the other side, stumbled, then righted myself, taking in the scene.

At the end of the cobbled street, Harry was standing with his wings stretched out, smiling warmly. "Amber Eldritch, welcome to the Old Magical Mews – the magical quarter of Windsor."

He flew down to meet me, his expression gentle and playful.

I held out his feather. "I think this is yours… Why have I never been here before?"

"Because you've never wanted anything to do with magic before."

"But my parents never brought me here."

"They were probably worried you'd think it was boring."

I glanced around. "I think it's anything but boring."

The main space looked like an old stable yard, but all the stone horseboxes around the perimeter had been ingeniously turned into little artisan shops. The large courtyard in the middle had been visibly weathered by hooves over the centuries, which was quite normal for Windsor. But unlike normal Windsor, Beings of Magic dominated the scene. Witches were selling magical potions behind wooden carts, elves stood chatting with wizards, and werewolves shopped for goods and groceries.

Harry held my hand. "Now that you've got your wand, you can come and explore."

He started to walk off, but I pulled him back. "I bumped into Miss Stern."

His expression flickered with anger. "Oh yeah, I see her around every now and again."

I glared at the ground. "I remembered something that I'd tried to forget."

He placed his hands supportively on my shoulders. "She was horrible, Bambi."

"*I* was. I left you in there."

"Not a bit of it, my darling friend. I wanted you to leave. I got your pendant back, didn't I?"

"You did!"

He hugged me tight – floating us slightly off the ground.

Marmalade Sandwich stuck his claws into my arm. "Tell him to put us down, Amber, meeeew!"

I chuckled. "Harry, my cat is unkeen to fly."

Harry floated us down and tickled Marmalade Sandwich behind the ears.

The cat spoke coolly. "It was *you* I was worried about."

I glanced over Harry's shoulder at the hustle and bustle of the street. "It's all magical?" I asked.

"Yep," Harry said. "This was once the magical mews of the Castle."

"For magical... horses?"

"Yeah, there *were* magical horses for royalty before the invention of the motorcar. But they fell out of fashion, so the Beings of Magic slowly moved in."

I wanted to know more about magical horses, but I was too captivated to speak. Harry – ever the tour guide – proudly showed me around. There was no electricity in the Old Magical Mews, but instead, everything was powered by magic and steam.

Harry explained that during the Industrial Revolution, a very bright witch had invented the Magical Crystal Steam Engine. "And here's one."

The device took up almost an entire stable. It was a huge iron box, containing intricate gears and vents. "This is how all the magical tools and machinery are powered around here," Harry said. "And that one there is the Levitation Harness. It combines steam power and magical crystals from Marvelton, to create powerful levitation spells."

"So heavy items can be lifted and carried?"

"Exactly."

The air crackled with magical energy. It smelled of steam and steel. It was incredible.

In one former stable, Wheelwright's Workshop was run by a burly werewolf, who had a wolf's head and furry body, but stood upright like a human. He was crafting a carriage wheel with meticulous precision. I didn't know people made wheels – I'd never thought about it before. But... presumably wheels had to be made somewhere. And if it wasn't in a factory, then it was by a person. Or a werewolf.

Nearby, the elf-run Fletcher's Fayre was a haven for archery enthusiasts, selling finely crafted bows. A large leather quiver held scores of handmade arrows. I picked one up. it tingled.

"Here," Harry said to an elf. "You can have this feather."

"Cheers, mate. You're an angel."

"Yes, I am."

I lost track of time as I gawped at stall upon stall of magical potions, crystal balls, and mystical runes.

I was drawn to a beautiful display of delicate wooden boxes, with jewel-encrusted lids.

"What are they?" I whispered to Harry.

The witch behind the stall leaned on her broomstick. "Pick one up and open it."

I gently opened the glistening lid. To my amazement, a mellow guitar track flowed out. "My favourite tune," I whispered.

She was an older witch with a warm smile. "It's powered by clockwork and magic. It plays whatever song you're in the mood for. Also, have a sniff…"

As I inhaled, my nostrils picked up the intoxicating scent of sweet peas. Then I watched in awe as red, orange, and yellow rose petals wafted around my head. "Wow..."

Harry draped his arm around my shoulders. "There's magic around every corner, Bambi. if only you open your heart to it."

I placed the box back on the stall and chuckled. "I bet if David was to open one of those, it would play *God Save the King* or *Rule, Britannia!*"

Harry nudged me. "I like that you're thinking of him, even when you're apart."

"Stop it. I was mocking him."

"Were you? It sounded like a compliment to me."

We walked back towards the main High Street, exiting the Old Magical Mews. On the corner, straddling the magical quarter and the human realm, was a crooked Tudor building with old wooden beams.

"*Ye Olde Antiques*," I read. "Is it magical?"

Harry squinted at the sign. "I think it's human. But there is something magical about antiques, don't you think?"

"I've never really noticed. Oh, look at that..."

I was drawn to a cool motorcycle parked outside – a black-and-steel hulk of mean-machine. And yikes, my legs filled with giddy helium as I saw who was standing inside the antiques shop, chatting to a lady behind the counter. "Oh fudge cakes."

"What, Bambi?" Harry asked.

"It's David. I wonder why he's in *there*. Do you think the shopkeeper has something to do with the murder?"

"No idea, why don't you go and ask him?"

My body tensed like a steel rod at the thought of talking to David again. "No, come on, let's go back to Paws. I want to see Vicky. Check she's okay."

Harry grinned. "Go and speak to David. I'll leave you to it."

Before I could protest, he pulled open the shop door and shoved me hard, making me stumble halfway across the worn carpet. I was tempted to turn and walk straight back out, but David rushed over from the counter and steadied me with a strong hand. Hopefully I could blame the flush of my cheeks and the quiver of my lips on my humiliating stumble, rather than the actual cause – his firm grasp on my arm.

"Hi Amber. I'm starting to think you might be *falling* for me." The smirk was back with a vengeance, gah!

"Huh, not likely. I only came in here because Harry…" The door was now shut and Harry had gone. "Because… um, Harry knows how much I love antiques."

David made a fuss of Marmalade Sandwich. "Really? I didn't know that."

"He's nice, Amber," the cat said, licking David's hand. "He tastes nice, he smells nice… he *is* nice."

I ignored the cat. "Well, I didn't know *you* like antiques either."

"I live here. Upstairs." He gestured to the older woman behind the counter. "Mrs Kettering's my landlady."

She sniffed snootily. "I trust your cat will be staying in the bag. We don't want any breakages."

I drew Marmalade Sandwich close and focused on David. "What happened to the three-storey Georgian mansion overlooking The Long Walk where you used to live?"

"As I told you at the time, my parents are rich. I'm not."

A phone rang out the back, so Mrs Kettering shot me a warning look, then slipped away, leaving us alone. Oh fudge cakes, this was the first time we'd been alone in ten years!

I resisted the urge to wipe my clammy hands on my jeans. But how did David always look so cool? Seriously, if *I'd* been wearing a suit, shirt, and perfectly done-up tie, I would've looked constrained, creased, and uncomfortable. How he always looked so fresh and relaxed was infuriating.

In an attempt to shift away from my nervous tension, I stepped over to a shelf crammed with household bric-a-brac and picked up a heavy candlestick. "I'm not usually so clumsy. It just seems to happen when I'm... um..."

"In *my* vicinity?" he asked, smirking smugly.

Right, that was it. I squared up to him. "What *is* with the smirk?"

He glanced at the candlestick I was unintentionally brandishing. "Put *that* down and I'll explain."

I laughed lightly, putting it back. "Sorry. I'm surprised you didn't say something about me holding a candle for you."

He fell serious. "That's because I know you *don't*. But... the smirk, yeah. It's a vampire defence thing."

"Really? How does that work?"

"It's so we can cover our fangs. Humans don't like fangs."

"But humans can't see your fangs, can they? I thought humans couldn't know about magic or it made their brains go funny."

"That's true, but humans aren't stupid and they can detect things unconsciously. When my fangs start extending, it makes them edgy."

I winced, remembering Judy's reaction to him earlier. "*So* does being smirked at. It does make you look a bit smug." *Very smug.*

"I need to get it under control." He rubbed his brow with dexterous fingers. "I've spent my entire life trying to get everything under control. I won't let being a vampire stop me."

I bent, trying to look into his downturned eyes. "You shouldn't be ashamed of who you are."

His eyes flashed icy blue. "Shouldn't I? *You* are, aren't you?"

Ouch. "That was a bit low."

"I apologise." He exhaled heavily.

In the swirling silence, I realised there was something I needed to say. "I'm sorry I outed you to Inspector Taylor. I shouldn't have done that."

"Thanks. I did try to explain everything to him, but he's so busy at the moment." He smiled lightly. "You'll have to tell me if I start smirking."

"All right. You're doing it now."

He groaned and theatrically pushed down his top lip, which made him look cutely vulnerable.

Blimey, I wanted to snog him. I stepped over to a shelf of vases, quickly deciding not to pick up any of them. My hands were still shaking from the shock of Harry's shove. *Not* because David was now standing rather close to me.

There was a mirror behind the shelf of vases, and I realised, as I pretended to be engrossed in a floral pattern, that David's gaze was fixed on me. If I was to turn around now, I'd get a faceful of fang.

He spoke in a dark growl. "Amber, there's something I've been wondering…?"

Oh fudge cakes, he was going to ask me on a date! Our eyes met in the mirror. "Yes?"

"It's just... how did you know about the arsenic?"

Huh? I did a double-take at this swerve ball. "What arsenic?"

"The arsenic in the green paint."

I turned to face him, taking a big step to one side. "Vincent's paintings contained arsenic?"

"They did. We've confiscated them all. And Vincent is in custody."

"He's been arrested?"

"He's helping us with our inquiries."

I scrunched up my eyes to focus. "So... Tony was poisoned with arsenic?"

David hooked his thumbs in his belt. "We're still waiting for the coroner's report. But, the truth is, when I first looked at Tony earlier, I did think he'd been poisoned – his eyes, his skin. But the police pathologist said she's never heard of anyone dying from chilli – not from the small amount he ingested from the heart pill anyway."

I gently lowered Marmalade Sandwich's bag to the carpet, as if the lighter load might help me think. "Are you saying that Vincent might've killed Tony with his paintings? I'm struggling to see how that would work. I mean, yes, the Victorians *did* die from being exposed to the painted wallpaper, but it took months to have an effect. If the paintings were the murder weapon, then surely all Tony's guests at the B&B would also be dropping dead?"

"I'm not saying that's what happened. We just want to know where Vincent got the paint."

"I promise you, David, I know nothing about it. I only mentioned it because it was the identical shade of green to the one I'd written my piece on. But until today, I'd never met Vincent. Or Tony."

He studied me for a moment. "Just don't leave Windsor, okay."

I resented his accusatory tone. "Well, I've just inherited a cottage, so I'll be here for the foreseeable."

He didn't hide his surprise. "You've inherited a cottage? Really?"

"Yes. My grandmother's been murdered."

"*Murdered?* Vermilitrude Eldritch? I didn't hear about that."

"I know. She doesn't want the police involved, in case it puts humans in danger. Or me, for that matter."

He pulled a notepad from his jacket pocket. "But still… Inspector Taylor knows about magic. I'm sure he –"

"No." I yanked the notepad from his fingers. "I definitely don't want *him* involved."

"Why?"

"We haven't exactly hit it off. He's not very friendly, is he?"

"He's all right, he's just very…" He abandoned the analysis of his superior officer and snatched back his notepad. "Did you say you were looking for a lost dog?"

"My granny's corgi, Colin. Apparently the last person to see Colin was Billy Royal – he was Colin's dog walker. Vermilitrude said, *Find Billy and you might find Colin.*"

He chuckled at my impression of her. "Well, we'd like a word with him too. But I can't imagine Billy staying hidden for long. He's the main beneficiary of Tony's will."

Here was my chance to probe for any Colin-related info. "Have you tried tracing Billy's mobile phone?"

"It seems to be switched off."

"Did... um... were there any text messages between Billy and Tony at all?"

The smirk swept back. "Ah, you were listening, were you?"

"You're always so suspicious. I simply stopped outside the gallery to tie my shoelace."

He glanced at my knee-high buckled boots. "Really?"

"Can't you just give me a hint of what the texts between father and son said? It might help me find little Colin."

He sighed wearily. "The one that really caught my attention was Billy's message to his dad saying, *Yes I'll come to your stupid lunch thing. I hope you choke on your food.*"

"Oh blimey." I glanced at the shelves crammed with antiques, trying to get everything straight in my mind. Then another idea struck me. "Have you checked Billy's social media profile?"

"Of course. No helpful death threats."

"Hm." I made a mental note to check Billy's online presence myself… "Why *were* they meeting up at Paws? Have you found out yet?"

"According to their witness statements, Tony was about to make an announcement."

"Yes, but he was waiting for Billy to arrive before he made it?"

"Exactly." David ran his fingers through his dark hair. "What was Billy bringing to the party – that's what I'd like to know."

"Not a can of Paris green paint, I assume… You're smirking again, Sergeant."

I took the liberty of prodding his top lip, which sent unexpected zings down my arm. Well, *that* had been much more flirty than I'd intended.

David wrapped his fingers around my wrist and smiled, exposing his fangs – which elongated.

I recoiled. *Oh no, sorry!*

The smirk became a snarl. "See? People don't like vampires. Even Beings of Magic."

"David, I'm sorry. I just wasn't expecting –"

"*You* don't like vampires – we all know that. But I would never hurt anyone. Especially not y… well, I wouldn't hurt anyone."

"I know." I smiled mischievously, breaking the tension. "*You* just ask innocent young women to lie to the police for you…"

He laughed lightly, holding up his hands. "Well, all right, I did do that."

I realised Mrs Kettering had finished her phone call out the back, and Marmalade Sandwich had curled up for a nap. The gentle silence in our private universe was lovely.

Feeling like David and I had come to a truce of sorts, I stepped over to a cosy corner of the peaceful shop, where china teapots, dainty spoons, and ornate cake stands were on display.

Hmm, this was what Harry had meant about antiques being magical. Each item had its own unique character – and probably a story to tell. I picked up an intricately designed silver spoon. The warm metal was comforting and I could feel the past tingling in its soul. What was I saying? Could a spoon have a soul? Perhaps it could, in its own way.

My eyes were drawn to a large teapot, decorated with several species of English butterflies – the red admiral, the peacock, and the swallowtail. Each picture was hand-painted, and it struck me that a stranger had poured their positive energy into this teapot – and now I was enjoying the fruits of their creativity.

I opened the teapot's lid with a rattle and gazed into its cavernous, tannin-stained insides. How many conversations over a cuppa had this teapot been privy to? In London, I'd chucked coffee down my throat for an instant caffeine fix, but I suddenly appreciated the intricacy of the tea ritual. It was good to slow down. My energy softened.

"How old is this?" I asked David.

He shrugged. "I'm not sure. I can ask Mrs Kettering."

"It's okay. I don't need any details. I can just enjoy it."

He stood beside me. "It's probably quite expensive. She's got some rarities here."

"Expensive, you say?" Remembering what I'd done to the teapot in Harry's photograph, I carefully slid it back. My eyes were drawn to a large orange stone beside it. "What's that?"

David picked it up and held it in his palm. "A paperweight, I guess."

I brushed my fingers over the smooth surface. "What's it for?"

"Holding down papers," he said, smirking.

"But isn't everything done on computers these days?"

"Well then, it has no function other than to *be*."

"I like that."

David put the paperweight back. He looked like he was about to say something poignant, but his phone rang, *gah*! "Yes, sir?"

I could hear Inspector Taylor's muffled voice at the other end of the line. "Sergeant Van Danté, I've emailed you a copy of the coroner's report, but allow me to precis it for you – a fatal dose of arsenic definitely killed Tony Royal. Get hold of Amber Eldritch, will you? I need her to come to the police station immediately, if not sooner."

David glanced worriedly at me. "Is she under arrest, sir?"

"Not yet. But I want a word with her about her intricate knowledge of Paris green paint and arsenic. And this time, I want the truth."

Chapter Twelve

I'd hoped David might take me to the police station on his motorcycle, but alas, my chariot was his unmarked police car.

I clutched Marmalade Sandwich's tote bag close as we stepped inside – dreading what might be about to happen. Was I about to be accused of poisoning Tony with arsenic?

Why hadn't I kept my mouth shut about my Paris green paint article? But Inspector Taylor and his competent sergeant would've probably found it online sooner or later anyway, and then I would've been in even more trouble.

I was, after all, the one who'd made the drinks for Tony and co at Paws for Tea.

Although, of course, my cousin Evelyn had assisted with the drinks. But presumably she was beyond suspicion for being the only person on this planet that Inspector Taylor seemed to actually like.

The shiny foyer of Windsor police station was a hive of crime-fighting activity, with uniformed officers moving purposely and talking loudly. At the front desk, David told me to check in with the desk sergeant.

"I'll be right back," he said – and then strode off, abandoning me.

The desk sergeant was a tall blonde officer, who – I now realised – was sporting an impressive pair of fairy wings. Real fairy wings. Gosh, being armed with my grandmother's wand was certainly an eye-opener.

The desk sergeant's wings fluttered urgently as she spoke into a police radio. "Okay, Constable, follow my instructions carefully. Proceed on foot along Broadway, then infiltrate building number fifty-four with stealth. Ensure no members of the public see you. Once inside, approach the proprietor and collect the loot – a deep pan, thick crust, extra pepperoni, hold the pineapple. Repeat, no pineapple! And I'll have a portion of garlic bread. You can take the money from petty cash on your return to the station. Got that? Right. Over."

She clicked off her radio and spoke casually to me. "I hope he's not too long; I'm starving. Right, love. What can I do for you?"

"Hi," I said nervously. "Sergeant Van Danté told me to check in with you."

"Okey-dokes. What's your name?"

"Amber Eldritch."

"And what time's your appointment?"

"I haven't got an appointment."

Her giant fairy wings drooped. "I'm sorry, you can't see Sergeant Van Danté without an appointment."

"But I arrived with him. He told me to check in with you."

"Oh I see." She perked up. "Do you want to *make* an appointment?"

"Er... okay?"

She hovered her fingers over her computer keyboard. "What's your name?"

"Amber Eldritch."

"And what time's your appointment?"

Fearing that I might end up in an eternal loop of nonsense, I edged away.

I noticed that Alex and David were now deep in conversation on the other side of the foyer. David gestured to me, and Inspector Taylor rolled his eyes, shaking his head. Oh fudge cakes, that didn't look good.

I lowered my head to talk to Marmalade Sandwich, who was lying at the bottom of his bag. "What do you say, puss? Perhaps it's time for a little magic?"

The cat didn't reply. I opened the bag and saw he was snoozing. Aww...

All right, I was on my own. I focused hard on fading, reminding myself of all the times the girls at school had ignored me, or worse. I instinctively felt I needed to hold my breath, so I took a big gulp of air – and my wand responded by tingling on my arm.

Had anything happened? Looking down, *I* could still see my body, but as I glanced at a chrome pillar, I saw that my reflection was transparent. And so was Marmalade Sandwich's bag. Oh my goodness, I was doing magic! Not completely invisible, but certainly not fully there.

No jokes about me never being fully there, thank you!

Holding my breath to retain the spell, I edged across the busy foyer, and stepped behind a convenient free-standing noticeboard to listen to Alex and David's conversation. I gently exhaled, fading back to visible, safely hidden.

Alex spoke in his usual deadpan tone. "Still no sign of Billy Royal, Sergeant?"

"No sir. We can't seem to find him anywhere."

"All right. Track down a list of Billy's dog walking clients, will you? Perhaps one of them's seen him."

"Already done that, sir."

"Oh. Carry out background checks on them, will you?"

"Already done *that*, sir."

"Right, I see. Find anything interesting?"

David spoke conspiratorially. "One of them's a lab technician at the local senior school."

"Really? I doubt they'd have arsenic knocking about at the school, but nevertheless, go and speak to him later. Or have you already done that?"

David laughed lightly. "Not yet, Inspector. I will."

"Good work. By the way," Alex sounded agitated. "What did you mean earlier when you said you can *smell* when someone's heart is beating fast?"

David's voice became tense. "I know I should've told you this before, sir, but like Amber said... I'm a vampire."

There was a brief pause. "I *see*. It won't interfere with your duties, will it? Will you need special days off or... maybe extra-strong sun block?"

David chuckled at what probably wasn't a joke. "Nothing like that, sir. I can function perfectly well in daylight. I just wanted to be honest with you. I know you're aware of Beings of Magic, and I heard from a relative in Maiden-Upon-Avon that your girlfriend had a nasty encounter with a rogue vampire last year."

Pride laced Alex's voice. "She's had a few nasty encounters with rogue *humans* too."

"Well, I just wanted to tell you the truth, sir. I've got into hot water before by not being up-front about what I really am. I'm sorry if I misled you."

Alex's voice softened a notch. "None of us can help who we are. And if people don't accept you, then that's their problem. Now, shall we get on with this interview? Where *is* Amber?"

I heard the swish of suit material as they turned to face the noticeboard.

"Ah," Alex said. "Here are her feet. Find the rest of her and bring her to the interview room, will you?"

The interview room was sterile and cold, containing one plastic table, three chairs, and a tape recorder. There was no bright lamp to shine into my eyes. With Alex and David sitting opposite me like that, such implements were not necessary.

To one side of the table, a long, high mirror was affixed to the wall. I avoided looking in it, in case I was being observed. I felt tense and squashed. But that was probably the intention of this entire set up.

I hooked Marmalade Sandwich's bag onto the back of my chair, leaving him to sleep. "Inspector Taylor, please just tell me, am I in trouble?"

Alex glanced at the tape recorder. It wasn't yet recording. "You might be. But first we need to take your witness statement."

I frowned. "I thought I'd already given Sergeant Van Danté my witness statement?"

Alex didn't take his eyes off me. "Well, that's what I would've thought too. Usually when I give an instruction, it gets carried out. However, it seems that Sergeant Van Danté forgot to take your witness statement earlier, because he was…" Alex read from a piece of paper in front of him. "… shocked and surprised to find you working back at the cat café after all this time."

David glared at the table. Oh dear, at some point earlier, David must've confessed to his boss that, instead of finding out my version of events, we'd had a quick catch up and he'd given me his phone number.

Alex pressed a button on the tape recorder and spoke a preamble into it. Then his laser-like eyes were back on me. "Ms Eldritch, you were the waitress on duty this morning at Paws for Tea. And your aunt, Victoria Sage, was down in the kitchen? Yes?"

"That's right."

Alex sat back in his chair. "Run me through the order that Tony and his guests arrived in."

"Okay." I closed my eyes and scanned my memory. "Hyacinth and Lydia arrived together first. Then Tony. Then Judy."

"Good. And what happened *after* they'd all arrived and sat down?"

I pictured the scene. I'd counted the cats... no, he didn't need to know that. "I took their order. And then Evelyn arrived, and we got started on the drinks before Vincent came bursting in all dramatically, saying he really needed to talk to Judy."

"About what?"

"I'm not sure. He didn't get the chance to say, because Tony invited him to join them, which rather took the wind out of his sails."

"And Vincent sat straight down?" David asked.

"Yeah. And then *Tony* said he had an announcement to make, but that he wanted to wait for Billy to arrive. I must say, there was a lot of tension between them. Tony and Judy were bickering, and it just felt like a bad atmosphere. Anyway, I made the drinks with Evelyn – and we were both extra careful not to accidentally slip in any arsenic, Inspector Taylor. And then Tony started choking... and he died."

Alex held up an evidence bag containing a bottle. "Exhibit A. A half-empty bottle of chilli oil found in the kitchen of Paws for Tea."

Oh fudge cakes, what was he implying?

I shrugged, or tried to – it was hard when I was so tense. "We use chilli oil in some of our dishes."

Alex stared at me for longer than I was comfortable with. I transferred my attention to David, who was also gazing at me intensely. I gulped and looked down at my hands.

Alex tried the slightly friendlier approach. "Speaking hypothetically, Ms Eldritch, if you wanted to kill someone at Paws for Tea, how would you go about it?"

David raised an eyebrow in my direction. If he was trying to tell me something, he'd need to be clearer than that. I didn't speak 'eyebrow'.

I held firm eye-contact with Alex. "I *wouldn't*."

The 'nice act' fell away as Alex leaned on the table. "Where's the arsenic, Amber?"

"I don't know!" My eyes darted to the door, where a uniformed officer was trying to blend in. I lowered my voice. "Do you maybe think Vincent did it? Via the paint? Sergeant Van Danté told me that his paintings *did* contain arsenic and Vincent was in custody."

David and Alex shared a look that I couldn't decipher. Then David spoke flatly. "We've let Vincent go."

"For *now*," Alex added. "He claims he had no *idea* that the paint contained arsenic."

I resisted the urge to reach for my reporter's notebook. "Where did he get it then?"

"He's conveniently forgotten," Alex muttered. "I did hope that a night in our cells without any dinner might jog his memory, but the superintendent kindly reminded me that's *not* how we do things around here."

"Wow… So, Tony was poisoned at Paws with arsenic." My thoughts shuffled around in my head. "But how? Was it the heart pills? Did the killer somehow get a fatal dose of arsenic into the pill that Tony took? And if so, how did they know which one he'd pick? Or perhaps they poisoned all of them, then swapped the bottles. And that means the pills must've been tampered with by someone who knew that Tony always took them with his lunch. And they must've been close enough to get a swipe of the bottle. What do you two think?"

Alex smiled humourlessly. "I think *you* ask too many questions."

"Have you tested all the glasses?" I asked. "Perhaps that's how they did it?"

Alex's voice dripped with sarcasm. "Blimey, Sergeant, why didn't *we* think of that?"

"No traces were found," David explained. "And Tony's tablets were only coated with chilli oil, which isn't deadly outside of a vindaloo curry."

I bit my lip in concentration. "So where did the poison come from?"

"That was going to be my next question," Alex said flatly.

"Not from *me*."

David tried playing 'good cop'. "Amber, just tell us how you knew about the arsenic, okay? Perhaps you overheard Tony's guests discussing it? Or you saw it somewhere?"

"I don't even know what arsenic looks like. I promise you both – and I do understand how it looks

– but it was just a lucky guess. Or unlucky. And not even a guess. I just recognised the shade of green paint. I have no motive, opportunity, or… what's the other thing?"

"Means," David said.

"And no means."

Alex clicked off the tape recorder. "All right, you can go."

Without hesitating, I scraped back my chair, grabbed Marmalade Sandwich's bag, and scarpered.

I wasn't sure if I'd convinced them of my innocence. But I really hoped the police would soon figure out who *had* killed Tony – because there was no way my nerves could stand another Taylor/Van Danté interrogation ever again.

Chapter Thirteen

There was only one place to go after that: Paws for Tea. The police had finally left, and it was closing time anyway, so Vicky was sitting at the table by the window, cashing up the day's pre-murder takings. At the back of the café, Harry was sitting at the desk that functioned as his office. Harry loved antiquated artefacts, so his *Windsor Magical Mystery Tours* workspace consisted of a clunky old typewriter, piles of leatherbound ledgers, and an old-fashioned inkwell. Perhaps they'd all come from the Magical Mews, or even Mrs Kettering's antiques shop.

As the café door swept shut behind me, Vicky and Harry stopped what they were doing and greeted me with a cheery hello. My heart fluttered with joy to be back with these two again. In London, I'd lived in a tiny one-bedroom flat, and had come home each evening to a half-dead potted plant. But here, Vicky and Harry seemed delighted to see me, despite it only having been a short while since we'd parted.

Marmalade Sandwich went out the back to play with his fuzzy feline friends – and to enjoy a bowl of well-earned food after all that snoozing throughout my police interview.

I grabbed a tub of clean cutlery and a pile of napkins and sat down with Vicky, explaining to them both about the ordeal I'd been subjected to.

Harry came over to sit with us. "That's incredible, Bambi – David's living above the antiques shop?"

I buffed a knife. "That's not the part I was expecting you to get snagged on, Harry. That police interrogation was terrifying."

Vicky counted out a pile of fivers. "They gave *me* a grilling earlier too. I think they might be trying to connect the chilli oil with me. But I'm really not in the habit of trying to poison my customers."

Harry grabbed a handful of pound coins to count. "I don't think anyone could accuse you of having a bad bone in your body, Vix."

They shared a smile. I loved how well they got along – my best friend and my lovely aunt. Now that my granny was gone, they were all I had left. Apart from Marmalade Sandwich, of course.

"I can't stop thinking about little Colin," I said, dropping a polished fork into the cutlery tray. "Oh – I had a thought earlier… I wonder if there's any info on Billy's social media profile concerning Colin's whereabouts."

I typed Billy's name into my phone, easily finding his online social media presence. Scrolling through, there were several posts advertising his dog walking services, and a few photos of him with his mates. But nothing about Colin jumped out – and there was no mention of his dad at all.

Oh well, it was worth a try. But Inspector Taylor was adamant that he wanted Tony's missing son found, so I knew David would be busy sweeping up clues.

But *I* had a different kind of sweeping to do. I'd always loved sweeping and mopping when I'd worked here before. Safe in the knowledge that the guests had enjoyed their tea, cakes, and lovely kitties, I could absorb myself in the mindful process of clearing up. It was like being a sailor onboard a galleon. Like a pirate!

As Vicky swept, I mopped the floor after her, swishing and swooshing my entire body from side to side, becoming at one with the mop, and fantasising about exploring the high seas with a pirate crew, shiver me timbers, arrr, pieces of eight...

In the middle of my swabbing-the-decks fantasy, my phone bleeped, bringing me back to this century. It was a text message from my cousin Evelyn, inviting me to join her and some locals on the village green for an early evening game of cricket. Oh, that sounded lovely – apart from the cricket.

I invited Vicky and Harry, grabbed Marmalade Sandwich, and off we set.

Now that the merry month of May was in full bloom, we could make the most of the lighter and warmer evenings. And almost directly opposite my new cottage was the village green and cricket club. The perfect location for a pre-dinner cuppa.

Despite finding cricket about as interesting as a boiled potato, there was admittedly something endearing about the game. Perhaps it was the nostalgia it evoked, reminding me of endless lazy summer days. And of course, the cricketers only came out when the sun did, so it was a sign that the rain had finally stopped!

The game was famously slow and steady, and the only excitement was when the spectators clapped politely at a jolly good shot. All very dignified. But crucially, cricket was the only sport I knew that actually incorporated a tea-break into its schedule. How terribly English.

The smell of freshly cut grass caressed my nostrils as I sat on a picnic rug with Evelyn, watching the impromptu cricket match. A pub called The Inn on the Green was a stone's throw away, and Vicky and Harry had disappeared inside to grab some tea.

I watched the players clad in their whites, sprinting across the green to catch out the batsman. It looked awfully civilised and gentlemanly – provided you didn't get close enough to hear what they were actually saying to each other.

David was currently bowling, and Inspector Taylor was up to bat. This should be interesting…

Evelyn watched him proudly. "Come on, Dimples!" she called out.

Alex took position and threw her a smile. A smile, wow! He must be feeling relaxed after a fun afternoon of grilling innocent women.

Marmalade Sandwich stretched lazily on the rug, arching his back and exposing his creamy, spotted tummy. Evelyn rubbed his fluffy down. "So, you *are* Amber's familiar, are you, little puss?"

"Mew, meow!" Marmalade Sandwich rolled over, laughing and purring at her gentle touch. Then, for no apparent reason, he engulfed her hand with all four legs, and nibbled her fingers – gently kicking with his kangaroo-like back feet.

"Hey, play nicely," I said to the cat.

Evelyn chuckled. "He's all right. You should meet my cat, Trixie. She's always attacking me. Alex calls her the velociraptor!"

"Takes one to know one," I said. "Your boyfriend's terrifying in police-mode."

She practically swooned. "He's good, isn't he. Always extra-hunky when he's angry. Hey, did he treat you to one of his looks? Never fails to make me weak at the knees."

I didn't hide my defensive tone. "He accused me of killing Tony."

"Oh bless him. He does get very into his job. But he's a big softy really. You just have to get beyond the steely wall."

I watched David bowl overarm to Alex, who thwacked the ball with a skilled *crack*. "I can't imagine him gushing *I love yous*."

Evelyn spoke with sincere affection. "He doesn't really talk about his feelings. But he shows them. And he wrote me a lovely little poem one Valentine's Day years ago. I guess some men find it easier to write down their feelings than say them. Especially English men."

I traced my fingers over the pattern on the picnic rug. "Well, *I'd* just like to talk to him without being accused of murder. Are you both coming to the pub tonight? It'll be great to see the old place again after all these years."

"Ah, I would, but Alex has got us tickets to see *The Mouse Trap* at Windsor Theatre. He's booked us a table at a nice restaurant. He's so romantic and sweet."

David bowled Alex another ball. As he swung the bat and cracked it hard, I tried to imagine him being romantic and sweet. Nope...

But Evelyn obviously saw something wonderful in him, and that was all that mattered. I leaned back on my hands, watching the fluffy white clouds scull past in the sky. The air was thick with the sweet scent of May blossoms. I exhaled peacefully.

Evelyn picked up on my relaxed vibe. "How are you enjoying being back in Windsor?"

I rolled my eyes and chuckled. "Apart from the murders – and being accused of murder? Er... it's the same as always really. *I've* changed – Windsor hasn't."

"Is that a good thing?"

I scrunched up my face as I considered this. "It's nice to have some stability here. London's always so hectic. I think I've become a bit disconnected from myself, if that makes sense?"

She reached out and squeezed my hand. "It makes perfect sense. I've lived in London too."

"But here..." I gestured to the rolling green fields in the distance. "Don't laugh, but I really enjoyed mopping the café floor earlier. How sad is that?"

She spoke kindly. "It sounds lovely. My waitress Leia always loves mopping at the end of the shift. Apparently she has pirate fantasies!"

Excitement swept through me. "*I* was having a pirate fantasy! Leia sounds cool – I'd love to meet her."

"She's playing at your aunt's Merrie May Ball tomorrow, so you can meet her then."

"Playing what?"

"Oh, she's a musician – a guitarist. She's really talented."

"Wow, that's so cool." I tickled Marmalade Sandwich's tummy. "I can't wait to hear her songs!"

Evelyn's face lit up. "Have *you* got any hobbies?"

I bit my lip, stifling my bubbling enthusiasm. A chat with Evelyn was like drinking a refreshing tonic on a hot day. "Er, I've always enjoyed baking. But I haven't done any for ages. I worked long hours in London, so I didn't have time."

"Then bake! How about reading? You're a journalist, you must love stories?"

"I haven't read a book for years." I fiddled with a blade of grass. "It's not good, is it?"

"Well, there's a wonderful little second-hand bookshop up the road."

"How do you know that?"

"Because I spent an hour in there this afternoon." Her smile was like a tender massage of the soul. "Who's your favourite author? Dickens?"

"Bit grim."

"Austin?"

"Too whimsical."

She spoke like a doctor prescribing a wonder-drug. "Then it surely must be Agatha Christie."

My energy soared. "I've never actually read an Agatha Christie. But I've seen a couple of Poirot films, which I enjoyed."

"There you go then. Grab yourself a Dame Agatha and have a murder mystery adventure!"

Her enthusiasm was wonderfully infectious – I wanted to go to the bookshop straight away and buy up all their stock.

But Vicky and Harry emerged from the Inn on the Green carrying a tray of tea things, so Dame Agatha would have to wait. As they handed out the cups and saucers, and placed the teapot, milk jug, and sugar bowl on the picnic rug, it struck me again how mindful the tea ritual was. We English liked to take our time over tea because it was worth the wait. It was important, like a work of art.

I focused on pouring the hot stream of golden liquid from teapot to cup, adding a splash of milk and a sugar cube – then stirring three times anti-clockwise, enjoying the charming *clink-clink-clinking*. How marvellous to observe the mini-whirlpool in my teacup… and then finally the first delicate sip!

Drinking tea like this, rather than glugging it out of a plastic cup, made this everyday event special. I realised there could be specialness even in the most mundane things – mopping the floor, drinking my tea… even in breathing. Sitting here with my friends and family was a common occurrence, but it was equally one of the most precious and special things in my life.

I thought about the antique teapot again. And the paperweight. All my possessions had fitted into one suitcase, because I tended to read e-books, stream music, and watch films online. Those things had their benefits, and I didn't want lots of clutter. But that paperweight, that antique teapot... I wanted to own them, for no other reason than to appreciate their uselessness. They were just beautiful, and that was enough.

Sipping my lovely cuppa, I started to feel warm, so I took off my cardigan. I'd almost forgotten that my wand was there, flush against my tricep in its lacy armband.

Evelyn spoke proudly. "That's the perfect place for it, Amber. What a beautiful armband. Did you make it?"

I tried to sound casual. "I fancied doing some sewing. That was another hobby I used to enjoy."

Evelyn's eyes sparkled with kindness. "*I* was reluctant to embrace magic when I first discovered it. But it's very cool."

Harry turned from watching the cricket. "This is what I've been telling her."

Vicky topped up her teacup. "Amber's spent a lifetime battling with magic. I think she sees it like… like a pain in the arse that pops up when she's least expecting it."

"That's precisely how I see it, yes." I twiddled my long hair around my fingers. "But perhaps I should try to befriend it, rather than fighting it all the time."

"Befriending it is a good start, but there's so much more." Evelyn rummaged in her handbag and pulled out her magic mirror. "Magic can actually help solve murders!"

My jaw dropped open. "Solve murders? Evelyn, I've no interest in solving murders. I'm just interested in finding Colin the corgi. *And* in making sure your boyfriend stops suggesting that I had anything to do with Tony's death."

Evelyn waved this away. "All right, but let's do this spell. It might help Alex, and a happy Alex is always…" She blushed. "Well, I won't say. But with your permission, Amber, I can cast a spell to project *your* memories of Tony's death onto the surface of my mirror. The spell can only see what your eyes saw at the time, but we can look around your peripheral vision at anything you might've unconsciously seen. Do you agree to that?"

I glanced at Harry who nodded eagerly. Vicky threw me an encouraging thumbs up. Feeling like I was on the cusp of something wonderful, I let out a nervous laugh. "Go on then, let's go for it."

With the sound of the cricket continuing in the background, Evelyn closed her eyes. "Here we go then. *Mirror, mirror in my hand, show Amber's memories, I command…*"

The surface of the mirror waved and wobbled like an old TV being tuned. Then, to my amazement, I saw a 'movie' of Tony, Judy, Lydia, and Hyacinth sitting at their table at Paws for Tea. The scene was being watched through my eyes, and 'the camera' – me – glanced at my waitress pad.

On the screen, Tony spoke gruffly. "We'd like to order some drinks."

"Uh-huh? And what are your top tips for beverage buying? You don't mind if I quote you, do you? What are your names, ages, and addresses?"

I cringed. This could get embarrassing.

Vicky pulled a face at me. "Amber, why did you ask them that?"

"Sorry, it was the notepad. I went into journalist mode."

Harry flapped his hand. "Quiet, I'm trying to listen."

"Oh look, there's me!" Marmalade Sandwich said with a mew. "What a handsome ginger hunk I am!"

I gazed agog at the scene in the café. Then an idea struck me. "Evelyn, can you adjust the speed? If we slow it down, we might be able to see if any of them tampered with Tony's pills?"

Evelyn paused the 'movie' on the mirror, then restarted the playback at ultra-slow-mo. I scrutinised the seating arrangement. The rectangular table had five chairs around it, and Judy and Tony were facing each other at the end nearest me. Hyacinth was in the middle of the table, and Lydia was at the other end. An empty seat for Billy had been left opposite Lydia.

We watched as the 'camera' moved away from the table, and I hugged Evelyn at the counter. After a bit of chitchat with my cousin, I took Tony his beer and Judy her water. But then nothing much happened, and certainly no one was tampering with Tony's pills on the edges of my vision. Vincent came bursting in, telling Judy that he needed to see her. He then sat opposite Hyacinth, and nothing much happened again until Tony started choking.

"Judy passed him the glass of water," Marmalade Sandwich said, flicking his tail.

I sat bolt upright. "Yes! *Judy* handed him the water."

Evelyn rewound that part, and we watched Judy passing her glass to Tony. "Quick, love, drink this!"

A brainwave flashed in my mind. "Was the arsenic in the *glass of water*? Was *that* how Judy did it?"

Harry squinted in confusion. "But then what was the chilli oil about? And how and when did Judy *add* the arsenic to the glass of water?"

"And," Vicky said, "why didn't the police find any traces of arsenic when they tested the glass? Did Judy take it away with her somehow?"

My brainwave was interrupted as the cricketers cheered.

Evelyn smiled wryly. "Oh look, David caught-out Alex."

Alex was laughing and shaking David's hand. He might be a bit grumpy, but he was clearly a good sport. Alex called over to us. "Oi, Eldritch, you're up next, come on!"

I froze. "Me? Oh no, I can't play cricket."

"It's all right," Evelyn said, clambering to her feet. "He's talking to me."

Chapter Fourteen

After the cricket and a nice dinner with Vicky, Harry and I headed for the pub.

Ah, English pub culture, where sticky floors and kitsch decor were as traditional as the Queen's corgis and our love for queuing.

My local pub, the Swan Uppers, was a beautiful old building that stood precariously across the road from Paws for Tea, like a stack of beer mats after one too many pints. It was delightful from the outside, with its whitewashed walls and old Tudor beams. Ivy grew up all four sides, as a constant reminder that Mother Nature would always find a way to reclaim even our oldest human structures.

Traditionally, all English pubs had been given names that could easily be depicted on a sign outside, such as The Coach and Horses, The King's Head, or The Crown. This was because these 'public houses' had been community focal points long before people could read. Churches had spires for the same reason, offering a similar community spirit of kindness, music, and a touch of magic. The sign outside The Swan Uppers depicted a cracked, faded river scene, which squeaked on rusty hinges in the gentle breeze.

As I heaved open the creaky door, I was struck with a wave of nostalgia – as well as the aroma of decades old ale. The interior hadn't changed since the last time I was here, encapsulating the 'faded charm' of English pubs everywhere – wobbly tables, peeling wallpaper, and food that ought to come with a government health warning. But, with its low ceiling and huge fireplace, it was cosy, nostalgic, and warm.

Tonight seemed to be open mic night, and the middle-aged man sitting in front of the dartboard was playing a beautiful folk song on his acoustic guitar. I spotted several familiar faces in the crowd – people I hadn't seen for ten years, but who were almost part of the furniture. They were still here! I was home.

And then I noticed Klaus the pub landlord, working hard behind the bar, serving drinks to the gathered punters. Wow, Klaus had aged like a fine wine. He was tall and broad-shouldered, with the sculpted muscles you'd expect from someone who'd spent years lifting barrels of ale and wrestling with his dual identity of werewolf and publican. We'd always got along well, and at one time I'd wondered if we might date, but it'd never happened for one reason or another. And then I'd left for London.

As Harry and I squeezed into the throng at the bar, Klaus's eyes lit up. He quickly poured a couple of pints and placed them in front of us. "Amber, it's awesome to see you. Welcome home. These are on the house."

My eyes welled with tears at this simple gesture of kindness. But sometimes it was the simplest things that could mean the world. Klaus was clearly more sensitive than his rugged outer shell might imply. He lifted the bar flap and stepped through to give me a hearty hug.

I resisted squeezing his bulging biceps, because that would've been a bit pervy during a friendly welcome-home embrace.

Still hugging me, he said, "Amber, is that a cat in your bag?"

I laughed. Marmalade Sandwich had insisted on coming along again. I thought he'd fallen asleep at the bottom of the bag, but the pub hubbub must've woken him.

I checked the cat was okay, and was about to pick up my pint, when a couple of women at the bar called over. "Is that Amber Eldritch? Oh Amber – you look just the same as when you left!"

And suddenly I was catching up with everyone. It seemed that Beings of Magic and humans alike came here to chat, drink, and enjoy the music – although of course, the humans knew nothing of magic. They probably just loved the magical atmosphere.

Immersed in the snuggly vibes, I was filled with a sense of belonging that I hadn't felt for years.

In London, the pubs I'd frequented with my newspaper colleagues had been corporate bars – all shiny wooden floors and chrome. The music had always been a little too modern for my liking – and far too loud to chat. I'd been one person lost in the crowd. But here, in the cherished Swan Uppers, people I hadn't seen for ten years were saying hello and asking me genuine questions about my life. They not only remembered me, but they wanted to *know* me. Me. Not some ideal of who I ought to be. But me. Amber Eldritch.

After I'd been hugged and gently interrogated by various groups and individuals, Harry and I sat down at a wobbly table. I wedged a folded beer mat under one of the table's legs. It was tradition.

"Cheers, Bambi." Harry said, as we clinked pints.

It was packed in here, so Harry folded his wings behind him and leaned forward to chat. "You said over dinner you wanted to think about the missing corgi. But where do you even start looking for a lost dog?"

I rummaged in my tote bag, making Marmalade Sandwich squirm and mew. "Hey, careful where you're rummaging!"

"I just need my reporter's notebook." I pulled it out and spoke to Harry. "Let's make a list of all the places Colin might be."

"Good idea." Harry sipped his pint. "I guess he might've run off and is frolicking in the Great Park?"

My heart filled with tender worry. "I hope not. I'm not sure how resourceful he is."

Marmalade Sandwich got comfy on my lap. "Poor little pup. Hey, better check the local shelters."

I wrote down *local animal shelters*. "Great idea, well done, puss."

Harry raised his voice against the guitarist massacring a perfectly nice Bob Dylan song. "What about posting something online? Or would that draw too much attention to our search?"

"If he's been kidnapped... dog-napped... we don't want the dog-napper knowing we're sniffing around."

"Yeah," Marmalade Sandwich said. "Because *we* might be next!"

Harry spoke pensively. "I suppose if he's been kidnapped, someone would've been in touch for a ransom by now?"

I was about to reply, when Judy stormed into the pub and halted at our table. Her palpable fury shattered my relaxed vibe. "*There* you are, Amber Eldritch! Is it true that you told the police that Vincent's paintings contained arsenic?"

I held out my hands. "Not exactly."

She frantically twisted her wedding ring. "Don't deny it – Lydia told me all about it. Well, the police have seized them all now – taken them away. My paintings! Isn't it enough that my husband has been poisoned? Now my exhibition and gallery are ruined too, and it's all your fault!"

She turned and stormed out before I could reply.

My ears rang as if I'd been slapped. All around me, the pub remained cheery and light, but my seat was now an island of tingling shock.

Harry squeezed my hand. "She's wrong to blame you, Bambi."

I exhaled heavily. "It's okay. I know she's upset because her husband's been murdered. But is she upset because she's about to get arrested for it?"

Harry's eyes widened. "The lady doth protest too much?"

"Perhaps." I drained my beer. "Come on, let's have another drink. It's my round."

On my way to the bar, I was 'accosted with kindness' by another group of locals, who wanted to hear all about my life. Their friendliness soothed me, dispersing the lingering grottiness of Judy's accusation. When I returned with two beers, Harry was gazing at a gold ring, as if he was auditioning for the part of Mr Frodo.

"What's that?" I asked, sitting back down.

He tore his gaze away. "I found it on the floor. I think Judy must've dropped it – I saw her twisting her wedding ring when she was talking to you just now."

"Give it to me." I held out my hand. "I'll return it. It'll be a good excuse to assure her I mean no harm."

"*And* to try to get more info out of her?" Harry said, raising a knowing eyebrow.

As Marmalade Sandwich slunk back onto my lap, I realised that perhaps Evelyn had been right. Perhaps I *did* want to solve this murder. I dropped the ring into Marmalade Sandwich's tote bag then, with my energy rising, I picked up my notebook. "Just for fun, let's write down everything we know about the murder."

Harry got comfy in his seat. "Right. Let's start with suspect numero uno. Tony's wife, Judy. She told us earlier that she'd made Tony's dream of owning a B&B come true, but then *Lydia* told us that he's recently threatened her with divorce. Did she kill him for spurning her?"

"Perhaps. But I do sense Judy genuinely loved Tony – and still does."

Harry smiled encouragingly. "Is that witch's intuition?"

I snorted. "Hardly. And it probably means I'm wrong."

"Anyway," Harry continued. "Judy was seen in the magic mirror giving Tony the water when he was choking, which could've been how she gave him the arsenic."

I jotted down a summary of Judy's motive and possible means. *Spurned after years of loving loyalty – arsenic in water.* "Okay next, Vincent, the local artist. We still need to speak to him to figure out his motive. But if he's been painting with arsenic-laced Paris green paint, did *he* somehow slip the poison into Tony's pills or glass?"

Harry raised a finger. "But let's not forget that none of the remaining pills nor the glass contained traces of arsenic when the police checked."

"Yes. And also, why did Tony invite Vincent to join them after he'd flounced in like that? I wish we knew what Tony's big announcement was."

Harry swirled his beer in his glass. "And *why* was he so keen to wait for Billy – his grown-up son and local dog walker?"

I vaguely listened to the song in the background as my thoughts churned. "David said that Billy is the police's prime suspect. I'm wondering about *his* motive: I guess dog walking might not pay the bills, especially in a town like Windsor – so did he need the money? Billy is the main beneficiary of Tony's will and, according to their text messages, father and son didn't get on."

"I think we should try and talk to Billy," Harry said. "Putting aside the death of Tony for a moment, Billy *was* the last person to see Colin the corgi. He might actually know something about your granny's murder."

Yes — he might've actually done it, yikes! "It would be good to chat with him. But why can't the police get hold of him? Has he absconded?" I played with Marmalade Sandwich's velvety ears. "From what Lydia and Hyacinth said, Billy Royal sounds like a bad sort. Although my *granny* didn't say that. In fact, she said he'd helped her with the microchipping of Colin, which is actually quite nice."

Harry's lips curled into a cheeky grin. "I only met your grandmother once as a teenager, but she definitely commands one's best behaviour. Even from the likes of Billy Royal."

I chuckled. "Fair point."

Harry gestured to my notebook. "Right, what about Hyacinth, Tony's hippy B&B-owning next-door neighbour? Tony wants to cut down her sacred tree and build another extension on *his* half of their shared garden. But that's surely not a motive to kill him?"

"And what was Hyacinth doing at the café? Why had she been invited along?"

I jotted down these questions.

"And finally," Harry said, "we have Royal Boutique B&B receptionist Lydia. She arranged the lunch at Tony's request, but he didn't tell her what his big announcement was going to be. And according to the ad we found online, he was possibly about to fire her – understandably as she seems to prefer painting her nails to working."

I swigged my pint, enjoying this 'armchair investigation'. "I wonder if Lydia knew about the arsenic in the paint? Just now, Judy said that *Lydia* had told her it was *me* who'd told the police about it. But did Lydia already know somehow?"

Harry gasped with realisation. "Lydia could've tampered with Tony's pills in advance – she had access to Tony all the time! Although, saying that, she was sitting furthest away from Tony at lunch, so *would* she have been able to poison his water?"

I tapped my notepad with my pen, trying to unravel my thoughts. "You know what I think? I think Judy added the arsenic to her glass of water while everyone was watching Tony choke. Then she handed him the water to drink, patting him on the back – all innocent."

"Yeah! Perhaps the Paris green paint *was* the murder weapon. All Judy had to do was crumble a little bit of it into the water, then hand it to Tony when he was choking. Maybe she then somehow smuggled the contaminated glass out of the café."

I sat up as a thought struck me, waking the sleeping cat. "Oops, sorry, puss. But is *that* why there was chilli oil all over Tony's heart pills?"

Harry frowned. "How do you mean?"

"I mean, what if the chilli was there precisely to *prevent* Tony from making his announcement? What if the person who tampered with the pills wanted not to kill him, but *silence* him?"

"But he died," Harry said.

"But not of the chilli. He died from arsenic poisoning."

"So who would want him to not say something?"

Before I could start speculating, Klaus came over to sit with us. "By the way, Amber, I heard about the murder at Paws. Is Vicky okay?"

"I think so. She's very resilient. But it's a shock to everyone."

Klaus scratched his manly stubble with strong fingers. "It's such a shame about Tony. He's been talking a lot recently about wanting to get away from it all to clear his head. What a pity he didn't leave sooner."

I leaned forward. "Tony's been talking about leaving?"

Klaus shrugged. "Yeah, just for a month or so. *I* suggested Thailand, because when I went there a few years ago, it helped me sort my head out – there's a lot of meditation and mystical stuff. I even said Tony could have the Bhats I had left over. You can't officially buy currency outside the country, so it's good to take a few notes with you. I dug them out for him."

Harry's wings unfurled and flapped in time to the music. "*That* was his big announcement then maybe? Tony was leaving for a bit?"

"Maybe." Klaus grabbed Harry's empty glass and stood up. He was about to walk away, but stepped back. "Tony told me he wanted to clear up a few home truths before he left. He said he was planning to gather everyone together and tell them over lunch."

"What sort of home truths?" I asked, itching for him to spill the beans.

Klaus lowered his voice. "Well, firstly, Tony said he knew his wife was carrying on with someone behind his back, and he was going to tell her to choose, you know? *And* there was someone else he was fighting with, who he planned to have it out with once and for all."

Hyacinth, perhaps?

I tried to sound casual. "Have you told the police this?"

"They haven't asked me. I didn't know Tony that well – just from when he used to drink in here. But I guess it really goes to show that you should do the things you want when you can, because you never know what might be around the corner." Klaus brightened up. "Hey, Amber, perhaps *you* could look into this? You could help the police with their investigation?"

"Me? Why me?"

"You're a journalist, aren't you? You surely must be good at investigating?"

"I'm not a journalist anymore. And I was only a tabloid journalist for a scurrilous scandal-sheet."

"Well then," he said. "Perhaps it's time to use your skills for good?"

Klaus strolled off to collect a few more glasses. I exchanged a look with Harry. Did I really want to get involved with this? Risk the wrath of Inspector Taylor?

It was appealing – exciting. I vowed to give it more thought tomorrow, but for now, I was going to have another beer and enjoy being home.

Chapter Fifteen

Day Two

I woke up in the comfy bed at my new cottage to the sound of birdsong, with Marmalade Sandwich snuggled up beside me. I wrapped him in my arms, making him purr loudly. Mmm, what lovely, cosy contentment.

I hadn't closed the pretty curtains properly last night, and the soft sunshine was now dousing my snuggly bed in a dappled shaft of light.

"Good morning, Amber," the cat said. "I expect you'll want to pour a drop of cream in a bowl to accompany my breakfast."

I stretched my arms over my head, making my body judder all the way to my pointed toes. "Come on then, puss, let's see what delights I can rustle up for us both."

Vicky didn't need me at Paws today, so I wrapped an old cardigan around the vest and boxer shorts I'd slept in, fed Marmalade Sandwich his kitty food, and enjoyed my toast and tea in the rustic kitchen.

I didn't have a teapot or milk jug yet, but I vowed to treat myself to a full tea service soon. My energy rose as I decided not to buy everything at once, but instead, it would be fun to select each item carefully. Perhaps I could visit Mrs Kettering's shop, and buy that beautiful butterfly teapot! And maybe I'd bump into her lodger while I was there…

Shoving that vampire out of my mind, I focused on the enticing idea of collecting antiques. Evelyn had suggested I needed a hobby, and the thought of learning about antiques made me feel zingy inside. Never ignore your zinginess, Amber. That was going to be my new motto. Oh, I knew life couldn't *all* be zings, but the bad times, the... um... the zongs, they just made the zings even sweeter.

Feeling ready to start the day, I shrugged off my cardigan and decided to explore the kitchen properly. There were cupboards crammed full of witch's paraphernalia, and my grandmother's iron cauldron and herb collection looked fascinating. But just as I was getting started, I jumped at the sound of a knock at the door. I grinned. This was probably Harry. He was a definite zing in my life and always welcome.

I opened the front door with a big smile. "Good morn—argh!"

"Hi Amb–"

I slammed the door in David's face. What the fudge cakes was he doing here?

Marmalade Sandwich trotted out of the kitchen. "What's wrong? What happened?"

I hopped from foot-to-foot. "It's David. He saw me..."

David knocked on the door again. "Amber, what's wrong?"

"Of course he saw you," Marmalade Sandwich said, sitting down. "What did you expect him to see when you opened the door?"

"I didn't expect *him* to be there. I thought it was going to be Harry. I'm wearing an old vest and men's boxer shorts!"

Marmalade Sandwich started to wash. "I don't understand humans. You look the same as always to me."

I straightened my hair in the mirror by the door, then opened it again.

David inhaled to speak. "Amb–"

Wait! I slammed the door. Did I have sleep-gunk on my face? I checked the mirror again. Phew, no. I was clean.

I opened the door.

David's fist was raised, ready to knock. I leaned out the way.

He unclenched his hand. "Sorry. Are you okay?"

I opened my mouth to reply, but oh yikes, I hadn't cleaned my teeth! I pressed my lips together as I spoke. "Yep. Sorry about that."

"What happened?"

"Oh, it's just I thought you were going to be Harry... I mean, I'm wearing what I slept in."

His eyes filled with kindness. "You look beautiful, Amber. You surely must know that."

Oh dear, I felt myself glow. And I didn't mean I blushed coyly. The trouble was, whenever I fancied someone, my aura always glowed with golden sparkles beyond my control. If the object of my desire had been human, he wouldn't have known. But David was far from human. It was embarrassing.

I composed myself. "Shall we start again?"

His face broke into a smile. "All right."

I closed the door again and grinned. Blimey, he looked handsome this morning. Was it my imagination, or was there something zingier about him today too? Even though there was now a door between us, I realised the smirk had faded. Was he making a special effort? Or had something changed? Was it because of—

David interrupted my thoughts. "Ready?"

"Yep!"

He chuckled, then knocked on the door again.

I laughed too, opening it. "Good morning, Sergeant Van Danté, *do* come in. Would you like some tea?"

"Sounds delightful." He stepped into my cosy living room, taking in the surroundings. "So this is the famous new cottage?"

I could tell he was impressed with the simplistic layout, the oak-beamed ceiling, and all the quirky knick-knacks in the glass cabinet atop the wooden dresser. The old, worn furniture gave the place a charming warmth, and I felt very proud of the cosy vibe my granny had created. I pictured David and I sharing pleasant times together in this room. Well, not *just* David, of course. All my friends and family.

David held aloft a gift-wrapped box. "You can use *this* for the tea."

"Oh…" Whatever this gift was, I felt touched by his kindness, but a nervous joke popped out. "If it's a severed head, I shall be very upset."

He laughed lightly. "Oh drat, I wonder if it's too late to get a refund…"

I placed the box on the writing desk, tugged off the ribbon, then opened it slowly. Ahh, how lovely. My nerves faded and my heart fluttered – it was the butterfly teapot!

I bit my lip to suppress my grin. "You must be psychic, David. I was just thinking about this."

He shrugged coolly. "House-warming present."

I turned to face him, wondering whether to give him a hug, but Marmalade Sandwich twined himself between my shins. "Better make the tea then. And I'll have a drop more cream."

"Hey, little cat…" David crouched to stroke Marmalade Sandwich, meaning his head was – yikes, I took a huge step back.

"Yes, I'll get the kettle on. I've got an unopened packet of chocolate biscuits in the kitchen."

David's smirk popped back. "You know the way to a man's heart."

"Er, well, I know the way to a *vampire's* heart."

He stood up. "Oh yeah?"

I rested my hand on his chest. *Wow, his pecs were toned.* "Yeah… with a sharpened stake."

"Hm..." He covered my hand with his, lowering his face to mine. "And what's the way to a witch's heart?"

I pulled my hand away. "Er… um… chocolate biscuits…"

"Of course." He fell serious. "Actually, Amber, I have a bit of a strange request."

"Uh-huh?"

"Would you... come with me to the magical library?"

"Oh. Um, why?" I gestured to the sofa.

David sat down, getting comfy. "Well, you know Vincent Varney? The artist who was dining with the others when Tony died?"

I perched at the other end of the sofa. "I could hardly forget. He was arrested because his paint contained arsenic, but he denied all knowledge of it and conveniently forgot where he bought the paint from."

"Exactly. Well, I want to talk to him again, but there's something... I need to catch him in the act."

Marmalade Sandwich leapt on my lap. "What act?" I asked.

"I'm *sure* I did just mention a drop more cream, Amber?" the cat said, padding his paws into my bare thighs.

"Ow, be gentle..."

"Pleeeeease!"

"Shh..." I glanced at David. "Oh not *you*. Sorry, what were you saying?"

"Creeeeeeam, pleeeeeease!"

"Not *you*. Carry on, David."

"I was..." David did a double-take at the cat, then continued. "I was following Vincent just now and he went into Windsor Public Library."

I pulled Marmalade Sandwich close for a hug. Despite his cream obsession, he purred contentedly. "But you said *magical* library?"

"That's right, Vincent went into the magical section." David frowned. "Haven't you been there before?"

"Not since I was seven."

Since my parents died. A memory surfaced like buried treasure. They used to take me there every Saturday morning to withdraw books. And... that's right, there was a special section where only Beings of Magic could go – and my mother used to make the books float off the shelves and flap around for me to run after like butterflies. I had such happy memories of laughing my head off as a book settled, before flying away as I went to grab it.

The witch librarian would always shush us and tell my mother that children should not be running around the place. "If you want to play, you can merely open a book."

And so the three of us, me and my parents, would get comfy on a beanbag, watching the scenes in the magical books come alive before us – travelling through history and into magical lands. How I'd loved magic back then. Why did the things we love have to leave us? When my parents had died, my magic had died. Or rather I'd killed it – or tried to – refusing to let myself ever be as happy as I'd been with them. I realised why now. It'd felt like a betrayal of their memories.

But my parents wouldn't want me to be unhappy – to cut myself off from my true nature. And what if by connecting with my magic, I could connect with the joy my parents had given me. What if magic could help me live again?

My grandmother's wand tingled on my arm. Oh... I'd slept with it there, in its lacy armband. I hadn't even felt it. Did *magic* make it feel comfortable there? Whatever it was, I was soothed by its presence.

I landed back in reality. "Vincent's a *witch*?"

That's *right*, you could get male witches. My dad had been one.

"He must be." David leaned forward, making the sofa creak. "The magical library is a sacred place, exclusive to witches. *I* can't go in there. But *you're* a witch."

"Not really. Not even a novice."

He spoke encouragingly. "But it's in your blood, Amber – you *can* access the magical library. The only snag is, to get inside, you need to be trained to a certain level. The guard on the door won't let you in unless you can recite a specific part of a complex spell."

Well, that was me out then. "What spell?"

"The Library Pass Codex." He raised an eyebrow. "Oh, don't look at me like that, I didn't name it. But when I was studying my magical theory M-Levels, I wrote my thesis on it, so I know all about it. The guard on the door will quote part of it to you, and you simply have to say the next part, to prove you know it off by heart."

"But I don't know it off by heart."

He rummaged in his duty belt and held up a tangle of wires. "But I do."

Excitement spiralled through me. "You want me to wear a wire for you? Is that legal?"

David couldn't suppress his playful grin. "The Beings of Magic council won't be happy. But it's a murder investigation, and I'm a copper first and everything else second. Don't you want to see Inspector Taylor smile?"

I hooked my hair behind my ear. "Er, that might be even more frightening than his default scowl. But, yes, I'll help."

Marmalade Sandwich propped his paws on my chest. "But first you'd love to give your cat a drop more cr–"

"But first, I need to give my cat a drop more cream."

I quickly showered and stepped into the magic wardrobe, which again dressed me in my new witchy attire – the purple top, black jeans, and buckled boots. Then David and I got wired up, which involved us each wearing an earpiece and a very small microphone, so we could hear and speak to each other from a distance. Marmalade Sandwich wanted to come, so the three of us left my cottage and made the short journey to the library on foot.

The public part of the library was fairly typical – a spacious modern building, with rows of bookshelves, and carpet-tiles covered with reading tables. But the far end of the space was much grander – and older. To humans, the door that separated the public library from the magical one just looked like a fancy bit of wall. But I knew better. The stone doorframe was wide enough to hold two magnificent ancient oak doors, which were carved with magical symbols. They shimmered faintly with a golden sheen, which was presumably a buildup of excess magic from the magical library on the other side. Like all old buildings everywhere, the magical library leaked – but instead of having leaky waterpipes, this place leaked sorcery.

Feeling like I was a gladiator preparing for battle, I drew myself up to my full five-feet-five height, bade David farewell, and strode towards the shimmering door.

"Are we going in there?" Marmalade Sandwich asked, popping his head out of his bag.

"That's the plan, puss."

"Amber?" David's voice crackled in my ear. "Can you hear me?"

I lowered my head to the microphone clipped to my collar. "Roger that, delta, alpha, v... er... victor... iglo–"

"Just speak normally," he said calmly.

"Right, sorry."

As another witch approached the huge doors, I slowed my pace to watch. The doors opened wide as they sensed her and she walked through.

"Is that all there is to it? I can do that."

David spoke into my earpiece. "There's a guard on the other side. When you see her, just repeat everything I say, okay? And try not to draw attention to yourself."

I turned and threw him a thumbs up, then stepped towards what I thought was the open doorway, realising too late that the doors were now shut.

The ancient oak thwacked me in the face. "Ow!"

Marmalade Sandwich mewed. "Careful!"

Right. I composed myself and approached the doors again. They swept open regally. I hesitated to check they wouldn't slam in my face... then I stepped through.

On the other side of the doors, I found myself in an ethereal corridor. The floor shone with black marble, and the walls were made of engraved stone. Wow, impressive.

The witch who'd entered before me was now chatting with the witchy guard, who was standing behind a desk of mahogany, dressed in the traditional witch's garb of a black cape and black pointed hat. The air tingled with magic, but also with the magic of books. There were no shelves here, but I sensed the magical library was just around the corner.

Hmm... if I focused on fading to invisible, like *this*, perhaps I could sneak past the guard while she was dealing with that other witch...

Creeping on tiptoes, I sidled past the two witches, holding my breath with anticipation. But partway through my stealthy manoeuvre, the other witch stepped away from the desk, exposing me to the guard, oh no! I tried to sneak behind her as she walked off.

The guard spoke in a booming voice. "Excuse me, you there!"

I froze. "Me?"

Oh blimey, she was as cool as a customs officer. She gestured with her gnarly staff. "Come back here and recite the Library Pass Codex."

David spoke into my ear. "Say, I'm sorry, I didn't want to disturb you."

I shuffled in front of her desk, wiping my clammy hands on my jeans. "I'm sorry, I didn't want to disturb you."

She peered over her glasses at me. "We'll do the recitation now."

"That's fine by me," David said into my ear.

I grinned like an idiot. "Fine by me."

David's tone was severe. "Repeat *everything* I say word for word. If you get even a little bit wrong, she won't let you in."

I hugged Marmalade Sandwich through his bag. "All right."

"Just relax," David said kindly. "You're doing great."

I smiled at the guard. "Just relax. You're doing great."

The guard cocked her head. "Pardon?"

"No!" David hissed.

"No!" I shouted.

David spoke through gritted teeth. "Amber, stop it!"

"*You* stop it!"

"Did you just tell me to stop it?" the guard spluttered.

David was getting exasperated. "Stop repeating everything I say!"

"But you said I should!"

The guard eyed me up. "Are you quite well?"

I lowered my face to my microphone. "Am I?"

David's voice was weary. "Yes!"

"*Yes*," I said defensively. "Can we recite this thing then?"

As the guard cleared her throat, her voice took on a theatrical tone. "In realms of magic, we drink dry sherry, give *me* some and you shall li-brary."

I frowned. "I don't have any dry sherry. And 'library' isn't a verb."

"Amber, will you just repeat what I tell you?" David recited the reply for me, so I said it out loud.

"*I would never stoop to bribery, just to see this lovely library. Alcohol I do abscond, for I have here my magic wand.* Well, that doesn't even make sense."

"It's an ancient rhyme," the guard snapped. "It doesn't have to make sense."

"And how long am I expected to give up booze for?"

The guard was losing her patience. "Just while you're here. Do you want access, my dear?"

I narrowed my eyes. "Do you always speak in rhyme?"

"All the time, all the time." The guard spoke theatrically again. "*If you seek to enter here, tell me who is training you, my dear.*"

"What!" David said in my ear. "That's not part of the Codex! She's gone off script."

"You've gone off script," I said, my panic rising.

"You're a novice, aren't you?" She leaned on her staff. "I'm impressed with your knowledge of the Codex, but to give you access, I must know the name of your sponsor."

That didn't rhyme! "Vermilitrude Eldritch," I blurted out. "She's my grandmother."

The guard smiled tightly. "And she's also dead – I heard the sad news earlier. So you don't have a sponsor. Well, I'm sorry, but –"

"David Van Danté!" I said urgently. "The vampire. He's training me in magic. He's got all his M-Levels and everything. And he's my sponsor."

The guard absent-mindedly adjusted her cape. "I shall need to check this with David Van Danté, which will take time. First I shall root out his address and write to him, then he will need to bring his written confirmation and put it into my hands. And I am sorry, but you won't be granted access until then."

The grand doors swept open as another witch stepped inside.

I smiled sweetly and pointed towards the public library. "He's over there."

Leaning against a pillar, David waved coolly.

The guard looked me up and down with scorn, but finally waved me through – possibly just to get rid of me.

But, oh wow. I halted to take it all in. The magical library was like a cathedral with its high walls and bookshelves that transgressed the laws of physics – they actually seemed higher than the ceiling! There were several studious witches in here, reading books and casting spells. Witchy librarians dressed in long cloaks with tight buns sat at desks or flew around on broomsticks, putting the books away.

And, ah-ha! Vincent was sitting at an old oak table, sketching with charcoal. I didn't recognise him at first, because he was wearing thick-rimmed glasses and his head was bowed. The tip of his tongue was sticking out in concentration.

As I halted at Vincent's table, I noticed that his charcoal sketch was of Judy Royal. Wait, why was he drawing her?

I glanced at the book open in front of him. The spell was for advanced art! Still oblivious to my presence, Vincent huffily licked his finger and turned the page. The next two pages were stuck together and he started to get flustered. Was this the behaviour of someone with a guilty conscience? He certainly seemed anxious.

David's commanding voice spoke in my ear. "What's going on?"

I whispered urgently to David. "I think Vincent's using magic to help him draw. He's doing a near-perfect sketch of Judy!"

A librarian shot me a sharp look. "Shh!"

Vincent glanced up and tried to cover his drawing with his arm, smudging charcoal over his shirt. "You?"

"Yes, me." I pulled up a chair. "You're not really an artist?"

"Shh!"

He closed the spell book with a slam. "I didn't know *you* were a witch."

"Shh!"

David spoke in my ear. "Amber?"

"Shh! Oh, sorry, David. Yes?"

"You'd better whisper or you'll never get through the conversation."

I focused on Vincent and lowered my voice. "And I didn't know *you* were."

He removed his thick-rimmed glasses and fiddled with them. "I'm a student witch. On a scholarship from Marvelton."

I gestured to his drawing of Judy, softening my voice. "Are you in love with her?"

He glared at me, then looked away. "Is it that obvious?"

"You're pretending to be a talented artist, and abusing your position as a student of magic in order to impress her. It's either love or money."

He sighed. "It's not money. Although she *is* wealthy…"

The suspicious part of my mind said: And with her husband out the way, she's free to marry you – and support your studies. She supported both Tony and Billy financially, so why not you? Is *that* why you killed Tony?

"Does she love you?" I asked.

"I've been hoping so. But... *I've* been doing the pursuing. She was unhappy, vulnerable. And I was there to lend an ear, to hug her... she took comfort in me. She loves my art, I know that."

I lowered Marmalade Sandwich's bag to the black marble floor. He wriggled out, then slid around on the slippery surface. "Hey, Amber, I can see another handsome ginger cat underneath me!"

"That's your reflection." I turned back to Vincent, who was frowning at Marmalade Sandwich. "How did you meet Judy?" I asked gently.

He rubbed his eyes wearily. "I work at Corporista Coffee as a barista part-time – just for extra money while I'm studying. Judy goes for a walk every morning, then pops in for a coffee. I always draw little doodles on her takeaway coffee cup. She likes those."

"You knew she was an art dealer?"

"Well, when she told me she was an art dealer, I blurted out that I was an artist. It was a lie. But she said she'd love to see my paintings. I panicked and used the magical library to create them." He winced. "I... yes, I'm in love with her. We started having... an affair. She said her husband wasn't very emotional, didn't show his feelings. Then she said she'd like to display my paintings! And that's where we are now. Only..."

"Only?"

"The trouble is, the paintings go bad after twenty-four hours, so I have to keep re-doing the spell. It's exhausting."

Marmalade Sandwich flopped down and started to wash. "Exhausting, indeed."

"Why?" I asked Vincent.

"Because with magic, you have to put something in to get anything out, whether it's your own energy or external ingredients." Vincent frowned. "But you're a witch, so surely you know about the witchy equation, blood/passion/sugar = magic?" Vincent blushed as he said 'passion', which hopefully distracted him from the fact that I had no idea what he was talking about.

"Just say yes, Amber," David said into my ear. "I'll explain later."

I smiled casually at Vincent. "Of course. But it's all a bit new to me. I'm only a novice."

"Oh right. When did you start training?"

"About five minutes ago. And you've been using Judy's sexual energy?"

He blushed again. "No. I love her. Love energy is the most powerful. You can't fake it."

I gestured to the Advanced Art spell. "But it's a lie. You're not the talented artist she thinks you are."

He exhaled heavily. "I'm not even a very talented witch. I can't get the greens right."

Paris green! "What do you know about arsenic?"

He groaned. "Not *you* as well. The police keep going on about that. Look, this is all I know: arsenic is a metal, chemical symbol As. It's a deadly poison that sometimes gets into the water tables of countries without good sanitation, leading to a long, slow, horrible death. Or it can kill almost instantly. It depends on the dose."

I sat back in my chair. "You have quite a *good* knowledge of it then."

"I studied natural poisons and deadly fungi last term. I got top marks."

"So where do you get your paint from? Specifically the green?"

He spoke quietly. "Look, I didn't want to tell the police this, but it's magic paint."

"Magic *paint*?"

"Yes. The arsenic must've been part of the spell. I wanted dark green, so that's the green I got."

"The arsenic *came* with the spell?"

"It must've done, because I didn't put it there. Look, you can see it here." He riffled through the pages of the spell book. "The spell goes: *Green of paint, and oil of chilli, I can paint like Botticelli.* I know it doesn't really rhyme, but... what?"

I closed my mouth. "Chilli oil?"

Vincent fiddled with his charcoal. "Yes. That was one of the ingredients in the spell. But I promise, I didn't tamper with Tony's pills. When would I have been close enough?"

Well, he did have a point. I gathered up my lovely cat and left Vincent to his sketching.

I left the magic library and found David leaning against a pillar in the human section. He threw me a crippling vampire smile. "Good work, Amber."

I shrugged, trying to pretend my heart wasn't skittering like crazy. Oh but of course, he already knew that, gah!

I spoke calmly. "Vincent loves Judy, which definitely gives him a motive for murdering her husband. Judy is wealthy, and with Tony gone, Vincent can keep giving her fake art forever and living off her."

David gazed pensively at me. "Yeah. And I'm wondering if Judy suspects Vincent too?"

"Do you believe Vincent about the magic paint?" I asked. "And *that* was the reason it contained arsenic?"

"It's as good an explanation as anything around magical Windsor." He removed his earpiece. "Thank you for helping me. I do really appreciate it."

"Oh... no problem." I handed him my earpiece and mic.

"Do you... are you going to the Merrie May Ball tonight?"

"Of course. It's Vicky and Harry's special event. I wouldn't dare miss it!"

He tickled Marmalade Sandwich's ears. "Can you put me down on your dance card?"

"I can probably find some space. Unless you're talking to my cat?"

"No, I'm talking to you." His eyes flashed blue as he stared exaggeratedly at me, making me laugh.

We shared a smile. "Hey, are you busy now?" he asked.

"I might be. Why?"

"I'd love to show you the garden here. I just know you're gonna love it."

Chapter Sixteen

The garden of the magical library was as beautiful as it was calming. Humans were allowed out here, but they wouldn't see it like I saw it – like a fantastical land from the pages of a fairy tale. The magic leaked constantly from the library, giving the sky a greeny-gold sheen, as exotic butterflies flittered around iridescent flowers. Hummingbirds zipped through the air too, visiting the lofty blooms that grew like giant beanstalks high in the sky.

I halted next to a normal-looking tree. "It's covered in apples!"

David smirked. "It's an apple tree, Amber."

"But… it's May."

He smoothed his smirk away with his fingers. "The magic plays havoc with the seasons."

I had no idea why David had brought me out here, but there was something I'd been dying to ask him since our reunion yesterday. "How *did* you get fired as a royal protection officer?"

He briefly looked offended at my candidness, then relaxed. "Well, I didn't exactly get fired. I got… transferred from royal protection to CID."

"Crime Investigation Department?" I translated.

"Yeah." He sneered. "My senior officer suggested quite forcefully that I'd *always* had a burning desire to become a detective. So after completing my training last month, I ended up here."

We resumed our stroll through the tranquil garden. "But what *happened*?"

David threw me a side-glance, and I expected a sarcastic reply about my sledgehammer journalist interview techniques. But as he gestured to a honeysuckle-clad archway buzzing with bees he spoke seriously. "Do you remember when we first met, my brother Ivan had just gone missing?"

"Of course I remember." I stepped through the archway and tried to act casual as a nearby magical fountain spouted rainbow-coloured water. "Did you ever find him?"

"No. In fact, I'd almost given up looking. His case was closed a few years ago, and he was... presumed dead."

"I am sorry."

He spun to face me; his expression intense. "But I saw him, Amber, in the crowd one day when I was guarding a senior royal. I know I did."

My heart rushed with empathy. "You were distracted by the sight of your brother? And that's why you... had to leave?"

My guess momentarily derailed him. "Yes, I was only distracted for seconds. But it was enough time for His Royal Highness to be grabbed by a bystander. She was just an admirer, and I quickly intervened. Everything was fine. Except nothing was. The whole point of me being there was to take a bullet if necessary. I failed in my duty."

I squeezed his arm. "Did they make a complaint?"

"Yeah. And when I explained to my boss that I'd seen my brother, all he could say was, *Ivan Van Danté is dead and you need to focus on your job.*"

Oh fudge cakes, poor David. I already knew a little of Ivan's history. "Did the police ever connect your brother with those diamonds?"

He lowered his voice. "No one else knows about that, Amber. As I told you at the time, if the police *had* discovered my brother's involvement, I would've been barred from joining the force."

Pride trickled through my chest. I'd had the chance to betray David's secret for my own journalistic gain all those years ago, but I'd done the right thing. "But despite your boss's sensitive and tactful words, you couldn't let it go? You were sure you'd seen Ivan?"

He rubbed his brow. "I became obsessed. I spent every spare moment searching for evidence and applying to get the case re-opened. Then I made another stupid slip up – again nothing terrible. But my mind was consumed with trying to find Ivan. I couldn't sleep; I could barely talk about anything else. And the worst thing was, no one believed me. I definitely saw my brother that day, and no one believed me."

I held his hand. "I believe you."

His gaze caressed my face. "I knew you would."

It was nice being here with him, knowing he trusted me. I gently expanded my focus to include the buzzing bees and chirping birds, taking solace in our soothing surroundings. "I know you're a good copper, David. You just need to… maybe lighten up a little bit. I know you want to find Ivan. But he wouldn't want you to ruin your own life in the process."

David's focus hadn't expanded. In fact, it was laser-like on me. "You're right. I've merely been existing. I've forgotten how to enjoy life."

I chuckled lightly. "You need a Harry in your life. He always makes me laugh and cheers me up."

David shifted his weight slightly, which decreased the already-small gap between us. "Amber, with your magic and journalist skills, *you* could help me find Ivan. I'm still a copper and I can access the database, but I need to be careful, because they've said one more muck up and I'm out. But *I* can train you in magic, just like you told the guard just now."

Marmalade Sandwich was clambering out of his bag. "Kiss him, kiss him!"

I popped the cat down on the grass. "I'll need to think about it."

Helping him or kissing him?

The trouble was, David Van Danté was complicated. I'd always known that. And the question was, did I *need* complicated in my life right now?

He took a step back and adopted a more professional air. "Anyway, you must let me investigate who killed your grandmother. I'm a police officer *and* a vampire."

"But Granny said something about the Beings of Magic committee needing to decide what action to take. She's warned me to stay out of it. She said it might be dangerous."

He smirked smugly. "Being told to stay out of something – especially if it might be dangerous – tends to spur *me* on."

"Yes, I had rather gathered that." I reached out and smoothed down his smirk.

He held my hand. "But you ought to learn to protect yourself really, just in case."

"Just in case what?"

"Let me teach you a spell."

"Oh, David, I'm not sure."

"Hey, I know…" He picked up an apple.

"Oi, what are you doing with me?" the apple asked.

David held it at eye height. "I just need to use you in a spell. It won't hurt."

"David, you're talking to an apple. And the apple's talking to you."

"You *know* it's a magical garden." He stepped behind me, making me tense like a tent pole. "Here, hold your arm out as if you're pointing over yonder. That's it. And you've got your wand, that's good."

It wasn't good. My knees had gone all wobbly. And my wand had started to shimmer with rainbow sparkles. Oh dear.

He jogged a few paces away. "Now, I'm going to throw the apple at you, and you're going to make it swerve with the power of magic, okay."

"This *is* going to hurt, isn't it?" the apple grumbled. "First I fall out of a tree, then I get nibbled by a squirrel, and now this…"

David ignored the apple. "The magic words are: *Time and space I will now curve, I will make this…* and then you say what the object is… *swerve.*"

I glanced around the magical garden. "Okay, I'll try."

"Here it comes." David threw the apple underarm.

"Waahhhhh!" the apple cried.

"*Time and space I will now curve, I will make this apple swerve!*"

As my wand tingled in my armband, the force of raw magic shooting from my hand shoved me backwards. I watched the apple swerve magically in mid-air then drop to one side. I'd done it! I'd successfully done a spell!

Not everyone shared my joy. "Ow, that really hurt!"

"Sorry, apple," I said grinning.

David picked it up and dusted it off. "Well done, Amber, you did it. Your first spell. Now you really are a novice witch – you can't deny it any longer." He held the apple to his lips and opened his mouth. Those vampire fangs were *sharp!*

"No!" I shrieked.

"Noooo!" the apple shrieked even louder.

"Oh sorry…"

We put the apple back under the tree. Marmalade Sandwich licked it, making it laugh.

Did that mean David was officially my tutor now? Oh fudge cakes, if so, I'd have to spend more time with him… what a pity.

"What about *your* magic?" I asked David. "You can fly, can't you?"

"You could too, if you learnt the Levitation spell. But until then, you can simply find a buddy to take you for a fly. What do you say?"

"Um, I think Harry might be working at the mo—wah!"

He wrapped an arm around my waist, pulling me close. I had no choice but to throw my arms around his shoulders, because we were already a few feet off the grass – and rising fast.

Marmalade Sandwich sat watching as we soared higher and higher, but then I lost sight of the cat, because I'd scrunched up my eyes with terror. I gripped David's muscular body with my jelly-like arms, wrapping my knees around one of his legs. If *I* fell, he was coming with me.

"It's okay, I've got you," David held me tighter. "I won't let you go, I promise. Look…"

I slowly opened my eyes and took in the spectacle below. I didn't know how far up we were exactly, but I could see all of Windsor as if it were a giant, living map. The solid stone towers of the Castle, which looked impenetrable from the ground, seemed tiny and fragile from my lofty perspective.

The wind was whistling in my ears up here, but I could just about detect the gentle peeling of church bells from the main square below, as well as the distant cars vrooming. The people were as small as ants, rushing around in a maze of twisty streets. Everything at this height felt as calm as the River Thames, which meandered through the town like blue satin. I felt my tension slowly ebb away – but continued holding tight to David.

Somehow seeing the world so small made it seem more manageable – it made my problems seem more manageable. From here, I could view them as separate entities that added to the rich tapestry of life, just like the rolling fields surrounding my beautiful hometown.

I glanced at David, who was watching me. Had he been looking at me the whole time? Was he trying to impress me? Was it wrong that I really hoped so?

He floated us back down to earth. As my feet touched the grass, I squeaked and giggled with elation.

David grinned. His fangs were now fully extended, and his eyes were crystal blue. Ten years ago, I'd seen him go full-vampire – which had admittedly freaked me out. But now he was showing a little vampire around the edges. And that I could handle.

I realised I was still gripping him, so I stepped away and checked on Marmalade Sandwich.

"I'd better get back to work," David said, turning formal.

"Yes, me too. I mean, not that I have a job. Well, I'm doing a few shifts for Aunt Vicky, but I think she's... sorry, I'm babbling. Thank you for that. It was spectacular."

"Thank you for helping with Vincent. I'd better report back to Inspector Taylor. I'm sure he'll be *very* interested in this new information. I'll tell him you helped."

I hitched Marmalade Sandwich's bag on my shoulder. "Can I ask you something, David? About the case?"

"I don't promise to answer, but ask away."

"I was wondering, what if *Judy* added the arsenic to her glass of water, and then passed it to Tony when he was choking? *That* could've been where the poison came from?"

He considered this for a half a second. "Impossible. I searched everyone's bags and pockets."

"Not Judy's. Because she threatened to slap you and you were told to leave her alone."

"Inspector Taylor would've searched her bag though. I don't see how she could've hidden an entire glass with traces of arsenic from us. But it was a good try."

Was it the patronising tone or the glint in his eye? Whatever it was, I was tempted to remind him *exactly* who'd solved our murder case ten years ago. Because I had. And I was determined to wipe that blooming smirk off his face.

My thoughts shunted into place. "Well, okay. Tony definitely died from arsenic poisoning, yes? And we know he took a heart pill and then started choking. But what if the two things aren't connected?"

Doubt flickered across his handsome face. "How do you mean?"

"I was just thinking of something Vincent said about arsenic. It can either kill you straight away or slowly build up over time. What if someone close to Tony has been poisoning him slowly?"

David's eyes widened. "And they gave him the 'straw that broke the camel's back' yesterday?"

"It's possible, isn't it? Tony wasn't feeling well at the table – he was clutching his abdomen and looking pale. Judy encouraged him to have one of his heart pills, because *she* believed it was his heart making him suffer. But what if it was arsenic poisoning?"

"Wait a minute, you think someone poisoned Tony *before* he even got to Paws?"

"Maybe."

"But then it could've been anyone."

"Ah, but would just *anyone* want him dead – that's the question."

Chapter Seventeen

I said goodbye to David and headed back to Paws for Tea, feeling excited that I'd just done my first proper magic spell. I did feel a bit tired now though, and I had a massive craving for sugar. Was *that* what Vincent had been talking about? The witchy equation where magic equalled blood, sugar, or… well, I could easily replenish myself with a slice of cake at Paws, no worries.

As I pushed open the door to the cat café, the bustling vibe hit me, and my excitement grew. It was like arriving fashionably late to your own party when it was in full swing. Every chair was occupied, and a few customers were up and playing with the cats. The music was muffled by nattering voices, which was a shame, because Vicky had brilliant taste.

Speaking of Vicky, I was struck with affection as I saw my lovely aunt standing near a table at the back, where she and Harry were busy working on the decorations for their Merrie May Ball tonight. Both of them were an integral part of Windsor – and they cared deeply about the town. I knew how much satisfaction they got from giving tourists and locals a good time.

Marmalade Sandwich peered over the top of his bag and started meowing at the resident Persian, who was called Jasper. Jasper mewed back, so I lowered the bag to let Marmalade Sandwich scamper out to greet his friend. They nuzzled their faces against each other, purring with joy. Aww…

Vicky was now en route to take an order, but she stopped to give me a hug. "It's lovely to see you, my darling."

I raised my voice against the hubbub. "Do you need any help?"

"No, my lovely. You go and help Harry untangle the fairy lights. We need to take them up to the Castle as soon as possible."

Harry greeted me with a kiss on the cheek. "Hey, Bambi. You look happy."

I glanced at the tangle of fairy lights on the table and a pile of homemade colourful paper streamers on the floor. "How are the preparations for the ball coming along?"

"Everything's running according to schedule," he said proudly. "Vicky and me will take this lot over in a bit, and we've got a team of volunteers to help decorate the public area of the Castle grounds later. *You've* volunteered too."

"Goes without saying." I picked up a strip of colourful paper. "What *is* Merrie Old England?"

"It's a mythical era between the Middle Ages and the Industrial Revolution, where everything in our nation was innocent and charming." He tugged at a knot in the fairy lights. "By the way, everyone's dressing up in Merrie Old England outfits, so whatever else you do this afternoon, make sure you get something to wear."

"Like what?"

"Anything ranging from a fairytale princess to a character in a Jane Austin book, or even a swashbuckling pirate if you like. Just make sure you get something. I know you've got a sewing machine, so have a rummage in a second-hand shop – and don't let me down."

I fluttered my eyelashes playfully. "I won't let you down."

"Good. Now tell me why you're glowing. Is it Van Danté-related?"

I grinned. "I've got something to tell you."

His wings fluttered excitedly. "You're going on a date with David?"

I snatched the tangle of fairy lights from his hands. "It's got absolutely nothing to do with David Van Danté – put him from your mind. It's about the murder case. I think I've worked something out."

Harry looked disappointed. "Oh. Do tell."

"Well, I went to the magic library just now and–"

"How did you get past the guard?"

"What?"

"The guard? You don't know the Library Pass Codex."

The background noise of teacups clinked in my ears. "I… um… had some help."

Harry frowned. "Who from? The ghost of your grandmother?"

"Look, do you want to hear my brainwave about the murder, or not?"

He took back the fairy lights. "Ah, so it *was* David who helped you then?"

I wrestled with my grin. "It might've been, I can't remember. Anyway, I was thinking, what if Tony was poisoned *before* he even got here yesterday?"

He paused, mid-untangle. "By whom?"

"That's exactly what I'd like to find out. But what if one of his nearest and dearest was adding a build-up of arsenic to his morning cuppa every day?"

"You think someone was slowly poisoning him?" Harry opened his mouth to add something, but one of our cute tabbies pounced on the pile of streamers in full attack-mode. "Stop that, Sneaks." Harry picked the cat up, resulting in an armful of streamers and a bundle of manically kicking fur. Harry tickled the cat's tummy, which was brave, because Sneaks simply transferred his attack to Harry's hand.

While Harry disentangled himself from the cat, I gazed at the table where the murder had taken place yesterday. Today it was occupied by another set of people who were, hopefully, blissfully unaware of what had happened.

I spoke pensively. "Tony *can't* have been killed here, because there's no trace of arsenic anywhere. So if Tony hadn't been slowly poisoned over time, I'm wondering, did someone give him just enough arsenic to *delay* killing him? He *was* rubbing his stomach and looking unwell. I'd love to know where all the suspects were just before they arrived here."

Harry gently put Sneaks down. "Only one way to find out. Let's ask them."

I laughed scornfully. "All of them?"

"Why not?"

"Judy?"

"Yeah, why not?"

"Lydia? You want us to ask Lydia?"

"We can."

"And Hyacinth?"

"She might let you hug her tree again."

I ignored this. "And the fraudulent artist Vincent."

Harry scrunched up his face in confusion. "Vincent's a fraudulent artist?"

I told Harry the whole story. He was extremely happy to hear how well I'd been getting along with David.

Marmalade Sandwich wanted to stay and play with his feline friends, so we checked that Vicky was okay for us to leave, then set off through the streets of Windsor to visit the suspects. If we could find out where they'd all been just before arriving at Paws, perhaps we could also deduce which of them might've been busy poisoning Tony at that time.

We found Hyacinth sitting cross-legged in the garden of Turret Sanctuary, meditating with her eyes shut. Several of her guests had gathered in a semi-circle around her, also oblivious to our presence.

Harry shoved me, whispering sharply. "Go and talk to her then."

I edged away. "Maybe we should come back. She's busy."

"*I'll* talk to her." Harry crouched on the grass and spoke in Hyacinth's ear, making her jump. "Sorry to interrupt. but can you remember what you were doing just before you arrived at Paws yesterday?"

Her windchime voice was laced with agitation. "Why do *you* want to know?"

"Because..." He smiled angelically. "Because I believe you're innocent and I want to help you prove it."

Hyacinth rubbed her crystal nervously. "Before I came to the café, I was finishing off a meditation session here in the garden. You can ask any of my guests."

Harry shot to his feet. "I will."

Hyacinth grabbed his hand. "Not now!"

But it was too late. Harry knelt down in front of a young man who was sitting with his eyes firmly shut. "Hi," Harry said, practically nose-to-nose.

The man jumped. "Argh!"

"Sorry," Harry whispered. "I was just wondering if you can remember what Hyacinth was doing just before lunch yesterday."

The young man glanced at Hyacinth, then spoke angrily to Harry. "She was out here with us, helping us find some inner-peace."

"Uh-huh? Until what time?"

The man had clearly been through this with the police already. "Until five to twelve, when she said she had to go and meet someone at Paws for Tea. Now if you don't mind? I'm trying to relax."

Next door at The Royal Boutique B&B, Harry picked up the ringing phone on the narrow reception desk. "Lydia's in a meeting at the moment," he said, then abruptly hung up.

Lydia thrust her hands on her hips. "That might've been important!"

Harry adopted a gravelly voice, straight out of a 1970s police drama. "Not as important as this, me old chestnut. Where *were* you just before you went to Paws for Tea for lunch yesterday?"

Lydia shrugged. "I was here – in the reception area of The Royal Boutique. You can ask Hyacinth. She came in the front entrance at around five to twelve, and we went together."

I tried the slightly saner approach. "And where was Tony before *he* came to Paws?"

Lydia gestured dismissively down the corridor. "Probably cleaning the kitchen or something. There are always carpets to hoover, bannisters to dust… Don't let anyone tell you running a B&B is glamorous."

Harry leaned on the small desk. "So you didn't see him all morning?"

"He's always busy first thing, setting up the dining room, cooking the breakfasts, playing his saxophone for the guests, then clearing up. I saw him for a quick chat on reception in the morning, but I can't remember what time exactly."

I helped myself to a complimentary chocolate. "But you didn't go to the café together?"

"I went with Hyacinth. I didn't know where Tony was."

That was *right*. Lydia and Hyacinth had arrived together, and then Tony had joined them shortly after. Then Judy.

Harry glanced at his watch. "Where would Judy be around about now?"

"Probably at the auction house. There's a big art sale on today."

Harry knew the way to the auction house. We stepped into the near-silent opulent room, where posh people were sitting on padded chairs opposite an auctioneer with a gavel. In her trademark pink suit, Judy was sitting in the middle of a row. There were a couple of vacant seats next to her, which were begging for *us* to take.

Disgruntled tuts followed as we apologetically squeezed through a row of well-dressed knees.

"Ow, watch it!"

Whoops, that was a man's toe. "Sorry!"

The man angrily yanked his foot from under mine, which threw me off balance, and I almost landed in another man's lap.

Harry grabbed my arm to save me, but I stumbled, meaning the woman I'd now stepped in front of had to crane around me. "Move out the way!"

"Sorry," I whispered, as we finally took our seats next to Judy.

"Hi... sorry..."

Judy shushed me, gesturing to the auctioneer at the front of the room, who was pointing to a large oil painting.

"I'll start the bidding at one hundred thousand," he said snootily.

"*Talk* to her, Amber..." Harry poked me in the ribs, making me jump and yelp.

The auctioneer spoke loudly. "One hundred thousand to the lady with the long red hair."

"What? No!" I waved at the auctioneer.

"One hundred and *fifty* thousand to the lady with the long red hair."

Harry laughed at my discomfort, covering his face with his hand.

"Two hundred thousand to the man sitting next to her."

"No!" I ran my hand across my throat to indicate he needed to stop.

"Two hundred and *fifty* thousand to the lady with the long red hair, who seems to be bidding against herself."

Thankfully, a woman at the back made a bid, so I was off the hook, phew!

"What are you doing here?" Judy hissed, as the next lot was brought onstage. "Not only do you accuse me of killing my husband with the paintings in my gallery, but now you're ruining my auction too!"

I sat stiffly, not daring to move in case it cost me. "I was just wondering where you were yesterday before you arrived at Paws for Tea?"

She straightened her suit huffily. "Not that it's any of *your* business, but I was with an art supplier in Datchet. I drove straight to Paws from there. The police can easily check."

"All right, thank you. We'll get out of your way now." I stood up and tucked my hair behind my ear.

"Fifty thousand pounds to the woman with the long red hair!" the auctioneer announced.

I patted my pockets. "I don't seem to have my chequebook. Er... do you know my name and address?"

The auctioneer eyeballed me. "I hardly think so, madam."

"Great." I grabbed Harry's arm. "Run!"

As we walked back into town, we speculated about where Billy might've been yesterday before *he* was due to come to Paws.

"And where is he now?" Harry said. "The police still haven't tracked him down."

"We'll have to make our own enquiries. Right, we've got one last person to talk to. And we'll probably find him at the magical library."

With no suave vampire to whisper sweet-nothings or access spells into my ear, we resorted to knocking on the window near Vincent's table.

Vincent opened the sash window and stuck his head out. "What is it now?"

I held up my hands appealingly. "Just a quick question. What were you doing before you arrived at Paws for Tea yesterday?"

"I was at work – at Corporista Coffee. I've already told the police that."

Harry slung an accusing hand to his hip. "You weren't invited to the lunch though, were you?"

"No. But when Judy sent me a message saying where she'd be, I decided it was time to declare my love for her."

I narrowed my eyes suspiciously. "Why so urgent?"

He chewed his charcoal-stained thumb. "I was worried that Tony was about to ask Judy to come back to him. To break it off with me."

Hmm… so killing off the competition with arsenic from Paris green paint would've been very timely.

We said goodbye to Vincent, then headed back to the cat café for lunch.

Wow, I was famished after all that! I tucked into my delicious black bean and cheese quesadillas, as we went over what we'd just learnt. "Right, they've all got alibis. Hyacinth was leading a meditation session, Vincent was at work, and Judy was in Datchet with a supplier. Ah but *Lydia* could've got close enough to drop a bit of arsenic into Tony's tea before she headed here." My phone bleeped. "Oh, it's my cousin Evelyn. She's invited me to meet her at The Long Walk at two o'clock."

Harry swallowed a mouthful of salad. "Perfect – just enough time for you to finish untangling those fairy lights. Come on, eat up."

Chapter Eighteen

The Long Walk in Windsor was one of my favourite locations anywhere ever. It was a magnificent tree-lined grassy avenue that began directly outside the Castle gates and continued for two miles to Windsor Great Park. And if the tree-lined grassy avenue wasn't enough, you could also feast your eyes on the wildflower meadows and lush countryside that rolled off to the horizon – making it easy to forget you were in a town.

May was a stunning month in Mother England, with so many different shades of green. But hopefully not Paris green, yikes! I turned my face upwards as I strolled along, relishing the warm sun on my skin. It was perfect to come here and simply *be*.

But my heart surged with joy as I spotted Evelyn sitting on the grass, playing with a huge German shepherd.

Marmalade Sandwich tensed in his bag. "Hold on, Amber, I don't like the smell of this."

I tickled his head. "It's all right, puss."

Evelyn shot to her feet to hug me tight. "Amber! Oh my goodness, you look so well."

I spoke into her ear, melting into her arms. "You only saw me yesterday."

"I know." She leaned back to inspect me. "But you look different. Sort of… lighter."

"Thank you." I hooked my hair behind my ear self-consciously. "Where did this dog come from? He wasn't with you yesterday."

"He's Alex's dog." Evelyn ruffled the German shepherd's oversized ears. "Amber, this is Fuzzball. Well, his real name's Max – short for Nautius Maximus. But I call him Fuzzball."

Fuzzball wagged his tail and barked. Then he sneezed and jumped around like a giant puppy.

"He does that when he gets over-excited," Evelyn said, stroking him. "Shh, calm down, you big softy. Sit down, boy."

Fuzzball sat obediently, but with his ears pricked forward as if he was keen to play.

I glanced at the rug that Evelyn had laid out, feeling as giddy as a gooseberry on a summer's day. "Is this picnic basket full of treats, by any chance?"

"Yes! I've got a flask of tea too – all courtesy of Magic Cakes Café."

I helped her unpack the picnic basket, which was full of homemade scones, strawberry jam, and clotted cream. "This is perfect actually, Evelyn. I did a magic spell earlier and I'm really craving sugar."

She almost dropped the plates. "You did some magic? *And* you know about the blood, passion, sugar replenishment thing?"

I chuckled proudly. "Perhaps that's why I'm looking a bit lighter today?"

"Yes, magic has that effect. Hey, is your cat all right?"

Marmalade Sandwich hadn't yet taken his eyes off Fuzzball. He lowered his head further into his bag under our scrutiny. "I'm not *frightened*," the cat mewed. "If *that's* what she's suggesting."

I tried to remove his bag from my shoulder. "Why are you sticking your claws through the material into *me* then?"

"To protect you."

I wrapped him – bag and all – tight in my arms. Fuzzball was now lying down, Sphinx-like, with his tongue hanging out. His tail hadn't stopped wagging since we'd arrived.

I rocked Marmalade Sandwich in my arms. "Come out and meet him."

Evelyn gripped the dog's collar. "How about if I promise to hold him tight until Marmalade Sandwich feels comfortable?"

This time the cat allowed me to remove the bag from my shoulder, so I placed it on the grass a short distance from Fuzzball. Marmalade Sandwich poked his nose out, gingerly followed by the rest of him. The dog didn't move, other than his tongue and tail. Then, pretending he'd never been afraid of anything in his life – *who me? No never* – the cat slunk fully out of his bag and sat a short distance from Fuzzball, blinking up at him.

Fuzzball's joy at meeting Marmalade Sandwich was evident as he sneezed with excitement, but he was a good boy, and continued to stay.

As Marmalade Sandwich crept a little closer to the colossal dog, Fuzzball gently lowered his head so they could sniff each other's noses. Then, to my delight, my adorable kitty switched on his purring and playfully batted the dog on the nose –claws in his paws. This gave Fuzzball the cue to play, so Evelyn let go, and Marmalade Sandwich scampered under the dog's legs, mewing with glee.

As our pets frolicked together, I slathered a scone with cream and jam, and took a big bite. "Oh wow, these are amazing. Did you make them?"

She poured the tea into two mugs. "They were made at Magic Cakes Café, but I had some help from my mother."

I stopped chewing. "Your mother… who you said had been murdered?"

"Yes. I'm so lucky that she materialised in Marvelton after I helped Alex catch the killer. She lives there now in a gingerbread house, and we talk regularly via our magic mirrors."

I swallowed my mouthful. "That's what my granny said *she* wants to do. Hey, I bet *you* embraced magic straight away as soon as you found out about it."

"Oh butterbeans, no! I was in complete denial. But I slowly accepted it when I realised how important it is." She sipped her tea. "It's wonderful that you've done your first spell, and you should be proud of yourself. But there's no hurry. You can take your time and let things unfold."

I gazed at my lovely cousin against the backdrop of The Long Walk, feeling overcome with gratitude and love. I knew Evelyn and I would be the best of friends for all eternity from this moment onwards.

How did I know? Because it felt like we'd already been firm friends since the beginning of time.

I dipped my knife into the jam jar and slathered it onto my scone. "I guess I've always felt under pressure to either be fully-human or fully-witch. But you've made me realise it's actually okay to just be... well, just be me."

Her face lit up with affection. "It's all you can be, Amber! And speaking of taking things slowly... this is for you."

She rummaged in her handbag and passed me a hard rectangular object wrapped in pretty tissue paper. Obviously a book. A spell book perhaps?

I carefully removed the paper, relishing the moment. Ah! It *was* a book full of magic, but not how I'd thought. "*The Mysterious Affair at Styles* by Agatha Christie. Thank you, Evie. I shall treasure it."

She smiled into my eyes. "It's only second-hand, but it's the first in the series. You should read them all. They'll help you heal."

A volcano of emotion whooshed up and I couldn't hold back my tears. How embarrassing! I threw my hand to my face, realising too late there was a splodge of jam on my finger.

Evelyn shuffled over and wiped the jam off my cheek – licking her finger and making me chuckle through my tears. She wrapped me in her arms. "Why don't you tell me all about it?"

I sniffed as *I* tried to understand what the matter was. "I feel like I've failed. I wanted to change the world with my words, but instead the world changed me. I lost my job, got dumped… and I was struggling at work anyway. That's probably why I messed up. I was frazzled. Not enjoying it anymore."

She passed me my mug of tea like a magic potion. "Were you thinking of leaving journalism before you were pushed?"

"Sort of." I sipped my soothing drink. "But I hung on much longer than I probably should've. I've always dreamed of being a journalist. I love words, I love investigating. I guess I had this romantic idea that I'd end up uncovering political scandals for a proper newspaper. Or as a foreign correspondent for the BBC! I wanted to help expose the bad guys – to make a difference. But actually, it was all about… well, money. I felt pressured to keep working harder and dumbing down my articles more and more, just to keep my job. It was heart-wrenching."

She tenderly adjusted my long hair. "And your ex-boyfriend was your editor?"

"Marcus Manning, gah!" I juddered with remorse. "I admit it was appealing that he was the editor of the newspaper. Does that sound really bad?"

"Not at all."

Fuzzball and Marmalade Sandwich jogged over to join us, so Evelyn broke off a bit of scone for the dog to snuffle up. I gave Marmalade Sandwich a scoop of cream to lick off my finger.

Evelyn stroked the dog's soft fur. "Amber, what did you want to be when you were a child?"

I answered straight away. "Normal."

Evelyn chuckled. "I mean, before you decided you *weren't* normal. When you were still living a life of magic with your parents. Before they died."

I closed my eyes and drifted back there. "I wanted to… I'm not sure."

"Don't think about it too much. Let your mind churn up some happy memories. What did you love doing?"

I grinned as a memory struck me. "I loved baking cornflake cakes! I used to beg my mum to let me make them every weekend. I loved getting gooey – my fingers all covered in chocolate."

Evelyn spoke eagerly. "It sounds like you need to make a cake, my dear cousin."

My eyes flew open. "I was actually going to explore my new kitchen earlier, but David Van Danté knocked on my door."

"Oh *did* he?" She raised a suggestive eyebrow.

"Stop that…" I battled to suppress my grin. "The truth is, I'm finding it hard to accept him… as a vampire. I know how awful that sounds."

She leaned back on her hands. "Not a bit of it – you have your reasons. And anyway, before you can accept *him*, there's someone *much* closer to home you must accept."

I cupped my hands around my tea. "You're going to make an excellent therapist."

"Thank you." She smiled tenderly at me. "Look, if you'd still like to work as a journalist, there are plenty of other options. How about local news?"

I winced at the thought. "I've done that. It was all *Man Dies From Natural Causes – Shocker!"*

Evelyn guffawed. "The Maiden Gazette's front page yesterday was, *Woman Finds Crisp Packet From 1980s in Attic!"*

I almost spat out my tea as I laughed. "Crisps in the *1980s*? Surely no one was *alive* back then!"

We chuckled together, lost in our silly bubble of playfulness.

"I wish we lived nearer to each other," I said, hoping not to sound too needy.

Evelyn started to pack away the plates. "Funny you should say that. I invited you to The Long Walk because I've got something special to show you."

"Evelyn, this is one of the main tourist spots in Windsor. Beautiful as it is, I've seen it from tip to tail."

"You haven't seen everything." She clambered to her feet. "Come on, Fuzzball, walkies!"

We strolled the pleasant two-and-a-half-miles to the end of The Long Walk, halting in front of the famous twenty-six-foot-tall bronze statue of King George III. For reasons I'd never quite understood, the regency monarch was dressed as a Roman, riding on his horse and pointing at Windsor Castle – apparently his favourite castle of all the castles he had to choose from.

The statue's large plinth had been constructed to look like an old dry-stone wall, giving the monument a nostalgic feel, With the statue towering regally, Evelyn led me around the back. I'd been here loads of times before, playing with Harry, but this time my wand started tingling on my arm. Was it picking up magical vibes? And why was there a shimmering doorway-like hole in the plinth that I'd never noticed before?

Evelyn gestured proudly to the large circular entrance. "This portal leads to Maiden-Upon-Avon, where I live. And see there's two pathways? If you take the other one, you'll end up in Marvelton."

I lowered my voice as a group of tourists strolled past. "Marvelton... wow... Is this how you and Alex got here from Maiden-Upon-Avon? You travelled 'portal style'?"

Evelyn gently eased Fuzzball back on his lead as he sniffed around the entrance. "I did. Alex took the train. He's slowly embracing magic, but when he's in police mode, he likes to stick to human transport."

I raised a cynical eyebrow. "He travelled by British Rail? Well, that explains why he's so miserable."

Evelyn laughed affectionately. "You've only met the Alex *he* wants the world to see... No, boy, sit down. Good boy!"

I leaned against the stone plinth. "But you know him better than that?"

"I tend to see people as they really are. And I saw him straight away." She basked in a grin of adoration.

I twiddled my hair nervously. "Can you see me as I really am?"

"Oh yes, Amber. That's how I know you're going to make a fine witch and a wonderful friend."

I couldn't suppress my own beam of happiness. "I'm so glad you're here."

"Me too. Whatever you do, be true to yourself, okay? Be who you really are. Because your true self will come out in the end whether you want it to or not. So you may as well embrace it." She stuck out her hand. "Deal?"

I shook her hand. "It's a deal."

Chapter Nineteen

Evelyn and I ended up having dinner together in a local restaurant, where we chatted about magic, men, and all the murders she'd apparently helped Alex to solve. It must be a family trait!

I returned to my cottage fizzing with zings. Wow, I'd had such a cool day since I'd left here this morning. And tonight was the ball, and – oh fudge cakes... my eye caught the clockwork sewing machine in my living room. I had nothing to wear.

Harry was going to kill me.

Was there a fairy godmother spell I could try? Although knowing my luck, my granny would appear and force me into a corset.

Ah, but who needed a fairy godmother when *I* had a magic wardrobe?

I ran up the stairs to my bedroom and stepped into the pine-scented closet, pulling the ornate handle and letting the magic swirl all around. What sort of outfit would this supernatural furniture come up with for a Merrie May Ball?

As the magical sizzles faded, I stepped out and nervously inspected my reflection. Oh wow! I wasn't usually one for dresses, but my beautiful sky-blue satin gown was a magnificent creation – with its long skirt and intricate embroidery on the bodice. The capped sleeves were a perfect fit for my lacy armband and wand combo. I tried a gentle swish in the mirror, making the long skirt sway. But what about shoes? I hitched up the dress and grinned at my delicate satin slippers, which were adorned with little bows. Harry should be impressed!

And as for my hair... my magic mirror skilfully styled it into a cascade of ringlets down my neck and shoulders. "I feel like I've just stepped out of a Regency drama."

Silence... Hmm, where had my lovely cat got to? Probably downstairs sleeping, washing, or postulating about quantum physics.

I wasn't sure if the cat would like to come to the ball, so I grabbed his Union Jack tote bag and was about to search for him, when a small gold object clattered to the bedroom floor.

Judy's wedding ring – oh fudge cakes, I'd forgotten to give it back to her. I decided to take it along to the ball, and if she was there, I could return it. I might redeem myself after the art auction fiasco earlier! I put the wedding ring on my finger and made my way downstairs.

Marmalade Sandwich was curled up on the sofa, snoozing. "Hey, puss, I'm going to the ball. Do you want to come?"

He opened an eye. "Nah, I'll stay here and keep guard. You have a good time."

I kissed him on the head, suddenly reluctant to be parted from him. But he flicked his tail at me, which I knew from the cat café was the international feline signal for 'bugger off'. I kissed him again, then left.

Vicky and Harry had sold hundreds of tickets for The Merrie May Ball – with all profits going to a local cat charity. Feeling my excitement build, I joined a crowd of tourists and locals making their way up the hill towards the public grounds of the Castle – all dressed in wonderful costumes. The women looked beautiful in their stunning gowns of bright coloured silks, satins, and velvets. And the men looked smart in breeches, waistcoats, and knee-high boots. It was like being surrounded by several hundred Mr Darcys!

With chatter and laughter all around, we made our way through the big iron gates and into the Castle grounds, ready to dance the night away. It was an honour to be granted access to a small part of this world-famous landmark. Harry had explained that this section of the expansive grounds was reserved for public events, and many-a grand garden party had been hosted here by Her Majesty Queen Elizabeth II.

And what a visual feast! With the ancient towering walls of the Castle providing a magical backdrop, the lush green lawn stretched lazily down to the peaceful riverbank. The manicured grass was crisscrossed with graceful pathways and stunning rose trellises, and several lofty magnolia trees stood in full bloom, with bluebells growing brightly beneath them.

A multitude of colourful tents were dotted around the perimeter offering food, drink, and entertainment and, at one end of the space, a stage had been set up. A band called *Leia Lucas and the Wyrd Boyz* were performing lively folk music with guitars, violins, and old-English lyrics. Oh, this must be Evelyn's friend Leia! I'd have to go and introduce myself later when she came off stage.

But for now, I greeted Harry and Vicky with tight hugs, and we danced to the lively music as the sun went down – turning the sky a glorious mix of pink, orange, and purple.

Harry grabbed my hands, and we span round and round, faster and faster, as the bouncy tunes flowed and swirled. My hands slipped from his, and I careened off – stumbling to the grass and bursting into giggles. It was wonderful and childlike. Trying to control my giddy laughter, I hitched up my dress, clambered to my feet, and we danced some more.

In the dusky twilight, I saw the untangled fairy lights twinkling among the ancient branches. "I just need to catch my breath," I said to Harry.

He knew this was a euphemism for a call of nature, so he grabbed Vicky and danced a lively jig with her instead. As I came out of the luxury porta-loos, I spotted Hyacinth and Lydia talking urgently in the shadow of a tall oak tree. Hmm, what was that about?

Ensuring I didn't tread on any twigs, I sidled behind the oak's hefty trunk and quietly listened.

Hyacinth was dressed as a pagan priestess. "Did you really think you'd be able to get away with this, Lydia? It was madness."

Lydia smoothed down her highwayman's mask "It was perfectly *sane* after what Tony did to me, How dare he advertise my job behind my back? Did he really think I wouldn't find out?"

Hyacinth's voice was sharp. "The *police* are sniffing around."

"Don't worry about them. I can wrap Sergeant Van Danté around my little finger."

This was news to Hyacinth *and* me. "Can you?" she spluttered.

"Oh yes. We're old friends."

"Well, I think you should tell your old friend about your corporate sabotage."

"It was committed on *your* behalf." Lydia sounded annoyed. "You said you wanted my help."

Hyacinth spoke through gritted teeth. "I didn't know Tony was going to end up *dead*."

They walked off before I could overhear anything else. Hmm... so, Lydia had committed corporate sabotage, had she? But *had* it included killing her boss? Well, she might be able to wrap *David* around her little finger, but she couldn't wrap *me* around any parts of herself. Eugh, what a thought.

Continuing my journey back towards Harry, Vicky, and the dancing, I squeezed through the crowd of merrie revellers, immersing myself in the vibrant thrum. It was impossible to think about murder surrounded by all this laughter and happiness. And the outfits were incredible! I inhaled the sweet aroma of fresh air, spring blooms, and fried onions, exhaling with joy.

But then, over by a beer tent, I spotted Judy and Vincent standing together, deep in conversation. They'd already seen me, so I couldn't stealthily eavesdrop this time. But I could be subtle and fish for information.

The beer tent was full of rowdy fairytale princesses, downing pints. "Hello, young lovers," I said. "Have you come here for a romantic tryst?"

Judy raised her voice above the boisterous singing behind us. "How dare you? My husband died yesterday and you're accusing me of having an affair?"

Vincent squeezed her shoulder. "She knows about us, Jude. She guessed earlier."

"Yes," I said. "Vincent was telling me *all* about his paintings. Weren't you, Vincent?"

Vincent suddenly grabbed Judy's hand like a praying mantis. "I love you, Judy – *that's* what I was telling Amber. Please tell me you feel the same?"

"It was just a fling, Vincent," she said snappily, wrestling back her hand. "Surely you must've known it wasn't serious between us?"

Vincent couldn't have looked more devastated if she'd punched him. Hmm... was he now regretting killing off the competition? But I wasn't sure if Vincent really had that killer instinct, especially now he was in tears and sobbing on Judy's shoulder.

I left them to talk things over and continued my way towards the dance area. But blast! I'd forgotten to give Judy her wedding ring *again*. I turned to go back, but froze as I saw Lydia air-kissing David in the middle of the lawn.

My heart sank. Just when I'd thought it was safe to swim in the warm waters of Sergeant Van Danté, they'd turned out to be shark-infested. Oh *no*, I'd started coming up with tortuous metaphors – my inner-journalist did that whenever I was nervous. But I couldn't drag my eyes away from him. He looked incredible in his black knee-length breeches, knee-high leather boots, fitted tailcoat, and red silk cravat. Most men would look ridiculous trussed up like that, but he looked even more smoulderingly hunky than ever. How blooming annoying!

I watched as he struggled to extract himself from Lydia's grip. He'd kept *that* quiet, hadn't he? His more than passing acquaintance with one of the murder suspects.

David glanced around for an escape route, and unfortunately saw me. He swiftly excused himself from Lydia and strode over.

I *could* just walk away... But we'd already made eye contact, and I was far too British, so I smiled politely – resisting the urge to check out his thighs in those tight breeches.

Before he'd even halted, I caught a whiff of his sandalwood and chocolate chip cheesecake scent, which did nothing to calm me. My nerves lurched further as he smiled sincerely. "Amber, you look beautiful."

I hugged myself self-consciously. "Fraternising with murder suspects, are we?"

"What? Oh, I've known Lydia for years. She's a friend of the family. Inspector Taylor knows."

I glanced over. Lydia was now on the phone. "Is she a vampire?"

"Yes. But that doesn't automatically make her a bad person."

"Are you two... together?"

He raised a flirty eyebrow. "Why, are you after a date?"

I held his gaze. "She's not my type."

"That's *right*. You don't like vampires."

I laughed, breaking the tension. "Not vampires who might be murder suspects, no."

I was about to tell him about Lydia's confession to corporate sabotage, but David was scrutinising me as if he was about to say something important.

"What?" I asked, twiddling a ringlet in my fingers.

The breeze gently blew his fringe across his forehead. He swept it back with his long fingers. "I didn't tell you this earlier, but I saw you a few years ago. At a royal event. You were reporting on it, I assume."

"*That's* who you were protecting? Wow."

"Yes. But I was distracted by the pretty journalist with the long red hair."

I playfully tilted my head. "It sounds like you get distracted rather a lot when you're supposed to be working."

He smirked and looked away. Wow, had I just won something there?

I started to ask him if he'd care to dance, but my insides wilted at the sound of a familiar male voice calling over from a short distance away. "It *is* you, Amber. I thought so!"

The joy drained from my heart like water down a plughole. "Oh fudge cakes, no."

"Who is it?" David asked with concern.

"My ex-boyfriend. He was my editor at the Daily Snoop. He must be here reporting on this event – he'd do anything for a free party."

David's voice was low and gravelly. "He's the one that fired you?"

"Yep. And he broke up with me too, because I'd apparently let the newspaper down. What a moron."

With the merriment and music swirling all around us, David stood firmly by my side. Marcus joined us, smothering me with his smarminess. What had I ever seen in him? He was all right looking, sort of a cheap version of David really… oh fudge cakes, *that's* what I'd seen in him. Before I could start comparing David to any *other* of my ex-beaus, I focused on my most recent ex-beau.

Marcus gestured to my gown. "Glad to see you've made an effort for once."

David reached for the ID tag hanging around Marcus's neck. "Press? Sorry, mate, Her Ladyship isn't answering any questions today. So back off."

Marcus and I spoke at the same time. "*Her Ladyship?*"

David snarled at Marcus. "Haven't you heard the news? I thought you were supposed to be a reporter?"

Marcus scoffed. "What news?"

"About Lady Amber here? And how her grandmother left her a fortune and a title."

I wrestled with my laughter. Ohhhh, the dumb look on his face was priceless!

"Amber, is this true?" Marcus asked.

David thrust an arm across me. "Mr Manning, I told you, she's not answering your questions, so back off."

"And who might you be?"

David produced his police warrant card from his back pocket. "Sergeant David Van Danté. Royal protection."

"But..."

David stepped forward, arms out wide. "You're invading her space, Mr Manning. I'm authorised to arrest you and I *will*. If there's one thing I hate more than tabloid newspapers, it's journalists who *work* for tabloid newspapers."

"But I didn't know she–"

"Off you go now. And make sure you bow properly. Show some respect for once in your life."

To my amazement, Marcus bowed his head sharply, then walked backwards three paces on the grass, before turning and striding into the crowd.

I burst into laughter. "That was very cool. Thank you."

The smirk was fully there as David shoved his warrant card back into the rear pocket of his breeches. I craned to look behind him – just to ensure his ID was safely snug, of course. *Phwoar...*

"Don't tell Inspector Taylor," he said coolly.

I rested my hand on his arm. "I hope you didn't mean it though. About hating tabloid journalists."

His eyes twinkled with sincerity. "That was just something you *did*. Not who you are. And I could never hate who you are, Amber Eldritch. Oh..." He touched Judy's wedding ring on my finger. "Did you get married?"

I laughed. I was about to explain, but the sound of squabbling drunk men seized his attention. "I'd better see you for that dance later."

Blimey, was that a threat or a promise?

He wasn't even on duty, but he swiftly threw himself into the melee, before leading the men away towards a couple of burly security guards.

Well, that was fun. But I probably ought to give Judy her wedding ring back. Now, where was she?

I couldn't see Harry or Vicky on the dance floor, so I drifted towards the perimeter of the large lawn. My spirits soared as the fairground vibe hit me. Interspersed among the food and drink tents were various entertainment stalls and, as I weaved through the merry revellers, I was enthralled by old-fashioned games – hoopla, hook-a-duck, and a coconut shy. A man dressed as a ringmaster was juggling batons, and a woman in a leotard was fire-eating, wow! Several tables had been set up too, for card tricks and fortune-telling.

Oh! That was Aunt Vicky. She was sitting behind a wooden table, offering psychic readings to raise a bit more money for the cat shelter. Hmm, that gave me an idea.

I waited for Vicky to finish with her current punter, then took a seat opposite.

She was about to begin her mystical spiel, when she realised it was me and smiled warmly. "Oh hello, darling. Would you like me to read your fortune? I saw you chatting with Sergeant Van Danté just now." She winked playfully.

I held out Judy's wedding ring. "Actually, I was wondering if you could get any vibes from this. It belongs to—"

"Don't tell me anything, it'll obscure my pure insight. All right, pop the ring in my palm and I'll see what I can detect."

She covered the ring with her other hand, then closed her eyes and focused. I jumped as she twitched suddenly. "Oh yes, there's a fragment of Judy Royal's angry energy embedded in this gold." She opened one eye. "Amber, where did you get this?"

I was about to explain that I wasn't a thief, when my wand tingled against my arm, and a hologram of Judy from the *ring's* point of view surged up from Vicky's hands. We both watched agog, as it played out a scrap of a conversation.

"Tell me you love me, Tony," Judy was saying. "You can't, can you! Even when we're about to split up! I won't let you leave me. If you divorce me, I'll take back everything I've ever given you, which is everything *you* own."

Tony's gruff voice flowed from the hologram. "Don't you understand — I don't care about money. I was happy busking under the arches."

Judy hurled the chilling words at her husband. "I'll kill you before I let you leave me, Tony. I mean it, I'll kill you!"

Vicky and I stared in stunned silence as the hologram vanished like a lightbulb popping. I tried to form words, but... where to begin?

But then our shock was shattered by a piercing scream from the river.

"Now what?" Vicky whispered.

I hitched up my dress and ran.

A group of people had already gathered at the tranquil riverbank, their faces etched with worry and confusion.

My heart pounded in my throat as I caught a glimpse of the body on the grass – legs still dangling in the water. Despite how bloated and blue this person was, I could tell it was the corpse of Billy Royal. I recognised him from his social media profile, when he'd been so full of life.

David pushed through the crowd and took control. "Police – get back!"

He crouched to check the body with one hand – making a phone call with the other. "Inspector Taylor, we've found Billy Royal. He's been dead for about a day, sir. Cause of death? Well, I've seen enough traffic accidents to guess he's been hit by a car. All right, Inspector, I'll cordon off the area and see you soon."

David hung up, then ushered back the crowd. "I want you all to stand over there. In a minute, I'll need whoever found the body."

Satisfied that his words were as good as reality, he crouched back down with Billy, searching his pockets.

There was, of course, one person who hadn't stepped back. My years as a journalist had given me the courage to hang around and ask questions.

I watched as David rummaged through Billy's wallet. "Someone ran him over then threw him in the river, Sergeant?"

"Looks like it. Which means we have no idea where it happened." David inspected a credit card and a few pieces of paper. "Oh, this is a ticket for the car park near the railway arches."

I gazed at the glistening dark water. "The car park near the river?"

"Yep." David stood on the slippery bank. "So did someone dump him in the river upstream, and he's drifted all this way with the current?"

I read the ticket in David's hand. "It was issued from the machine on Thursday at five pm."

"The day he was last seen." He frowned at me. "You all right?"

I exhaled heavily. "Better than Billy Royal. But at least we can eliminate him from our inquiries."

"We?"

"Yes that's right, *you* can eliminate him from your inquiries."

A dreadful thought struck me. If Billy was dead, which he definitely was, then where did that leave little Colin the corgi? Wherever he was, may he be safe and well.

Inspector Taylor arrived quickly and told me to go away. And the truth was I had no desire to hang around Billy's corpse. But I was wondering, with Billy dead, would Tony's possessions now go to Judy as his next of kin? Was *that* what this had been about? Money?

But Judy seemed to have plenty of money. This was a confusing case indeed. I yawned, feeling exhausted, so I decided to find Harry and Vicky, and go home to bed. Perhaps after a good night's sleep, things might seem clearer – especially after a cuddle with my magic cat, and a nice cup of tea.

Chapter Twenty

Day Three

There was a heavy, pendulous feeling pressing on my chest.

"Amber, wake up, quick!"

Like a squirrel on rocket fuel, I went from snugly snoozing to sitting upright in a split-second. "Whassit!"

"Meeeeew!" Marmalade Sandwich slid from my chest to my lap.

"Sorry, puss. What is it?"

"It's urgent, Amber, you have to come quickly!" He hopped up and down.

I froze with fear. "It's not David at the door again, is it?

The cat shook his head. "Worse."

"Not another murder?"

"Even worse!"

"Not… it's not my granny, is it?"

Marmalade Sandwich leapt off the bed. "It's even worse than that. It's my food bowl – it's empty!"

He opened the door with his nose and rushed downstairs. I loved how he automatically assumed I'd follow. But I did of course. He'd only come back again.

I fed the cat, checked the time, vowed to get him some sort of auto-feeder, then went back to bed for the next few hours. Ah, yes… nice comfy pillow…

Just like how food has no calories when eaten straight from the fridge, it's a well-known fact that if you get woken up too early by your talking cat, you're allowed to lie-in for even longer. Otherwise the universe gets out of sync, and I couldn't have that on my conscience.

As I floated down into a deeper sleep, my nostrils breathed in the succulent scents of sandalwood, chocolate biscuits, and spring blooms – the unique smell of the man of my dreams. My soul fluttered with pleasure. What a nice surprise! His reassuring presence was like slipping into a warm bath. He'd left me ten years ago, after David had broken my heart, but now, on the edge of consciousness, his voice filled my mind. "*Hello, Amber…*"

Oh fudge cakes! I jerked awake – my heart thumping hard. I'd forgotten over the years, but that smell – my dream man's smell – it was the smell of David Van Danté.

Anger flashed through me and I was suddenly tempted to climb out of bed and push my dream man away – just as *he'd* left *me* for so many years. But he enthralled me; I yearned to be with him.

"*I've missed you, dear one,*" he whispered.

"You left me!"

"*No… you left me.*"

Trying to understand how this could be true, I inhaled and relaxed, drifting once more into a snoozy sleep. And there he was, fully with me again.

His commanding presence had always comforted and empowered me. Being with him in my dreams had secretly been my favourite thing in my teens – lying half-asleep, watching the movies in my mind, and drowning in his warmth. The man whose face I'd never seen, but who I knew so well. I couldn't *see* his smile, but it soothed me all the same. His strong hands caressed me, making me feel 'complete' – and making the word seem okay.

In some ways he was a stranger to me – a shadow or a whisper. Yet he was so familiar – a part of me. I knew for sure that we'd always been together – for time immemorial. We were stardust; beams of sunlight reunited after a billion years apart across the universe.

But was he really David Van Danté?

I woke up peacefully a few hours later in my cosy cottage to the sound of birdsong and… silence. How lovely compared to the honking horns and pneumatic drills of London. There *was* a rhythmic rumbling nearby, but that was the soft purr of Marmalade Sandwich, who was now curled up by my side with a tummy full of kitty food. Aw, he was just too cute, for goodness cake.

I stroked his soft fur, wondering why the man of my dreams had decided to re-appear after all this time. Perhaps it was because I was back in Windsor? Perhaps it was the influence of my grandmother's wand? Perhaps it was just a perfectly normal dream, where my brain was trying to make sense of everything. But why couldn't my brain show me his face? Tell me who he really was? *Had* it been *David* with me? Was he *really* the man of my dreams like Harry thought?

I started to smile, but my heart crunched with sorrow. Surely it couldn't be. Not only was David a vampire, but he was complicated. And did he even fancy me? Perhaps it was better if he didn't. Then I wouldn't need to worry.

Right… this called for a distraction to get my teeth into – metaphorically and literally. Carrying the sleepy cat in my arms, I padded downstairs, and decided to bake that cake I'd promised Evelyn. The ingredients were simple, and I'd already stocked up.

Baking had clearly been a hobby of my granny's, because the kitchen was equipped with all the essentials – a wooden rolling pin, ceramic bowls of various sizes, and a rack of copper pots above the aga. There was even an old-fashioned larder – a stone room that had been used to keep food cool before the invention of the refrigerator.

Despite the kitchen having a stone floor and granite surfaces, the rustic vibe made it warm and snug. It was much smaller than the industrial basement kitchen at Paws for Tea, but it was plenty big enough for me. A large window near the ceramic sink overlooked the lush overgrown garden. Hmm… the grass needed a mow. But it could wait.

In the centre of the kitchen stood a large wooden table surrounded by padded chairs. Hey, I could invite Harry over for tea and cake. Vicky and Evelyn. Alex… hmm, perhaps not. David? Well, he'd need to sample a cuppa from the teapot he'd so kindly bought, wouldn't he?

But for now, with Marmalade Sandwich curled up on a chair, I put on some music, and gathered the ingredients together.

I danced around the kitchen. "As if by magic, I'm going to transform this butter, sugar, eggs, and flour into a Victoria sponge!"

His ear twitched. "You doing some magic, Amber?"

"Yes. But it's a long, slow spell. Observe, young puss."

I grabbed a big bowl and enjoyed creaming up the sugar and butter. In went a fingertip, slurp went my lips. Mmm...

And now, to get cracking! The two eggs made the mixture light and fluffy, and the sweet aroma of vanilla essence made my mouth water. Jigging on the spot to the music, I folded in the flour, remembering how my mum had always taken care over this part, so as not to get in too much air. And she'd always folded in extra love. I folded in an abundance of love for her, then poured my creation into two round cake tins, before popping them into the old-fashioned oven.

I did some of the washing up, then sat with Marmalade Sandwich. "And now the best bit," I said. "Licking out the bowl together."

I scooped up some mixture onto my finger and sucked it off, then did the same for him. The feel of his tongue on my fingertip was fuzzy and cute.

"Like that?" I asked.

He licked his lips, blinking and purring, which made me want to give him more. He knew that very well, of course, and I was glad to fall into his little trap of cuteness.

After the two cakes had cooled, I spread a thick layer of raspberry jam on one, and whipped cream on the other, then sandwiched them together. And for the finishing touch, I dusted the top with a sprinkle of powdered sugar and – hey presto – a cake fit for a witch!

Recipes really were like magic spells.

"Hey puss, where do you stand on cake for breakfast?"

"I'll stand on anything as long as you give me some of that cream filling."

As I took the first bite, the soft cake melted in my mouth, and the sweetness of the jam and cream lingered on my tongue. Arhhh, perfect. All I needed now was some tea.

As if handling a precious relic in the Natural History Museum, I carried David's teapot towards the table. But I almost dropped it as my granny appeared in a puff of smoke. "Wah!"

She looked disorientated. "Oh… good morning, Amber."

"Granny, you can't just appear like that!"

She straightened her hat. "It's my cottage!"

"Not anymore… apparently."

"Well, I can't knock, can I? I don't know if you noticed, but I'm dead."

I gently placed the teapot on the table. "Yes, you did mention it."

"Oh I am sorry to keep harping on." She composed herself. "Now, have you found Colin yet?"

"Not yet, I'm sorry." I wondered whether I should tell her about Billy's death, but I decided to find out why she was here first. "Did you want something? I'd offer you a slice of cake, but…"

"Never mind that." She floated after me as I grabbed a box of loose-leaf tea from the cupboard. "Amber, I didn't tell you this yesterday because you seemed shaken about… everything."

"About your murder?" I poured the tea-leaves into an old tin caddy. "And Tony's murder?"

"Yes, precisely. Er…"

I focused on spooning the tea-leaves into the teapot, waiting for her to elaborate. She seemed uncomfortable, and I could put money on *that* soon resulting in my discomfort too.

"My dear, you know you were asking why your parents aren't ghosts, but I am?"

"Yes?" I paused mid-spooning.

"Well, brace yourself, Amber, but…" She fiddled with her lacy collar. "I believe your parents are still alive."

A tidal wave of shock washed over me. The teaspoon dropped from my fingers. I froze like a rusty bike chain – and even my brain cells held their breath. My mouth opened and closed, then my mind slowly juddered back to life, shooting raw energy into my limbs, turning my flesh to jelly.

I sat down.

I wanted to ask her if this was some kind of sick joke, but Vermilitrude Eldritch didn't joke. My shock surged to anger. "Where have they been all this time? It's been twenty-five years!"

Her voice was as tender as her Edwardian sentiments would allow. "I'm not exactly sure. I've only found out myself very recently. You see, about a week ago, your mother spoke to me in a dream."

My heart spattered with confusion. "She spoke to you in a *dream*?"

"She told me things that only the two of us would know."

I tutted. "That's because dreams come from your *head*, Granny."

Her expression tightened. "You must never ignore the dreams of witches or psychics, Amber."

Oh fudge cakes, I couldn't even begin to think about my *own* dreams. So it *was* magic that had switched my dream man back on?

I crouched to pick up the teaspoon. "And what did my mother say in this dream?"

"She said, *Tell Amber I'm alive and I love her*."

I slowly stood up, trying to make sense of all this. But... she was alive and she loved me... could this really be true? Oh, please let it be! "Why only now?"

"I believe your parents have either been kept captive or in hiding for all these years. Not harmed. But not free to live their lives normally."

"But...why did you think my parents *had* been killed?"

She pursed her lips primly. "Even though their bodies were never found, we all assumed they were dead, because... You know it was vampires who did it, don't you?"

"Yes, Vicky told me."

"Well, there's something she *didn't* tell you..." Vermilitrude cleared her throat. "Your mother and father were vampire hunters."

I was in the middle of filling up the kettle from the old-fashioned tap. "What!"

She held up a finger. "Only of *rogue* vampires. They worked for a top-secret government agency that tracks down and neutralises Beings of Magic who've gone bad. Not all vampires are bad, of course, but sometimes they get tempted and... turn rogue."

"So... this rogue vampire *kidnapped* my parents? But who was he? And where are my parents now?"

The kettle boiled furiously. She raised her voice. "I don't know the answer to either of those questions, my dear. Only that your mother finally got a message to me last week."

"In your dream?"

"That's right. And naturally, straight after your mother made contact, I started researching who this rogue vampire might be." She gestured to her ghostly form. "I wonder if perhaps I got a little too close for comfort. You see, I was asking around in magical circles, digging into your parents' disappearance, going over old magical newspapers in the library..."

My thoughts squirmed, trying to understand. "Someone killed you because you were about to find out what happened to my parents?"

"I think so." She tried to pat my hand. "Amber, dear, do close your mouth, it's terribly undignified."

I stared at the stone floor, feeling like a trapdoor had swung open and swallowed up my entire life. There was only one thing for it. "I need to find them."

"Then you must train in magic."

I poured the boiled water into the teapot, trying to stop my hands from shaking. "Magic is... I've always wanted to be normal."

Vermilitrude floated towards the window. "I understand, my dear. And I believe you'll find inspiration in the garden once you've tidied it. *That's* where the answer you seek lies."

I scoffed. "What? Is that some sort of *Karate Kid* exercise? I'll paint the fence and become a skilled fighter by honing my arm muscles?"

"I've no idea what you're talking about, dear, but I've always found gardening very relaxing. The lawnmower's in the shed."

Chapter Twenty-One

My mind clattered like a rickety rollercoaster as I drifted through the cottage's pretty glass sunroom and out to the small but overgrown garden.

It looked like *I* felt; a wild, tangled mess. The lawn was covered with meadow grasses and tall daisies, and the flowerbeds were overflowing with bluebells and dandelions. The out-of-control lilac bush smelled incredible – as did the honeysuckle that climbed the wall in a frenzy. The entire garden was a riot of colour, with bees buzzing around, gathering pollen for their honey. Hmm, perhaps a wild tangled mess wasn't so terrible after all.

I stood on the patio and basked in the mid-morning sun. "I actually quite like it overgrown like this."

Marmalade Sandwich had ventured into the long grass – only leaving the tips of his ears and his tail visible. "*I'd* like to be able to see what I'm chasing."

I scooped him up and held him close. "Leave the little furry folk alone, young puss."

"On one condition..."

"Does it involve cream, by any chance?"

He licked my neck, making me laugh. I assumed that meant, yes.

It was so peaceful out here – with the grass ticking my shins, holding Marmalade Sandwich in my arms, and standing in a sunbeam. But this wasn't going to get the garden tidied – and apparently that's where the answers lay.

Although, perhaps I should've first got clear on what the *question* was.

A memory of the film *Mary Poppins* drifted into my head. That bit where the darling little kiddies click their fingers and the nursery gets tidied up by magic. Was *that* what my granny was trying to tell me? If you train in magic, you'll never need to bother with housework again?

Unlikely.

I kissed Marmalade Sandwich on the head. "I'll never get this tidied. She can't be serious."

The cat wriggled to get down. "Try not to think of it as one big tangled mess. More like, lots of little tangled messes."

"Is that supposed to make me feel better? It just multiplies my problems."

He blinked up at me. "No, Amber, it breaks the mega-tangle into manageable strands. One mess tidied here; one strand combed there. It stops you from drowning in the foliage." He paused to chew a long blade of grass.

The cat had a point. Apart from the chewing the grass part. Trying to look on the bright side, I opened the door of the rickety wooden shed and found a mechanical lawnmower. It was heavy, cumbersome, and rusty. "I might leave the grass for now. Make a start on the weeds."

Marmalade Sandwich flopped onto the patio. "That's what I'm talking about, Amber. One thing, then another. First fish, then cream."

I found an old pair of gardening gloves in the shed and pulled them on. "I suppose this is how David feels when he's working on a murder case. He figures out one clue at a time, slowly combing out the tangles."

The cat sniggered. "Funny how *he* always comes up in the conversation."

Actually, I had more pressing things to think about. After my granny's bombshell about my parents, a tsunami of emotions was swirling in my chest. I was trying not to think about it, which was classic *me*. Or perhaps it was a symptom of the stiff upper lip. But, whatever it was, I always numbed myself like this – stuffed my feelings down to my knees.

But there was no way I could escape *this*. Not out here, alone and raw with nature.

Okay, anger seemed to be topping the bill. I knelt in front of a flower bed and started ripping out the weeds in frenzied handfuls – throwing them behind me, and unleashing decades of pain on the poor plants. My parents had been alive for twenty-five years, and no one had told me! *Why hadn't anyone told me!*

Poor little plants. I gazed at the weeds in my hand, looking so innocent and tender. My anger dissipated and I felt a shift within me. I took a deep breath, inhaling the soothing fragrance of the lilac. Right, this wouldn't do. Going berserk wasn't going to help anyone.

One weed at a time, that's what my beautiful little Marmalade Sandwich had said. I gripped a thick stem between finger and thumb and delicately eased it from the soil, respectfully laying it down.

And then, like the clouds parting to reveal a sunbeam, I finally understood the most important part of my granny's message. *My parents were alive!*

This was the best thing I'd ever heard. I shot to my feet, determined to get them back by any means possible, even if that meant training in magic and begging David to teach me. Not that I needed to beg – he'd already offered.

Marmalade Sandwich trotted over and sat on the soil I'd just cleared. "You're grinning like a Cheshire cat. What's happened?"

"I took your advice, puss."

He spoke sagely. "Ah. You'll probably want to reward me with some sort of fish-based treat."

"I will." I gathered the uprooted weeds in my gardening-gloved hands. "My granny will be pleased that I've decided to take up the wand. It was strange seeing her so uncomfortable just now, but…"

Sometimes people acted guilty when they hadn't done anything too bad. My mind churned up Judy Royal. *She'd* been acting shifty ever since Tony's murder. She'd even begged Hyacinth not to tell the police about something. What was *that*?

A flashback unfolded in my memory. At Paws, straight after the murder…

Judy sounded frantic. "Hyacinth, they think Tony was poisoned! You won't tell them anything, will you?"

Hyacinth squeezed Judy's trembling hand. "Your secret's safe with me. Although I am surprised you went through with it."

What had she done?

"She's feeling guilty about it, whatever it is," I mused.

"About killing Tony?" the cat asked.

"Maybe. But if *not* that, then what?" And she'd certainly *threatened* to kill him during their argument. But... had that been an empty threat borne from desperation?

The breeze picked up, wafting the scent of honeysuckle into my nostrils. I shivered.

The fur prickled on Marmalade Sandwich's back. "It is a bit chilly, isn't it? Why don't you put those weeds in the green bin and find me that fish you mentioned."

"Yes, all righ— wait a minute!" *Chilly... bin... chilli oil. Rubbish bin...*

Like a toaster launching the breakfast across the kitchen, a brainwave struck me. "*That's* it – that's why she went back to Paws straight after the police had let everyone go. But where exactly did she put it?"

"Put what?" Marmalade Sandwich asked.

I didn't even dare *think* my idea fully through, just in case I was wrong. But if I was right... there was only one way to find out. I grabbed my gardening gloves, said goodbye to the cat, and set off.

The litter bins in Windsor were quaint and old-fashioned, with sturdy hinged lids. Thankfully, there weren't too many bins between Paws for Tea and The Royal Boutique B&B and, after rummaging through several layers of food packaging, old newspapers, and a few banana peels, I found what I was looking for in the second bin. Yes!

Now, would Inspector Taylor be pleased or furious? It was hard to tell.

At the police station, the fairy desk sergeant and a uniformed officer were involved in a high-stakes, high-speed game of cards, so I snuck past and eyed up the shiny corridor that led to the offices.

When I'd been here the other day, I'd noticed that the interview room was a few doors down from Inspector Taylor's office – he'd emerged from it to march me to my interrogation. I halted outside the office door now, and *yes*, I could hear David and Alex chatting inside. I glanced at the nameplate on the door: *DI Fletcher*. Oh fudge cakes, I'd met her ten years ago when she was still a sergeant. This must be who Alex was covering for.

The office door was only half closed, so I silently stepped into the doorway and observed both detectives, sitting opposite each other at a desk near the window.

This office was as shiny and light as the rest of the police station, but Alex looked like he had the weight of the world on his shoulders. "We don't have enough evidence to charge her yet, Sergeant. Let's give her a minute to catch her breath, then try again."

David's dark hair looked dishevelled today, as if he'd had a late night followed by an early morning. He spoke in his gravelly growl. "I hope you didn't mind me suggesting this break, sir. But Mrs Royal was finding it hard to carry on when she kept bursting into tears like that."

Alex shifted uncomfortably. "She wasn't the only one."

David picked up a folder on the desk. "Oh, look, sir – we left this behind. We can ask her about these finances when we reconvene."

I cleared my throat and stepped inside. "Hi..."

David sat to attention. "Amber?"

Alex was far more relaxed. "Well?"

"Hi, Inspector Taylor." I held up the bottle of chilli oil I'd found in the bin. "Exhibit A, I think."

He stared at me, waiting for more information.

"I'm sure if you check, you'll find Judy's fingerprints all over it."

He gave David a small nod.

David shot me a look of admonishment, then pulled on some disposable gloves and disappeared into the corridor with the bottle.

I flopped down in the chair where David had been sitting. "So..."

"Yes," Alex said, holding eye contact. "Very clever. *If* you're correct."

"Thank you." I glanced around the office. The clock ticked on the wall. "How was *The Mouse Trap* the other night?"

His voice was flat. "Same as always."

"You've seen it before?"

"Evie's a little obsessed."

"So… you keep going with her?"

His tender smile made him look ten years younger and infinitely lighter. "It makes her happy. That makes me happy."

Aw, there *was* a decent man under that gruff exterior after all.

Alex tightened back up as David strolled in. "Judy Royal's prints are all over it, sir."

"Go and get her, please, Sergeant."

David put down the bottle and went off again.

"You've just been interrogating Judy?" I asked, wondering how far I could push my luck.

"We arrested her this morning on suspicion of murdering Tony and Billy. I haven't charged her yet." He fiddled with a pen. "We were in the middle of her interview, when she burst into tears and got very distressed. So I asked a more sympathetic officer to get her some tea."

I raised an eyebrow. "A female officer, you mean?"

"Don't start accusing me of sexist tactics, Ms Eldritch. I won't apologise for doing my job."

"Not sexist tactics, Inspector Taylor. I think it's sensible to see if a friendlier approach might work. *I've* also been subjected to your sledgehammer techniques."

He was about to reply, when Judy walked in carrying a mug of tea in one hand and a box of tissues in the other. Her face was puffy and tear-stained.

"Ah, Mrs Royal, feeling better? Do come in. Pull up a chair."

David positioned a chair in the middle of the office, then stood behind it. Alex perched on the edge of his desk. Judy sat alone, yet sandwiched between the detectives. She glanced warily at the shiny floor as if it might swallow her up. It was possibly an option she'd choose, given the amount of tension that was zapping around the room. And *I'd* thought we were trying the friendlier approach?

Alex held up the chilli oil bottle. "Recognise this?"

Judy almost dropped her tea. "Where did you find it?"

"Where you left it," I said kindly. "*After* you'd covered Tony's heart pills with the chilli oil. I guess it's psychological that we think anything we chuck in the bin will disappear."

She spoke directly to me. "I didn't dare put it in our kitchen bin."

"So you got rid of it on the way to Paws?" I asked.

Alex sounded annoyed. "Do you *mind*? This is my interview."

"Sorry, Inspector Taylor."

"So," Alex said. "You got rid of it on the way to Paws?"

Judy plucked a tissue from the box on her lap. "Yes, but *not* on my way to lunch. I drove there from my meeting in Datchet, remember?"

She bit back her tears, so I took over the explanation. "Yes, *that's* why you returned to the café after the police had dismissed everyone – when Harry and I rescued you from that journalist." I closed my eyes and focused. "You tampered with Tony's pills that morning, but left the chilli bottle at home, because at that point no crime had been committed. But then, after Tony's death, you panicked, secretly retrieved the bottle, shoved it in a bin – and shortly after, picked up the journalist. In your desperation to get away from the press, you ended up back at Paws, and we rescued you. You then went inside the café when Harry and I dropped you off, because I'd actually asked you why you'd gone back there, and you wanted to cover your tracks."

"You *said* you wanted a silent moment with your husband's spirit." Alex treated Judy to a withering stare. "Why am I only hearing about this 'bottle in the bin' thing now?"

She sat up urgently. "Because I thought I'd killed him! I thought he must've had some allergy that I didn't know about."

David was still standing behind her. "But if you didn't want to kill him, why tamper with his pills?"

She twisted awkwardly to look at him, then turned back. "When I was standing at the reception desk last week with Lydia and Hyacinth, we were chatting – girl talk, you know. And I was complaining that Tony kept droning on inanely in the mornings before I'd had my caffeine fix – he was getting on my nerves." She spoke sadly. "How I'd love to hear his voice again now. We should be careful what we get upset about."

Alex wasn't interested in platitudes. "Yes, very profound, Mrs Royal. And the chilli oil?"

"Well, one of the girls – Lydia or Hyacinth – pointed at the chilli plant on reception and suggested I could silence him by making him cough. *Pour chilli oil on his cornflakes*, type thing. It was just a stupid joke. But when I discovered he was about to make an announcement that lunchtime, I... I did it."

Alex leaned forward. "You wanted to stop Tony from announcing your divorce?"

"I wanted to *disrupt* his announcement." Judy fiddled with the tissue box. "I was so worried he was going to tell everyone he was leaving me. I loved him; I couldn't bear it. He's threatened divorce more than once. I couldn't let him say it out loud in front of everyone like that. Then it would be real."

My heart surged with compassion. "Did part of you want to humiliate him? Teach him a lesson?"

"No! The opposite. *I* wanted to be the one to give him the glass of water. To save him. To remind him that he needed me."

David stepped over and handed Alex a report. "And there's *this*, Inspector."

"Oh, *yes*. Mrs Royal, did you know that your late husband was using the company credit card for extra perks? You might have the Inland Revenue contacting you about that."

Judy seemed genuinely surprised. "What perks?"

"We've been looking over the finances for The Royal Boutique," David explained. "And the company credit card was regularly used for expensive massages, beauty treatments, and designer clothing."

"That's so strange..." Judy shook her head, trying to comprehend. "Tony wasn't the sort of bloke to spend money on massages or beauty treatments. *I* can't think why the company credit card would've been used for anything like that. But anyway, he wasn't very financially savvy, so Lydia did all his accounts for him. You could ask her?"

Yes, ask her if *she'd* been treating herself to a few perks courtesy of the company credit card. No wonder she was so keen to hang onto that job!

And there was something else about Lydia, wasn't there? I cleared my throat.

"What is it now?" Alex asked wearily.

I refused to be brushed off. "This is important. Last night I overheard Lydia and Hyacinth talking. Lydia was saying she'd committed corporate sabotage."

"Corporate sabotage?" David sounded surprised. "In what way?"

"She didn't elaborate. But I guess you could talk to her?"

David glanced at Alex who nodded his agreement.

I gazed at Judy. After her interrogation and confession, she seemed limp and watery, which made me think of something else. "And what about Tony's last words? Fine lettuce? What did that mean?"

"Well, Mrs Royal?" Alex asked.

Judy twisted a tissue in her fingers. "Don't ask me. He didn't even like salads."

Poor Judy. I regretted now not bringing her wedding ring along, but I hadn't known she'd be here. Aunt Vicky still had it, so I vowed to return it when this was over.

David's phone bleeped. "Oh, sir, it's a text message from that American tourist who was staying at The Royal Boutique – the one who checked out on Friday morning."

"Well, what of her?" Alex asked.

"She's been away in London all weekend, but she's kindly returned to Windsor – apparently she's got some information. I'll go and meet her now."

Alex stood up. "Right, I want everyone out of my office. Sergeant Van Danté, process Mrs Royal, then go and talk to this American tourist. *And* to Lydia."

"Yes, sir. This way, Mrs Royal."

David ushered her out. I was about to follow, but Alex called me back.

"Yes, Inspector Taylor?"

"Stay out of this case, but…" A smile skirted over his face. "That was good work."

I left his office feeling pleased to have finally penetrated his steely wall – even if this murder case still seemed as impenetrable as ever.

Chapter Twenty-Two

Well, that was a turn-up. Apparently, Judy was guilty of nothing more than having a fling with a younger man and lacing her husband's pills with chilli oil. Unpleasant, yes. But not illegal. And certainly not murder.

So who had killed Tony?

Inspector Taylor had told me to stay out of it, and the truth was, I was keen to go to Paws for Tea to see Vicky and Harry for my daily dose of kindness. I wanted to check they were okay after Billy's surprise appearance at their lovely event last night. And I needed to tell them my amazing news. My parents were alive! My body fizzed with excitement. Vermilitrude had no idea where they were, but I was determined to train in magic and find them. I couldn't wait to hug them both!

I headed towards the cat café with a spring in my step. The streets of Windsor were bustling with tourists as usual, but today I seemed to be *wearing* my hometown like a comfy coat. Three days ago, I'd returned a stranger, but now, this was *my* town – my sanctuary. I glowed with pride as I said hello to tourists, welcoming them to Windsor – even though they'd possibly been here longer than *I* had this week.

As luck would have it, my scenic route to Paws took me down the street that contained The Royal Boutique B&B. I was itching to know more about Lydia's corporate sabotage, especially in light of this info about her abusing the company credit card to fund her extravagant lifestyle. Was that a motive for murder?

Last night, she'd bragged that she could wrap David around her little finger. Ha! I couldn't imagine anyone manipulating that steely-willed vampire. I'd pay money to see her try!

As I approached The Royal Boutique, I spotted David's unmarked police car parked outside Turret Sanctuary. It was a beast of a vehicle that I'd had the misfortune of seeing from the inside only two days ago, but now David was standing beside it with his back to me, chatting to a middle-aged woman – who had silver hair and a pleasant smile. Her combination of sunglasses, umbrella, and raincoat suggested she was planning some outdoor sightseeing.

Ah, this must be the American lady who'd messaged David just now. Curiosity swept over me. What new evidence did she have about the murder? Luckily, she was speaking loudly in a Texan accent, so I ducked down the side of Turret Sanctuary to eavesdrop.

Peering around the corner, I watched David take out his notebook. "Mrs Jackson, you said in your text message that you saw Hyacinth and Tony chatting first thing on Friday morning – the day he died?"

She replied in her distinctive Southern lilt. "That's right, I was sitting in the dining room at The Royal Boutique, surrounded by those beautiful paintings, and enjoying my delicious breakfast." She gestured animatedly. "I saw Hyacinth walk across the lawn to the outside door of the dining room, then wave at

Tony through the glass. He put down his saxophone and they chatted quietly."

"Did they argue?" David asked, pen poised over notepad.

"I couldn't hear exactly what they were saying, but they looked like they were getting along okay. Hyacinth gestured to the old oak tree and I *think* she said, 'I'll give it to you'."

David raised his voice above a noisy group of tourists. "She was going to let Tony cut down the oak tree? Is that what she might've meant?"

"Could be," Mrs Jackson said. "And then Hyacinth left, saying she'd see him later."

"What time was this?"

"Umm, 'bout eight a.m."

David pensively scratched his stubble. "And they were meeting at twelve o'clock at the cat café for lunch, so *that's* presumably where she planned to see him later. Did she give Tony anything to eat or drink?"

"No, officer, she did not – not as far as I could see."

A traffic warden crossed the road, shouting angrily. "Oi, mate, you can't park there."

As the traffic warden squared up to him, David leaned over and told him to get lost, which he did pretty sharpish – looking rather stunned. Perhaps David had flashed him a bit of vampire. It was a nifty way to get out of parking fines! Although being a police officer probably helped.

David focused back on the American lady, softening his tone. "Did Tony seem unwell at all after that?"

She pushed her sunglasses up her nose. "No, sir, he seemed fine. He continued to play his saxophone through breakfast, and a couple of guests even got up to dance!"

David thanked the lady, wrapping up their impromptu interview, so I darted back behind the wall.

Hmm, *that* was interesting. Hyacinth had chatted to Tony on the morning of the murder. Had she somehow slipped him the poison when no one was looking? But that really *would've* been slow-acting arsenic! Eight o'clock was far too early. And besides, the Texan lady hadn't seen Hyacinth *give* him anything to eat or drink, so... what an anti-climax. It just sounded like the two neighbours had had a chat which, in all honesty, they possibly did most mornings. And then Tony had carried on playing his saxophone during breakfast as he famously did.

I had a vision of Tony turning the pages of his music book... licking his finger.

Oh fudge cakes, maybe *that* was it!

I peered around the corner and saw David gazing up at The Royal Boutique B&B. He took a step towards the building, but I had a theory to share. "David, psst!"

He joined me down the side of Turret Sanctuary. "Amber, what are you doing here?"

His face flashed with annoyance. And now that we were alone, I could see he looked tired.

"Late night?" I asked, wincing.

He stifled a yawn. "I don't know if you remember, but a dead body floated down the river last night. And what are *you* doing getting involved? You could've just told me about the 'bottle in the bin' theory. I would've taken care of it."

"No way. Inspector Taylor said he was impressed with my amateur sleuthing. I wouldn't have given that away for anything."

He rankled. "It's not a competition. And anyway, you need to stay out of it now."

"What happened to…" I put on a deep and gravelly voice… "*Hey, Amber, you could use your magic and journalist skills to help me.*"

"To help find *Ivan*, not to get involved in a murder case. I was grateful you helped with the magical library to speak to Vincent. But I shouldn't have encouraged you."

Fine, if he didn't *want* my help… I held up my hand. "Message received and understood. You haven't encouraged me, so you can stop worrying."

"But I *am* worried. Don't you realise how dangerous this is? What if it's all connected to your grandmother's murder? What if *you're* in danger? Seriously, when I finally got off duty last night – well, this morning – all I could see when I closed my eyes was *you* being…" He shook his head and glared at the ground, but swiftly transferred his glare to me.

Woah, *that* was probably the expression that had so spooked the traffic warden just now. It was a look that contained a word *so* unprintable, that even my tabloid newspaper would've hesitated. The icy blue flash was what made it so forceful, as well as the intensity behind his eyes. It was raw, pure vampire. But unfortunately for David, it was lost on me, because *I* thought he looked even *more* snogable than ever.

And perhaps it was a bit mean, but I had the perfect way to disarm him. I couldn't hide my smile. "By the way, I have some news. My parents are alive."

As expected, the glare surged to confusion. "What?" he spluttered. "How?"

"I'll explain all when you're not on duty." I playfully folded my arms across my chest. "But while you're *on* duty, Sergeant, I have a theory, if you'd care to hear it?"

He wrestled with his grin. "Oh for goodness sake, go on then."

"Um… Well, did you check Tony's *music book* for arsenic? When I was in the dining room the other day, I noticed a jam fingerprint on the page that the book was open at."

"So?"

"So *maybe* Tony had a habit of licking his finger to turn the pages? It's quite common – I saw Vincent doing it at the library when *his* book pages got stuck together."

David spoke as if he was playing a winning hand. "Impossible. I checked the whole dining room for traces of arsenic but, other than the paintings, there was nothing. Not on the saxophone or anywhere else."

"Can we check the music book again?"

"We?"

I groaned. "My instincts are screaming at me, David."

He ran his long fingers through his hair. "Well, it's never wise to ignore a witch's instincts."

"Really? Is that a thing?"

"Unfortunately, yes."

I inhaled sharply as a strong odour wafted into my nostrils. "Can you smell garlic?"

"Very funny, Amber."

"No, seriously. Sniff…"

He sniffed, making his nostrils flare. "So what? Someone's cooking with garlic. It's not against the law."

Squeezing past Hyacinth's battered old Volkswagen Beetle, I stepped further down the side of Turret Sanctuary. David followed, but gently grasped my arm, sending tingles through my soul. "Mind the muddy puddle," he said into my ear.

Blimey, he had a strong grip. I yanked myself free from the magnetic tension that drew me towards him. Then, on trembling legs, and avoiding the muddy puddle, I edged along the side of Hyacinth's property and peeked in the window.

Hyacinth's office contained the usual desk, filing cabinet, and bookshelf crammed with paperbacks. But more importantly, Hyacinth was in there, standing with her back to the window. She wasn't cooking with garlic, but rather she was burning something in a metal bin on her desk!

The office window was ajar. A plan struck me. "David, go and ring the doorbell. As soon as she leaves, I'll climb in."

He spoke quietly. "You can't break into her house!"

"Whatever she's burning is *burning*. Don't you want to know what it is? Surely there's *something* you need to ask her? Go and ring her doorbell."

He raised an eyebrow that clearly said, *I'll go because I want to, not because you're telling me.* Then he jogged around the corner.

Oh, apparently I did speak 'eyebrow' after all!

As I'd hoped, Hyacinth left the office at the sound of the doorbell. Right, action stations…

In all my years as a journalist I'd never climbed in a window, and it was harder than it looked. I hooked my foot onto the six-inch wide window ledge then, using the frame for purchase, tugged myself inside. Whoops, I used too *much* purchase, and ended up landing in a heap on the carpet. "Oof!"

I scrabbled to my feet and pulled the metal bin towards me. Ow, it was hot!

It was *also* too late. Only a fragment of a wad of paper and a bit of envelope remained in the ashes.

I jumped as I heard Hyacinth's voice. But she was just answering the front door. "Detective Sergeant Van Danté, what are you doing here?"

His voice was curt. "I could smell burning, madam."

"Everything's fine."

"I'd like to check. Excuse me."

"Hey, you can't go in there!"

I froze as the office door was flung open and David darted inside. He slammed it shut and leaned against it. "Well, Amber? What was it?"

Hyacinth banged on the door. "You can't do that!"

"It was mostly burnt," I said, showing him the bin. "Just a little fragment left."

Leaning backwards on the door, he rummaged in the charred remains. "Looks like printer paper. It could've been anything."

Hyacinth banged angrily from the hallway. "Let me in. Who are you talking to?"

"You'd better get out of here," David whispered.

"Yes!" I rushed to the window.

"Amber, leave the bin *here*!"

"Oh yes." I plonked it on the desk, then climbed outside – splashing into the muddy puddle as I landed. Yuck, wet socks! I pressed myself against the external wall.

David stepped away from the door.

Hyacinth stumbled inside.

She huffily straightened her kaftan. "You'd better tell me what's going on, DS Van Danté, or I'll make a formal complaint!"

Hyacinth was standing with her back to me, so I watched through the window as David took control. "You were overheard telling Tony on the morning of his death that you'd decided to *let* him cut the oak tree down after all."

She shoved the wastepaper bin under the desk, trying to hide it. "I wanted to discuss everything with him like an adult. To put all those applications and counter-applications behind us and try to figure out a compromise."

"Why did you change your mind?" David asked, flipping open his notepad. "About letting Tony build his extension?"

"I *didn't* change my mind. As I said, I wanted to talk to him calmly. My angels told me it was better to be a good neighbour than a fighting neighbour. Now, if that will be all?" She held open the door.

"Actually, madam, the inspector has asked me to follow up with everyone, with regards to the death of Billy Royal."

Her voice was strained. "Billy's dead too?"

As David started to explain, Hyacinth paced nervously to the other side of the office and David followed, meaning I couldn't hear them.

Right, I needed to get closer. As I checked that she still had her back to the window, I hitched a knee onto the ledge. But, because the window was the outward-opening sort, I shifted forward and accidentally knocked it shut. Oh fudge cakes!

Balancing precariously, I tried to ease it back open. But... ah good, David was coming this way, perhaps *he* could help. Unfortunately, he was so entirely focused on Hyacinth that, as he shoved the window open, I was flung into the muddy puddle. "Wah!"

Well, I hope he hadn't done *that* on purpose!

I sat shivering in the cold, dirty water, with my sodden jeans clinging to my skin. But at least the window was now open.

David was talking about Billy. "You knew him when you taught at Hurley College?"

"Not especially," Hyacinth said flatly. "I knew *of* him – that he was a troublemaker. I'm sorry he's dead, of course. But our paths never crossed."

David's voice was granite-hard. "Any idea why he was at the railway arches on Thursday night?"

"Why should I know?"

"Anything you can think of *would* be helpful."

Hyacinth's voice moved away from the window, so I clambered to my feet, hoping to stealthily watch. But my wet trainers slipped underneath me and I yelped out loud.

Hyacinth turned suddenly. "Did you hear something out there?"

I ducked down, sloshing my feet in the puddle. My trainers were soaked, my jeans were soaked... But at least my upper half was dry. At the moment.

"I don't think so," David said dismissively. "Now, madam..."

"Wait, I just need to feed the birds. Hold on, Sergeant."

Hyacinth stuck her head out the window, looking anxiously from side-to-side – while *I* squatted a few feet under her nose. Hmm... why was she acting so paranoid? Who did she think was out here?

Whoever it was, they weren't here. But she clearly felt the need to keep up the pretence for David, because a handful of seeds suddenly landed on my head. Oh for goodness cake! I brushed the assorted bird treats out of my hair, just in case a flock of ravenous seagulls swooped down. An aerial avian attack would fit *right* in with the nonsense of the last five minutes.

"Billy Royal, madam?" David said, his voice straining with impatience.

Hyacinth exhaled heavily and turned to face him. "Look, if you want my honest opinion, Detective Sergeant, *I'd* guess Billy was at the arches selling drugs. Or buying drugs. That's what people usually do there, isn't it? Maybe he was murdered by his dealer. Perhaps *that's* how he acquired the arsenic that killed his father."

"Why would he want to kill his father?" David asked suspiciously.

Her voice went up a notch, getting frantic. "*I* don't know. I'm just guessing. A bit like you."

"I'm not guessing, madam," David said, supercool as ever. "I've been gathering evidence and speaking to people. And I have it on good authority that you and Lydia discussed corporate sabotage at the ball last night."

I watched as Hyacinth shuffled a pile of papers on her desk. "Look, it's nothing to do with me. Lydia was helping Tony with the tree protection order, because apparently he wasn't very educated – and Lydia studied law at university. Anyway, when she found out that Tony was planning to replace her, she switched her allegiance to me. I *refused* Lydia's offer, of course."

"Why didn't you mention this to the police before?" David asked.

"I didn't want to get her into trouble. Now if you'll excuse me, I've got a crystal-healing presentation to prepare for."

She turned to face the window and, in my haste to duck, I fell flat on my face, drenching my t-shirt, hands, and head – and thus completing my all-over mud bath.

Okay, that was my cue to leave. Dripping and muddy, I squelched back towards the street, making a mental note that, from now on, David could do his own dirty work!

Chapter Twenty-Three

David's top priority now was to catch a cold-blooded killer. Mine was to find a nice hot shower.

I squelched back to meet him outside The Royal Boutique B&B, where he was leaning against his car, unable to suppress his laughter at the sight of me covered in grime, looking like a swamp monster.

It was a pleasant sunny day, so my mud was already starting to set.

His smirk was back with a vengeance. "I, er, I wasn't able to get any *dirt* on Hyacinth. How did *you* get on?"

I laughed wryly. "I listened to your interview with her, and there seemed to be a lot of mud-slinging between you."

David opened his mouth to continue with the mud-based banter, but he stood straight as Vincent plodded out of The Royal Boutique B&B, wearing his pointed witch's hat and long black cloak. He was carrying a battered old suitcase – as well as the weight of the world.

David stepped into his path. "Where do you think you're going?"

Vincent gripped the handle of his suitcase tightly. "I'm leaving. I've just said goodbye to Judy."

I glanced at the beautiful Victorian frontage of The Royal Boutique B&B. "Is Judy in there?"

"I gave her a lift back," David said. "Vincent, you're not supposed to leave Windsor."

"I'll be in Marvelton, at the university." He rummaged in his cloak pocket. "Here's the name and address of my sponsor and tutor. You can follow me through the portal anytime."

David hooked his thumbs in his belt. "You're still a suspect in this murder inquiry."

"I didn't kill Tony." Vincent lowered his suitcase to the pavement. "But I need to get away from Windsor. If Judy doesn't want me, then I'm going to stop being a fraud. I don't even enjoy painting."

"*I* still want to know why there was arsenic in your paint," David said accusingly.

"As I told this novice w–" Vincent frowned at my muddy clothes, but decided not to ask. "As I told this novice witch at the magical library, the spell created the paint."

David's tone was sceptical. "But magic doesn't create arsenic unless *you* instruct it to."

Vincent waited for a nearby courier to walk into The Royal Boutique B&B, then spoke pleadingly. "Honestly, Detective Inspect–"

"Sergeant," David interjected.

"Detective *Sergeant*, it was the ingredients of the spell that created the poison. You see, along with the chilli oil, the spell required copper, iron, and nickel to be melded at a high temperature. I suppose when the magic mixed everything together, the arsenic was created." He perked up. "Hey, perhaps that's how Paris green paint was originally invented all those years ago."

David scrutinised him for an uncomfortable few seconds, then stepped aside. "Off you go. But be aware, I've reported you to the Beings of Magic committee. They'll decide what to do with you for abusing magic."

Vincent's face flashed with worry. "Not the Beings of Magic committee. I've heard they use torture!"

David grinned. "Worse. They use a giant rulebook, an agenda full of local issues, and boring presentations with more slides than a waterpark."

Vincent's cheek twitched. "Please, Inspector, I throw myself at the mercy of the human police."

"It's *Sergeant*." David held up his hands. "And there's nothing *I* can do. You've committed no human crime."

Like a man approaching the gallows, Vincent picked up his suitcase, nodded tightly, then plodded off up the road.

"You're sure he's innocent?" I asked, brushing some crusty mud off my t-shirt.

David watched him disappear into the crowd. "I don't feel he's killer material."

"I agree. Poor guy. I hope he'll be okay."

"He brought it upon himself. He was pretending to be something he's not, in order to win the affection of the woman he loves." David pinned me with his gaze. "*I* could never do that."

Well, *that* was clear. I raised my chin. "You shouldn't have to."

Oh blimey, the sizzling friction between us was making my mud crackle. Perhaps I could lighten the mood by asking him to train me. I grinned as I remembered about my parents! But clashing voices from inside The Royal Boutique B&B made David groan and rush inside.

I followed.

The luxurious foyer dripped with tension as Lydia and a courier squared up to each other in front of the narrow reception desk, practically nose-to-nose with rage.

The poor chap was trying to defend himself, but she was furious. "You're utterly incompetent, you stupid little man!"

"Now look 'ere, sweetheart—"

"Don't you call *me* sweetheart. This is absolutely—"

David thrust an arm between them. "Stop this now!"

Lydia and the courier glared at each other around David. The courier blinked first and stepped away.

Facing Lydia, David spoke over his shoulder. "Sir, tell me what's happening?"

The courier gestured to a large cardboard box perched on the edge of the small reception desk. "When I was here this morning, I accidentally took *that* box, because it was underneath my actual collection. Anyway, this lady phoned my company and had a right go at my dispatcher, so I've brought it back. But it wasn't my fault. *She* put the boxes on top of each other."

Lydia huffed. "But only *one* box had your company's label on it, you stupid little man. This other package is a delivery for *me*. Why didn't you check before you left?"

"You were on the phone. It's not my fault the reception desk is too small to hold more than one box."

"Well, it *is* your fault that I won't be using your courier company ever again."

David eyed up the box in question. "Lydia, what's in here that's upsetting you so much?"

Guilt flashed across her face. "I don't have to tell you that."

"This is a murder investigation and you're a suspect. Open it. Now."

She folded her arms across her chest. "Not unless you can produce a warrant."

He pulled his warrant card from his back pocket. "This gives me the right to stop and search any member of the public if I'm suspicious. And I'm suspicious. And if you don't open this box *now*, I'll seize it and open it at the police station."

Lydia adopted a whiny voice. "David, how long have we known each other? You can't seriously suspect me? What would your parents say?"

The courier was getting agitated. "Look, can I go? I *have* actually got other things to do today."

Lydia waved him away. "Yes, go and ruin someone else's day."

David spoke sternly to her. "Pass me those scissors."

She thrust them towards him – blades outwards, which was just rude.

As David sliced open the box, I braced myself to see a stash of gold bullion, a haul of cocaine, or at least some designer shoes. But Lydia smiled smugly as David pushed back the flaps to reveal a pack of brown envelopes and two reams of paper.

His voice was low and flat. "It's full of *stationery*."

She glanced at her fingernails, unable to hide her satisfaction. "What did you expect?"

But it didn't change the fact that she probably *had* been using her employer's credit card to treat herself to luxury items at the B&B's expense. All David would need to do was cross-reference her online shopping accounts with the offending items on the company bank statements. She struck me as someone far too smug to properly cover her tracks.

But I was wondering, had Tony or Billy found out about this blatant theft? And so she'd killed them? Or had it been enough that Tony had wanted to replace her?

For now, she was enjoying a little power trip. "Are we going to apologise, David?"

He pushed away his anger, pulled out his notepad, and spoke in a far-too-calm voice. "Tell me what happened with the tree protection order. You switched allegiance? Decided to sabotage Tony's side of things?"

Lydia glanced at me, wrinkled her nose at my muddy clothes, then replied breezily to David. "Yes, I decided to help Hyacinth prevent Tony from cutting down the oak tree. He'd annoyed me after I saw my job advertised online. But I didn't kill him."

I stepped forward. "No, he was worth *much* more to you alive. Because you were using his credit card to fund your lifestyle."

She scoffed. "Spare me the lecture, Swamp Girl. Tony didn't know anything about running a business. He was more suited to busking. Perhaps if he'd stuck to that, he might not have got himself killed. Now, if that will be all, Sergeant Van Danté? I'm actually rather busy myself."

"No it will not be all. I'm here for another look in the gallery. And, let me assure you, after this murder enquiry is over, I shall tell Judy *exactly* what you've been up to with her husband's company credit card." He glanced at me. "Come on, Amber. I need you."

I suppressed my grin and strode past Lydia, hoping we'd find a conclusive clue in the dining room –and finally find the killer together. Oh please let it be *her*!

Chapter Twenty-Four

Without Vincent's paintings to brighten up the stark magnolia space, the gallery/dining room felt soulless. Perhaps the room was missing Tony and his early-morning saxophone renditions. The buzz of guests and the mellow music would've truly been a fun way to start the day. Lydia had said that Tony wasn't much of a businessman, but he'd clearly been a great entertainer, and sometimes that was all you needed.

David was already flicking through the music book with gloved hands. "Oh, here's the jam fingerprint. I *have* already checked this book for arsenic, but if your witchy instincts are saying there's a clue here, then I'd better take a closer look."

"Are you all right?" I asked gently. "After that confrontation with Lydia? I know she's a family friend."

"Yeah, fine. I have a job to do, and she's a suspect in this case." He scrutinised me. "What are your instincts saying? Anything about this room?"

"David, I'm not psychic. Maybe you should ask my aunt Vicky to do a scan, or whatever she does."

"Come here." He removed his gloves and stepped over to the far wall. "Stand here next to me and take in the whole space. Just take your time."

I stood next to him, wishing I could provide some pertinent information. Nothing was coming up so far, but if *he* believed my witchy instincts were failsafe, then maybe I should give it a try. My wand tingled in its armband, but *that* didn't give me any tangible clues. I should've asked Granny if the wand came with an instruction manual…

Letting the wall take my weight, I gazed at the pretty garden through the large glass expanse opposite, hoping the greenery might inspire me. It *was* a beautiful outside space, with the ancient oak tree – which I'd hugged – as well as the quirky turret embedded in the wall, the disused well, and the large lawn where Hyacinth led her meditation classes. The truth was it *would've* been a shame if Tony had built on it. Hyacinth–

David's urgent whisper interrupted my thoughts. "It's Hyacinth!"

I watched her walking cautiously across the garden, carrying a small bundle. Could she see us in here? Possibly not. We were firmly pressed against this far wall and, in my limited experience, if you looked into a window from the outside, the view quickly trailed back to darkness.

So, we could see her, but she possibly couldn't see us.

My muscles tensed as she approached the French windows and peered inside.

David spoke quietly. "She's checking there's no one in here. Keep completely still. She can't see us if we don't move."

"She's not a tyrannosaurus rex, David. And she *might* be able to see us. So…" I grabbed his hand and focused on fading. Even if I couldn't turn us invisible, at least we could blend in.

I hadn't actually intended for this spontaneous contact to be anything more than a camouflage technique. But, of course. David and I were now holding hands, and my heart fluttered at his strong, masculine touch. His fingers wrapped around mine far more snugly than was probably necessary for the magic to work. I stole a glance at his face and saw that, while most of it was maintaining a professional air, his lips had gone off on a little holiday with a sunny smile.

Through my layer of mud, I felt myself glow.

Thankfully Hyacinth couldn't see *that*. In fact, she seemed satisfied that no one was in the dining room, so she stepped away.

David and I continued to hold hands, totally unnecessarily, as Hyacinth made her way over to the disused well. She leaned in and hoisted out some sturdy branches.

"They're not *growing* over the top of the well," David said in disbelief. "Someone's put them there to make it *look* like it's overgrown."

"And the question is… what's down there?"

Hyacinth glanced around again, then lifted the plant-entwined metal grille off the well, before hooking a leg over the rim and disappearing inside.

"Should we go and investigate?" I asked.

"*We* shouldn't do anything." David retrieved his hand. "But just give her a minute, I want to see if anything else happens. Then I'll go and check."

After a tense couple of minutes, which is a long time when you're standing in the shadows with a handsome vampire, Hyacinth emerged and hefted the grille and foliage back into place.

We watched her stride off to her B&B. After waiting a moment to check she wasn't coming back, David stepped over and wiggled the handle of the French Windows. "Locked."

I wilted. "We'll have to go all the way back through reception and past—"

The lock clunked. David held up a thin piece of metal and grinned. Oh yes, he could pick locks, couldn't he. I'd discovered *that* ten years ago. "Is that a standard-issue *police* lockpick?" I asked, raising my eyebrows.

"Stay here," he commanded, slipping into the garden.

Er. *No*.

I caught up with him at the disused well. He wasn't surprised to see me, and coolly grabbed his torch from his duty belt. "Stay back, let me look."

He shone his torch down onto the foliage. There was nothing interesting on top of it. But there must be something interesting below. Or at least interesting to Hyacinth.

We reached in together and removed the branches, then David lifted off the rusty grille, chucking it on the grass.

My heart pounded hard as I glanced at Turret Sanctuary, fearing that Hyacinth might be watching. It was thrilling in a terrifying way!

I gazed down into the well's deep shaft and, as my eyes adjusted to the darkness, I realised there were several rows of missing bricks leading into the abyss. *That's* how she'd climbed down there. The missing bricks formed a ladder of sorts.

David grasped my shoulder. "Stay here. I *really* mean it. I can fly down."

He slung a leg over the rim of the well, and dropped into the darkness.

Even though I was worried that Hyacinth might be lurking, it was actually lovely out here in the sunshine. I relaxed as I gazed at the beautiful old oak tree. Hmm, all right, after this, I would go straight to Paws for Tea and tell Vicky and Harry all about my exciting morning. My tummy rumbled. Tell them over *lunch*. But before that, of course, I needed to have a shower and check on my lovely Marmalade Sandw—

Yikes! I froze like a sunbather at the English seaside. Hyacinth was heading this way, deep in thought, and carrying several folding chairs.

Oh fudge cakes, she'd *said* she had a crystal-healing presentation to prepare for. She must be giving it out here! I glanced around for somewhere to hide.

The only way was down.

With my heart thrashing in my ears, I clambered over the rim of the well, vowing to learn that Levitation spell David had mentioned. Okay, come on, I could do this. There was thankfully *some* permanent foliage flowing from the old bricks, so I grabbed a handful and carefully lowered myself down, tentatively shoving one foot into a gap, then the other – descending into the darkness.

I dropped the last few feet, then stood there listening to a faraway water outlet, drip, drip, dripping.

"*David?*" I whispered sharply.

He grabbed me, making me jump. "Arrrggh!"

"Amber, what did I just tell you?"

Oh fudge cakes, he'd gone 'fully vampire'. "Arrrggh!"

Actually, the only thing that terrified *me* was how gorgeous he looked. As a vampire, his features were even more handsome – his chin was chiselled, his cheekbones sharp, and his canines long and pointy. His brown eyes had turned sapphire blue and were full of passion. The whole effect made me want to don a negligee and run around a haunted house in the dead of night... *Ahem*. Sorry.

I composed myself. "Hyacinth's up there. She came outside."

His voice was primal. "All right. Stay close."

If you insist....

He shone his torch into the darkness. I'd expected to simply see the bottom of a well, but we were apparently standing in an underground tunnel. "How far does it go?" I whispered.

He held up a hand. "Shh, what was that noise?"

My irritation at being shushed was replaced by sickening terror as I saw the flash of golden fur in the shadows. I braced myself to be savaged by a wild animal, but oh! Bounding towards me on stubby legs was a thick-set, small dog, with a gaping mouth that appeared to be smiling with glee. The only wild thing about this animal were his wildly flapping ears.

"Hello darling." I tried to stroke his soft fur as he scampered around. "Are *you* Colin? Do you belong to Vermilitrude Eldritch?"

He yapped at the sound of his name, excitedly licking my hand. He was the type of corgi with a bushy tail, and it swished joyfully as I tried to persuade him to sit.

David patted the dog's back, which swayed in time with his tail. "What's he doing down *here*?"

"And why did *Hyacinth* want him?"

"Let me check his collar." David inspected the silver tag. "Not much to go on. Is he microchipped? We can scan him at the police station."

"Yes, Granny said that Billy had sorted that out for her. Oh, she'll be so glad to see you, won't she, boy!" I laughed with delight. "I'm surprised that naughty old Hyacinth didn't attach a crystal to your collar – she's obsessed with crystals, isn't she, Colin? Yes, she is, *isn't* she, boy!"

David was now on his feet and searching the tunnel with his torch. "Oh blimey…"

With little Colin trailing behind, I stepped over and saw a rack of glass bottles in the shadows, each labelled with a skull and crossbones motif and bearing a chemical symbol. There was *$N2O$*, which I had a feeling was nitrous oxide or laughing gas. I had no idea what *$NaCN$* was. But the bottle that really caught my attention was the one labelled *As*.

Arsenic.

"Stay back, Amber. Don't touch anything."

"Don't worry, David, I wasn't about to start drinking the—"

Glass crunched beneath my feet. I bent to pick up whatever I'd trodden on, but David pulled me back. "What did I just say about not touching anything?"

He pulled on some disposable gloves, and picked up a smashed mobile phone.

My thoughts clicked into place. "Do you think this might be *Billy's* missing phone?"

"Could be. I can't turn it on. I'll see if the tech team can salvage anything – they're always really good at doing what I ask." He raised an eyebrow. "Unlike some people."

I was about to defend myself but, as his words clicked into my brain, I was assaulted with a flashback of Judy at Paws for Tea on that fateful lunchtime.

She was sitting at the table in her pink suit, glaring at her husband.

Tony slapped the table hard. "I just don't understand you, Judy. I've done what you wanted."

"Have you?" Judy asked. "That would be a first!"

Why had *that* come into my mind? But then another fragment surged up... Tony staggering into me and coughing out his incomprehensible phrase. *"Fine lettuce!"*

More memories bobbed. Klaus at the pub. *"Tony's been talking about wanting to get away from it all... I suggested Thailand... He wanted to clear up a few home truths before he left. To gather everyone together and tell them over lunch..."*

Then an image of Hyacinth rubbing her crystal. *"I'm a certified level three crystal healer and reiki master. All fully accredited from the ashram I attended in Phuket."*

And then her meditating guest talking to Harry on the lawn. *"She was out here helping us to find inner-peace... then at five-to-twelve she had to go and meet someone at Paws for Tea."*

David's voice sounded far away. "Amber, are you okay?"

It was like trying to rouse myself from a dream. *"Jam fingerprint. Reception desk too small..."* My eyes swept open. "Oh, I've got it!" I grabbed David's suit jacket. "Have you spoken to the headteacher at Billy's old college? The one Judy paid for him to attend?"

He leaned away from me. "He's on my to-do list. Why?"

I frantically gripped his lapels. "We... *you* need to ask him a few questions. And *then* can you contact the post office? I think there's been another mistaken collection at The Royal Boutique B&B. And it's a fine lettuce!"

Chapter Twenty-Five

One hour – and one shower – later, it was time to shine a light on this now crystal-clear case.

I swaggered with Harry, Alex, and David into the garden of Turret Sanctuary, where Hyacinth was delivering her crystal-healing presentation on the lawn. We hung back unnoticed behind the audience of her B&B guests – as well as Judy, Lydia, and my Aunt Vicky, who'd taken their seats for the showdown.

Hyacinth was in full flow, gesturing to the projector screen behind her as she extolled the benefits of each crystal. There was pink amethyst for boosting confidence, green beryl to inspire creativity, and deep amber to invoke happiness. The irony being that *this* Amber was about to bring Hyacinth anything *but*.

David stood beside me, watching with interest.

"Nothing about arsenic for anger," I whispered.

He grunted. "She'll need more than crystals to deflect *me*."

I eyed up a table near Hyacinth, where her laptop was installed, along with a delicious-looking cake for the break. There was a sharp knife nestled with the plates, and I started fantasising about cutting myself a big slice. This was the trouble with trying to execute a plan at teatime.

Shoving the cake from my mind, I glanced at the USB stick in my hand. When David had checked Colin the corgi's microchip earlier, he'd found a website address oddly entered in the 'Dog's Name' field of the online record. This peculiar link led to a private webpage, which hosted just one photo – a photo that Billy had intended to use for blackmail.

It was time to share it with the world. And for that, I needed access to Hyacinth's laptop. Stealth was required.

Harry was standing by my other side. I spoke to him quietly. "Distract her. I'm going in."

"My pleasure, Bambi." Harry raised his hand. "Excuse me, can I ask a question?"

Hyacinth stopped, mid-presentation. "Er. Yes?"

Harry's voice was flat. "Do crystals help you sleep soundly at night when you've got a guilty conscience?"

She transferred her gaze to Alex and David, who were stern-faced and ready to make an arrest. She staggered as she saw them, but regained control and chuckled nervously. "Whatever do you mean?"

Harry ambled to the front of the seats, revealing Colin on his lead. "Sit down, boy... Well, I was just thinking, if you'd kidnapped a dog, and were having trouble sleeping because of the guilt... would rubbing a crystal help?"

Hyacinth gaped at Colin in shock – giving *me* time to rush behind the greenhouse, where I pressed myself against the glass. Ah, bit of a snag here. Glass was transparent... Checking that Harry was still distracting Hyacinth, I threw myself down to the grass and crawled soldier-like towards the laptop.

Harry spoke angelically. "And do crystals bring people back to life after you've killed them brutally in cold blood?"

Her hippy act turned nasty. "I think you'd better leave."

"Nobody's going anywhere," David said gruffly. "Let's talk about your time as a chemistry teacher, shall we, Hyacinth? You were sceptical about crystal healing back then. What made you change your mind?"

She laughed tensely. "What makes you think I ever doubted the power of crystals?"

With trembling fingers, I shoved the USB stick into the laptop's port, fumbling to open the file. Then, as the image on the projector screen changed, I flopped to the grass with relief.

The stunned audience couldn't drag their eyes away from the social media post that Billy had dug out. Hyacinth's name and profile picture were as clear as her bragging statement: *Only childish idiots would believe such nonsense as crystal healing. I'm a scientist and always will be. But it would be easy for me – or anyone with half a brain – to set up a business to con people. In fact, perhaps I will.*

Hyacinth was still arguing with David, but as she noticed her audience's stunned reaction, she fell silent and slowly turned to the screen. "Wh... what... where did that come from?"

I smiled sweetly. "It came from your fair hand, Hyacinth. *You* posted those words online and, when Billy found them years later, you killed him."

She gripped the crystal around her neck, rubbing it frantically. "This is all lies – completely fraudulent!"

"Are we talking about your *business*?" I asked.

The man whose meditation session Harry had interrupted yesterday spoke with bewilderment. "What's going on? Someone tell me, what's happening?"

"I'm so glad you asked." I manoeuvred the shocked Hyacinth to one side and took over the presentation. "It all started a few years ago, when Hyacinth picked a fight with a group of students at Hurley College. The students were keen on crystal healing, but as a chemistry teacher, Hyacinth was on the side of science…"

I thought back to the interesting chat I'd had earlier with the Hurley College headteacher in his office. He'd remembered Hyacinth very well. "The final straw was when Hyacinth started attacking the students online," he'd explained. "It reflected badly on the college. I'm afraid I had no choice but to fire her."

I sipped the tea he'd kindly made me. "She *said* she'd left due to stress."

He steepled his fingers. "Yes, I allowed her to say that to prevent a scandal…"

Back in the garden, I continued the story. "After that, Hyacinth decided to go travelling in Thailand, where she realised she could *become* the very thing she'd been fired over. And so she returned to England as a crystal healer, albeit a fraudulent one."

Alex called out from the back, making everyone turn to look. "And Billy Royal presumably dug out this incriminating social media post in order to blackmail Hyacinth?"

"That's right," I said. "Billy remembered Hyacinth because of the very public disagreement she'd had with the students. And, although Tony and his son didn't get along terribly well, Billy decided to help his dad fight the tree protection order. He scrolled back years through the posts on Hyacinth's social media profile and found exactly what he was looking for. The incriminating post that undermined Hyacinth's position as a crystal believer." I pointed to the projector screen.

David was already gripping his handcuffs. "On the day before Tony's murder, Billy sent Hyacinth *this* photo and invited her to meet him in a secluded place – the car park near the railway arches. She drove straight there."

"Hyacinth met Billy at half-four by the arches." I gestured to where little Colin was now sitting on the grass. "And Colin was with Billy, because Billy had taken him for his daily walk. When he met Hyacinth, Billy presumably said something like, "Let my dad build his extension or I'll tell everyone you're a fraud."

I pictured the whole thing in my mind. They would've undoubtedly argued. But then Billy must've said something confusing about Colin holding all the information. Hyacinth had no idea what that meant, but she knew she needed to get rid of both Billy and Colin.

Hyacinth had probably said, "Let me just park the car and we can talk." Who knows if she'd planned it on her drive there *or* if it was simply too good an opportunity to miss, but she ran Billy over in her battered old Volkswagen Beetle – knowing one more dent and scratch wouldn't look out of place. Then she stole Billy's phone and dumped him in the river.

Later that evening, Lydia messaged everyone on Tony's behalf, inviting them to his lunch thing at the cat café, saying he had an announcement to make. Hyacinth panicked. Why would Tony want *her* at the lunch? They were rivals locked in a dispute over the oak tree. Had Billy shared her incriminating social media post with his dad? If Tony *did* know about it, it wouldn't take a genius to realise *she'd* killed Billy – his body was bound to resurface at some point. She had to act fast.

The next morning, Hyacinth knew Tony would be in The Royal Boutique B&B's dining room, so she went across the garden and knocked on the French windows – as witnessed by the nice Texan lady.

Taking Tony to one side, Hyacinth must've asked what the meeting at Paws for Tea was all about.

Tony would've said something like, "I've got an announcement to make."

"About what? My tree?"

"You'll have to wait. By the way, have you seen Billy?"

"No. Why?"

"He was telling me all about your past…"

Tony didn't elaborate because he was keen to get back to his guests. But for Hyacinth, this was *proof* that Tony knew about her social media post – and her fraudulent crystal healing business.

Actually, she'd been completely wrong. Tony had been referring to her past *travels* in Phuket, Thailand, where he was planning to go. He was probably going to ask her for some good places to visit. My proof for that was in my back pocket...

Standing in the sunshine, I concluded the gruesome story. "Panicking that Tony would guess *she'd* killed Billy when his body was inevitably discovered, Hyacinth realised Tony also had to die."

David strode up the garden towards her. "Hyacinth Meadows, you're under arrest for the—"

In one swift movement, Hyacinth grabbed the sharp knife from the cake and hurled it at David. *No!*

Reality warped into super slow-mo as he tried to recoil, but the blade was set on a collision course for his chest – a lethal shot, even for a vampire. In a split second between terror and action, I thrust out my arm, shouting the only spell I knew. *"Time and space I now curve, I will make that knife swerve."*

Inches from David's chest, the magic flared, throwing the knife off course, and missing him by the width of an eyelash.

Relief washed over me as the blade swished past Alex's ear, then plunged into the grass.

"Sorry, Inspector Taylor!"

The side of his mouth twitched. Was that a *smile*?

Not even pausing for breath, David clapped the handcuffs on Hyacinth and plonked her down in a chair.

Alex folded his arms across his chest. "But how did she kill Tony?"

"Ah yes, Inspector." I rummaged in my back pocket. "First, I need to give Judy a letter. It's from Tony."

Sitting on the front row, Judy was rigid. "What?"

I brandished the letter in its envelope. *"That's* what fine lettuce meant. I'd misunderstood because he was choking, but it was *Find letter!* You see, Inspector, like y— *some* men, Tony wasn't good at saying his feelings out loud, so he wrote it all down."

"But why didn't I get the letter?" Judy whimpered.

I smiled kindly at her. "He'd left it for you on the reception desk, but it was accidentally picked up by the postman – thinking it was out-post. Sergeant Van Danté managed to track it down and get it back earlier."

"It would've been missing forever if Amber hadn't thought of it," David added with a nod of approval.

I handed the letter to Judy, who tore it open and read it out loud:

My darling Judy,

You say I never tell you how I'm feeling. It's hard for a bloke like me to express myself, but I do love you and I want to save our marriage. I know what's been going on with your artist and I need you to choose. I hope you choose me. I've invited everyone to Paws for Tea to tell them my plans, but I want you to know first. I've decided to go travelling in Thailand for a month, to gather my thoughts and get some headspace.

I'm going to promote Lydia to manager of The Royal Boutique. I've advertised for a new receptionist. Lydia can carry out the interviews. I've decided I want to be a saxophone player again. That made me happy. The B&B's too much pressure and it's affecting our marriage. All I care about is you, Billy, and my music. Yours always, Tony.

Lydia was frozen in shock. "He was going to promote me to manager?"

Judy stared at the note in her hand. "But how was he murdered?"

"Right, yes. We left Hyacinth and Tony chatting at breakfast, didn't we? Just before he went back to playing his saxophone for his guests, Hyacinth quietly told Tony to meet her back there at ten to twelve. Louder – and to get him on her side – she said she'd changed her mind about the tree. *That's* what the nice Texan lady overheard."

It was all so clear in my mind. Tony went back to playing his saxophone, but his would-be killer was still watching. Hyacinth saw him licking his finger before turning the pages of his music book, and she realised *this* was the perfect way to poison him. Spread a little poison on some paper for him to read and he'd lick it off! And what better poison than arsenic? Because Vincent's paintings had made *her* think of Paris green paint too – her former headteacher confirmed to me earlier that she'd taught the students about it as a warning not to misuse chemicals.

Alex held up a hand. "Wait, wait. When did she give him this poisoned paper to lick? She was leading a meditation session for an hour before she left for Paws for Tea. There wasn't time."

I grinned at her audacity. "Yes! But the great thing about meditation is that people keep their eyes closed. So all she needed to do was ensure the meditators were sitting with their backs to the dining room with their eyes firmly shut, and she could slip off at ten to twelve to talk to Tony unnoticed."

So when Hyacinth popped over at ten to twelve, she entered the dining room through the French windows, and no one knew she was there. All Tony's guests had gone out and Lydia was on reception, getting ready to go to Paws. Hyacinth handed Tony a fake contract to read – pretending she was signing over the oak tree. And, as she'd hoped, he licked his finger as he turned each page. She even told him to pop the contract in the envelope she'd brought along. "*You'll* have to lick it. The glue is bad for my chakras... I'll take this and send it to my solicitor."

There was arsenic on the envelope seal *and* on each page corner. That's why it smelled of garlic when she was burning it. Arsenic smells of garlic when burnt!

I gestured to Hyacinth, who was staring unfocused at the grass. "Hyacinth expected the arsenic to kill Tony straight away so, taking the envelope and contract to hide down the well, she left him there and finished off the meditation session, making a show of noting the time and saying she was off to Paws for Tea – the perfect alibi. She made her way through her own B&B around to Tony's reception, where Lydia was waiting – giving Hyacinth an extra alibi if needed."

"Hyacinth assumed Tony would die in the dining room." David sneered at his prisoner. "She must've been amazed to see him turning up at Paws for Tea. But Tony was a big chap, and Hyacinth was a chemist, not a biologist. She hadn't given him enough arsenic to kill him straight away."

Judy was still staring at Tony's letter. I reluctantly explained *her* part in Tony's death. "The arsenic *would've* killed him that day, but it was the spike in his heart rate from the coughing that finished him off so quickly. Without the chilli oil, Tony would've been able to make his announcement. And then he would've died soon after."

"That's why he was feeling unwell," Judy whispered.

"Where did she get the arsenic?" Alex asked. He muttered an aside to me. "Don't tell me she *also* magicked it up."

"No, Inspector." I pointed at the old greenhouse. "Hyacinth regularly runs crystal-making workshops for her guests – she's got all the equipment already. I've been doing a bit of crystal studying myself, and the crystal around her neck is probably arsenopyrite. It's not toxic until you crush and distil it, which you *can* do if you're a chemist and have the right equipment."

David spoke directly to his boss. "I discovered bottles of various poisons stashed down the well, sir. Hyacinth clearly enjoys making deadly concoctions as a little side hobby."

My gaze rested on a patch of wild garlic. "And presumably Hyacinth overheard Sergeant Van Danté speaking to the nice Texan lady earlier, and decided to get rid of the murder weapon. But unluckily for her, we were in sniffing distance."

"Well, that seems to cover everything." Alex gave David the nod, so he hauled Hyacinth to her feet, read her her rights, and led her away.

And that was that. A complex and clever murder solved. Hyacinth would surely get life in prison for her crimes.

In the ringing aftermath, Hyacinth's guests drifted into a stunned discussion about what had just happened. Aunt Vicky was chatting to Judy – giving her back her wedding ring. And Lydia was already on the phone.

I made my way over to where Harry was playing with Colin on the lawn, feeling excited that my life in Windsor was only just beginning. After all, even the grandest castles were built one stone at a time.

Chapter Twenty-Six

My English country garden contained all the ingredients for a perfect afternoon. But *not* because I'd taught myself a nifty spell for growing chocolate-biscuit bushes.

Appealing as that sounded, *this* was even better than chocolate biscuits.

Clutching the bunch of flowers I'd handpicked from my own little patch of paradise, I found a vase in my kitchen and arranged the blooms proudly – their vibrant colours brightening the space and filling it with a sweet soothing fragrance.

Pleased with the floral display, I flicked on the kettle and surveyed my neatly mown lawn through the window. Yesterday, David had spent hours writing up his paperwork; today he'd volunteered to mow my lawn 'for a nice relaxing break' – *his* words. He was welcome to have a nice relaxing break vacuuming my living room too if he wanted.

As I tipped a packet of chocolate biscuits onto a dainty plate, I watched Marmalade Sandwich and Colin the corgi frolicking on the grass outside. My heart surged with tenderness as Marmalade Sandwich reared up on his hind legs, then stretched his arms out wide – presenting his spotty tummy to Colin for a boisterous 'tongue hug'. The pup's enthusiastic licking threw the cat off balance, and the two tumbled together, mewing and yapping with glee.

My cousin Evelyn was out there too. She'd found a hosepipe and was squirting Alex, chasing him and laughing. Alex tickled her playfully, then directed the stream towards his dog Fuzzball, who bounced and sneezed in the sunshine, eagerly trying to bite the water.

The water hit my granny – and flowed straight through her. She was floating near Harry and Vicky, supervising as they planted a punnet of perennials that my cousin had kindly given me. Harry and Vicky chatted animatedly as their earth-covered fingers patted pansies and petunias into place.

The kettle boiled, so I filled up my teapot, stuffed a chocolate biscuit in my mouth, and carried everything outside. I set the tray on the wooden patio table, soaking up the succulent scents of springtime in our fair land.

David looked relaxed as he strolled over in his jeans and t-shirt. There were several chairs dotted around this large table, but he sat right next to me – breaking a chocolate biscuit in two, and offering me half. "Present for you."

"Why thank you." I dunked it in my tea, relishing the melty chocolate, which tingled on my tongue.

David poured himself some tea. "Glad to see the teapot's come in handy."

"I love it. Thank you."

He fell serious. "Thank *you*. For saving my life."

"Oh... oh, I'm sure you would've dodged the knife in time."

"No." He munched his biscuit. "Hey, we should go to the pub to celebrate your first successful magic spell."

Was that a date! "Speaking of magic, David, there's something I need to ask you."

He stirred his tea. "You want me to investigate Vermilitrude's murder?"

"Er, well... sort of. Would you... would you train me in magic?"

His warm smile was sincere. "I should be delighted."

We clinked our teacups together, and I sat back in a sunbeam. "It's good to be back home in magical Windsor."

"Agreed," he said. "There's certainly no place like it."

For all my books, scan the QR Code

Or visit **amazon.com/author/rosiereed**

Printed in Great Britain
by Amazon